The Cold Truth

Michael Horton

Printed in the United States by
Independent Publishing Corporation
Chesterfield, Missouri 63005

Dedication

*This book is dedicated to
the strongest woman I've ever known!*

MOM

Special Thanks To

Andrew Wamboldt: Technical Skills

Ironworker's Local 396: St. Louis MO

Beer & Susan: You know why!

Elizabeth: 😊

The USA: What a Great Country!

Very Special Thanks To

Artist

Nicole Horton

For Her Contribution

To the Cover of this Book

You can see more of her excellent work at

MindWorks Gallery

Chesterfield Mall, Chesterfield, Misouri

Contents

Monk

"Hey, Monk, let's go get ice cream for everyone."

Even to a ten-year-old, this seemed a strange offer on the night before Christmas Eve in ice-cold St. Louis; but off we went. We brought it back home and everyone had ice cream. There were four of us kids: Sis, Monk, Johnny, and Cheeks in that order. That was our family, one girl and three boys, and Mom and Dad.

That was the last time we saw Dad for a long time. As I write this, 52 years later, I don't remember all the details; but what I do know is that I only saw my dad again three more times in my life, and I do not believe Sis or my brothers ever saw him again.

Two days after the ice cream, the day after Christmas, Mom was crying, there were neighbors at our house, and police were reassuring us that all would be well. "We will find your husband and father... . Monk, you are now the man of the house... . Be strong; we will find your dad." I was sitting in a large stuffed chair trying not to cry, but the burden was unbearable.

Now, Dad up to this time had been a good father. He had a good managerial job that paid well and required a degree of responsibility. But a higher position that he wanted and thought he should get was given to someone else. He never told anyone at the plant that he was leaving, he just never showed up for work the day he left us.

We found out many months later (that social security number can find anyone eventually) that dear old Dad had taken off with the redhead and her two children. ("The redhead" was a woman who worked in the plant with Dad.) He moved to Florida, a state that has no laws to make fathers pay child support.

There were numerous times I would overhear Mom on the phone, explaining to the many creditors how she would make everything right. "Yes, I will pay, but you must realize that I have four children and am five months pregnant." (You see, Dad took our paid-for car and left us a spanking new car he had recently purchased that hadn't been fully paid for; another little gift to go with the ice cream, I guess.) Another creditor; "Yes, I will make that good, but I must have some time." (Seems like Dad needed a whole new wardrobe while exiting stage right; he put it on credit with Mom's address—such callousness!) I don't think there were credit cards back then, but you could purchase on credit. Spouses are responsible for each other's debts, and Mom eventually paid off all of Dad's.

Many months after he left, I remembered having overheard my dad talking to the doctor. It had been late summer, about four months before he'd left. He'd been sitting at the breakfast bar on the phone. I'd been in my room, which was right across the hall from the kitchen. "Doc, that can't be so! There must be some mistake! I can't afford another one!"

Like I said, it took me many months after Dad left to remember that conversation; but to this day I can recall every word just like it was yesterday. I also remember one night a month or so before he left when he came home drunk. I had never seen him drunk like that before, as he was not a heavy drinker. I just remember him throwing up in the bathroom and saying he was sorry and would never do it again. I guess that should have been a hint of what was to come in the near future.

Dad did show up at our doorstep about a year after leaving. I was the only one home and I am not sure why he even stopped by. He just stood there for a time—I honestly can't remember any words being exchanged—and then he was gone.

Aunt Dottie and Aunt Edith

"Dot, you must take Sis and Cheeks; I am pregnant and I want my children to have a good home. I don't know what the future will hold, but I will get back on my feet and in time you can send them back to me."

Wilmington, North Carolina was a long way off, but that was where Sis and Cheeks went. Aunt Dottie was barren and the thought of children was very appealing. Uncle Al, a good man but a rather strange father figure, found much joy in the following nine years, when Sis and Cheeks were with Aunt Dottie and him.

Uncle Al was big on Germany, German cars, and, I got the feeling, sex. "This is my sanctuary, Monk," he once told me in his private room at the back of the garage. "I come here for privacy; that mat is where I do my pushups." "Unk" was a frail man at best, but he did have a workout regiment. I noticed *Playboy* magazines everywhere. (At the time, I wasn't really sure what they were, but I recognized what the photos were of immediately.)

I did visit Sis, Cheeks, Aunt Dottie, and Unk once in those nine years, and we wrote to each other from time to time, but I don't really know what it was like for them, as Johnny and I were not there. I do know that much later, when I was in my early thirties, Dot and Al came to St. Louis to visit. I told Al on the phone that I would take him to a strip club on the East Side (don't know why that came out of my mouth). He was in very bad health at the time but was quite excited at the prospect. I will always regret that I did not actually take him.

The only time Johnny and I visited Sis and Cheeks in Wilmington was a good time.

"Monk, our neighbor Shirley and her son Trevor are going to the ocean to fish. Would you like to go with them?"

"Yes, Aunt Dottie!" I have always liked fishing. Ocean fishing off a pier at twelve years of age was exciting. We purchased a bucket of shrimp for bait and found a spot on the pier.

"That's a bluefish! We'll keep it," said Shirley, eyeing my catch.

"I've got a big one!" Trevor shouted. "Wow… what is that?" That was my first look at a stingray.

"Don't touch that tail!" cautioned Shirley, and Trevor threw the stingray off the side of the pier like a Frisbee. There was a *splat* as the ray hit the water and scurried off to freedom.

We caught many more blues and some sheepshead. I was very impressed with Shirley, as she was a real fisherman. We headed back to Shirley's and started cleaning the fish. I guess they were eaten; I'll never know, as I did not stay for dinner.

Aunt Dot's home was very nice. They had a large yard, there was a huge lake, and the community had a swimming pool. I always figured life was good for Sis and Cheeks during their stay. Sis was probably more negatively impacted by Dad's leaving than us boys were, but we all at least had a good home life while separated from Mom.

✳ ✳ ✳

"Edith, I need to send Monk and Johnny to you. I cannot take care of them, as I am pregnant and in debt."

Off to Powder Springs, Georgia we went—on the Greyhound bus. Now, a Greyhound bus was quite an adventure for a ten- and eight-year-old. There were stops in many small towns along the way. For most of the trip we were in the two seats right behind the windshield, across from the driver, so we got to see everything.

I remember we were stopped at a railroad crossing and a police car was in front of our bus. The officer had lit a cigarette and thrown the empty pack out on the road. There was a TV commercial at that time of an Indian chief in a headdress looking across our nation at all the litter with a tear running down his cheek. A woman sitting behind the driver said, "Did you see that? A police officer littering the road." She told the driver if he would open the door she would go out and give the officer his trash back. To my surprise she did just that and the whole bus gave her a round of applause.

Aunt ET, as we called her later in life (her full name was Edith Tiggins, hence "ET"), was very good to Johnny and me. Uncle Wilbur was also a very good man. He had a lot of patience, though we could at times get him riled up.

I remember when Johnny and Lynn were doing something that got Uncle Wilbur really mad.

"All of you come here!" Uncle Wilbur was at the carport with a leather belt. We took turns holding on to the round metal post and running in circles as he swatted us. I told Unk I hadn't done anything. "Well, this is for the next time you do!" he said. But it didn't hurt too badly; Unk wasn't a mean man.

Johnny would at times rile up Aunt Edith too, and she would say, "Johnny, you go out to the switch tree and bring back a good one!" I never got switched, though.

Cousins Will and Lynn were like brothers from the moment we arrived.

How neat it was to live on a small farm (although Uncle Wilbur had a good job in town to provide some actual income). We raised pigs and had a large garden, a lake to fish in, and woods and fields for hunting. We also raised shiners on our second stay; more on that later. Mr. and Mrs. Ward, the Scoggins, and the Lovinggoods were our distant neighbors. Our closest neighbors I only knew as the tenant farmers.

✳ ✳ ✳

This was 1960-1964, and at that time segregation was pretty rampant in the South. I do remember on that first bus ride we would occasionally get off and there would be signs stating "Whites only". I did not understand what that meant until we had been in Georgia for a while.

Johnny and I had never witnessed anything like it, but we soon grew accustomed to not interacting with our closest neighbors across the creek bottom. There were around ten coloreds (as they were called in those days) living in that little house. When passing, I always noticed that they seemed happy, playing and such. I never once met even one of them during my whole stay.

Now, Anna was a different story. She was our housemaid, around eighteen years old and very pretty. "Now, Mr. Tiggins, you get out of this kitchen with that manure on your shoes!" That was one of Anna's favorite lines, as Uncle Wilbur never took off his shoes after tending to the pigs.

"Anna, I'm going to have a glass of tea. Do you want some?" I asked.

"Thank you, Monk, but I can't drink out of that glass."

"Why, what's wrong with it?"

"Oh, nothing, but Mrs. Tiggins would have a fit. That glass up there is my glass." I looked to where Anna was pointing and saw a brown plastic glass with a picture of a cow on it.

I never said anything, but I always thought it was kind of cruel that Anna could only drink out of that glass. Anna loved us, so I just figured that was how things were. Those "Whites only" signs were all over—on bathroom doors, water fountains, and restaurant entrance doors. Yep, that is how things were; the coloreds even had their own schools (I guess—I just know we had no coloreds in our school in Georgia).

Thinking back, I realize that if you grew up in the South at that time, what I saw as racism was just normal. It's kind of like religion; if you are raised to be a certain religion, then you think that is the way to live. As you get older, your beliefs may change, but change comes about slowly.

I have a good friend, Oscar, a black man that I worked with in St. Louis for many years much later in my life. He also had family in Georgia, and we discussed the racial thing from time to time.

"Monk, I remember going to see my cousins in the '60s. They got real excited one day and told me we were all going to go out in the fields to pick beans and make some money. I spent seven or eight hours picking those beans and at the end of the day we each got $2.25!" He was amazed that his relatives thought that was a satisfactory amount, and acceptance of segregation in the South was just a normal way of life.

Of course, this would all go to the wayside in the very near future.

But the white people in the South were good people. I remember there was a poor family whose home burned down. Families from miles around gathered in front of the charred house and decided that day to build them another one. Within two weeks they had a new home. It was a rather plain rectangle of a home, mostly made of cinderblock, but it had a nice wood porch attached. Yes, the whites were good people who had just been raised to accept the unfairness faced by their colored brothers and sisters.

I thought a lot about this during my time in Georgia. I would think to myself that it would be a good idea for the races to mix, marry, and become as one. Then, a few years later, I would think maybe that would not solve the problem because even if we all mixed and married there would still be different colors of people; the strongest genes would take over. We would not all just become the color of coffee with cream. And there would always be good and bad people, regardless of color.

I do think people of color in many instances have a tougher go in life… the exception being if you are a track star, football star, boxer, or especially a basketball star; then people of color more than likely have a slight advantage.

※ ※ ※

"Let's go visit Mrs. Ward," Lynn yelled as he trotted down the long gravel driveway.

Now, this was the country, so we had to walk two miles to the Wards' gravel road. Mrs. Ward was in her nineties and made homemade biscuits every morning. We visited her at least once a week and gobbled down those biscuits. They were so good and so fresh you didn't even have to put anything on them. To this day I can't pass up a good biscuit.

Everything there was so different from St. Louis. Mrs. Ward kind of reminded me of Old Mother Hubbard, and Mr. Ward was thin and always wore bib overalls. I don't know if I ever heard him say one word. He would just wander about, occasionally looking our way. He was probably wondering who these younguns were who came every week to eat his biscuits.

The kitchen had a wood stove for cooking and a water pump with a handle on the counter. You had to put a little water in the pump to prime it and then pump the handle to get water to come out; it would go *squeak, squeak*, as the handle went up and down.

There was a clapboard barn and stable with chickens running everywhere. The smells were foreign to me but I liked them, even the barnyards.

Along the front of the Wards' house was a wood porch, worn but sturdy. At the side was cut wood with a splitting maul, and a hatchet for splitting small pieces of wood for the cook stove. The roof was metal, and when it rained, man was it loud.

I don't think the Wards had an automobile, just an old beat-up pickup truck and mules. Almost everyone had mules.

* * *

Raising pigs meant one needed a breeding boar (a male hog). Bobo was our breeding boar, and Uncle Wilbur and Lynn would always say, "It looks like Bobo has a new girlfriend," when they saw him doing his thing.

One night at dinner, I looked out the window and saw Bobo with a new girlfriend. I said, "Look, everyone, Bobo has a new girlfriend." Uncle Wilbur let me know that that was not something to be said at the dinner table. He was stern so I knew he meant business, but that was all he said.

And then—such a ruckus! Bobo and our new breeding boar were going at it, with tusks flaring, hair flying, squeals of death piercing the air. Bobo didn't like this new boar.

"What are you carrying, Uncle Wilbur?"

"This is an electric prod to keep Bobo off our new Boar. Bobo is getting old and we must use this new boar for breeding, but Bobo will kill him unless I separate them."

Uncle Wilbur was not scared of Bobo, but I was very respectful of him and always kept my distance. Unk got in the middle and fought his way between them. He finally got Bobo in a pen by himself. The next morning a big colored man showed up with a huge knife strapped to his side and carrying a rope.

"Say, Unk, what is he doing?"

"Well, Bobo must be castrated to calm him down and to get the musk taste out of his body." Poor Bobo would eventually be ground up into sausage, which is something we had for breakfast every morning, unless we had salted ham or bacon. Yep, fried eggs, sausage or ham or bacon, grits, and toast every morning except Sunday. Sunday was usually a quick bowl of oatmeal and off to church. The ham and bacon was quite different from city folks' ham and bacon. Ours was cured and always tasted salty but at the same time had a twinge of sweetness to it. This was to be Bobo's fate.

Well this big colored man tied poor Bobo to a fence post and had him all stretched out. I don't know how he accomplished this, as Bobo was about 800 pounds of mean hog. The man then castrated Bobo, who took it like a man—not one squeal out of him.

Bobo had another few months of life to live to clear out the musk from his body and then it was off to the Scoggins. They know how to butcher and boil a hog. All of this was very interesting and very new. After shooting poor Bobo in the head, Jerry and Gary Scoggins tied his back legs to a tree limb and hoisted him upside down. Gary stuck him in the neck.

"Why are you doing that?"

"Well, Monk, that bleeds him out."

There was a huge vat of boiling water heated with burning wood to boil old Bobo in. This softened up his hair, which Jerry and Gary shaved off.

"Why are you shaving his hair off?"

"Monk, you can't have a nice ham with hair all over it." They also made chitlins; I think Yankees call them pork rinds. I've never eaten either. Johnny and I were enthralled.

Later, it was off to the barn. "Monk, bring those burlap bags over here. Now fill them up about one third with this curing salt." The curing salt was kind of a reddish orange and it was sticky. I think it had sugar in it, too, to give the ham and bacon that salty sweet taste.

"What are we doing?" I asked.

"We're going to put the hams and bacon in the burlap bags and tie them up to hang in the barn so they can cure." I was amazed, as they were hung in the barn—with no refrigeration—till we decided to eat them. I always wondered why the critters never got to them, but they never did.

⁂ ⁂ ⁂

Baby pigs were our commodity. Uncle Wilbur was king of the baby pig business in these parts. Lynn was second in command, learning the trade from his dad. People came from miles around to purchase our pigs to raise and slaughter. I asked Unk how much we charged for each pig.

"Well, Monk, a ten-week-old pig is $10, and a twelve-week-old pig is $12. If you are going to be born a pig, you might hope to be a female pig. You have a longer life expectancy as a female, as it only takes one boar to service a bunch of sows. Not to mention that whole castrating thing; a male pig raised for food purposes needs to be castrated before being sold, if you want top dollar.

"Boys, lets get out to the pig pen and rustle up those baby pigs."

We had a small pen next to the feed lot that enabled only the baby pigs to enter through small openings. Over time the little piglets would learn to go in that pen, where there was some nice slop for them to eat without having to compete with the grown-ups. Pigs can get pretty mean when eating.

Well, round-up time meant castration for the boys. We closed the openings in the pen and started throwing the girls out. Then us boys held down each little guy, one at a time, while Unk did the job. Unk then slathered something that looked like tar and smelled like linseed oil over the incision.

Usually there was much squealing during this process (not like with Bobo, who took it like a man). All of this squealing caused the sows to get pretty excited. Our pen was surrounded by angry mothers coming to the rescue. But Unk had made the enclosure well; it was a double fence with twice the normal amount of fence post. I had always wondered why it was so sturdily reinforced; then I knew, and boy was I glad.

❋ ❋ ❋

Now, we had a pet piglet that lived under the screen porch. Merf the Morf was its name.

"Will, why did you give him that name?"

"Monk, Merf is not a him. Merf is not a her either. Merf is a morphidite!"

"What is a morphidite?"

"Look, when you turn Merf over, you see that ole Merf has kinda two sets of organs."

I never knew if "morphidite" was a real term, but I did see that ole Merf was definitely different. Merf the Morf only lived about two years. We did not eat Merf, but gave him/her a decent burial.

In fact, we buried Merf in the same corner of the backyard where Uncle Wilbur used to relieve himself. He always wore nice brown slacks, usually a cream or tan shirt, brown wing tips, and a cloth hat—you know, like every white-collar man wore back in those days. Well, Unk would get home from work, walk to the side of the porch, and pee. He never knew it, but I took a picture of him peeing with his nice clothes and hat on. I still have that picture somewhere.

❋ ❋ ❋

"Okay, boys, we have some fence in need of repair. You three will string the barbed wire along the side of the fence, and later we will come back and attach it to the fence post."

Off we went through the weeds; Lynn was in the lead, followed by me, and then Will. Uncle Wilbur was on the side of the road directing us. Lynn walked right through this bush that had a huge wasps' nest he stirred up. I saw the wasps emerge from the nest and surround Lynn.

Now, wasps seem to know when someone is scared or a threat to the nest. Lynn never even saw them, as his back was to the nest. I, on the other hand, was seeing it all, and I was concerned. So all of a sudden they forgot Lynn and focused on me. They were merciless and one after another they attacked me.

I ran out to the road, pulling wasps off my head and running around in circles. A car came by, and to this day I can still see the look on the woman's face: a look of horror that mirrored exactly how I was feeling.

Lynn yelled, "Monk, get down low, as wasp cannot see below themselves." I got down on my belly in the road and they seemed to go away. I don't know if they can actually see below or not, but if you ever get chased by wasps, I would suggest lying down.

Lynn also told me that only bumblebees or carpenter bees with black faces can sting you; some have a white face and supposedly they cannot sting you. I had seen Lynn handle the white-faced ones and not get stung, but I passed on checking that little fact out for myself.

✳ ✳ ✳

Now, being from Missouri—not "Missourah", as some people pronounce it; it still gets to me that some people, mostly politicians of a certain political party, pronounce the "i" as "ah"… ticks me off! Anyway, being from Missouri, I know what ice on a lake can do. I know that it takes a few days of sub-30-degree weather for a lake to freeze up enough to walk on. Georgia is not a state you normally associate with frozen bodies of water. But that year Georgia had a two-day cold snap, sunny but arctic-like. Lynn suggested we go down to the lake and off we went.

"Lynn, where are you going?"

"I'm headed out to the island."

"I think we'd better stay close to the shore where the ice is thicker."

"I'm going to the island. You coming or not?" Before we got ten feet from shore the ice started creaking. Cracks were appearing all around us; I was scared, but Lynn didn't know any better. We made it to the island and back to shore. Surely God was looking over us that day, and performed a miracle!

The island was always our goal, be it summer or winter. We had an aluminum rowboat that Lynn and I would take out to the island in the summer, or sometimes we would jump off our dock and swim there.

On one swim to the island I got a sudden urge to poop when we were about halfway there.

"Monk, you can't poop in the lake!" Lynn objected. But it was too late, as I had already taken my shorts off and everything was good again.

Afterward, Lynn told his mom I had pooped in the lake. But I lied to her: "No, Aunt Edith, I had to go but I held it."

Bad News

"Monk, your mom lost her baby a few months ago."

Aunt Edith always had a warm way of talking, so I'm sure that wasn't quite what she actually said. But she told me that Mom wanted us to come back home.

I later learned from my mom what had actually happened. She had such a hard life, and this was really just the beginning of the tough times. Abortions were pretty much unheard of in those days, but a friend of Mom's knew someone who gave abortions and sold concoctions that aborted babies. Mom told me she'd taken that concoction and then had the baby on the toilet at home. It had still been in the fetus stage, but an advanced stage. She'd seen that it was a boy. She told me she had gone to the Chain of Rocks Bridge over the Mississippi River and thrown the fetus over the rail. She then told me she'd thought about jumping in herself, but thought of us children and wanted us to be a family again. Such anguish.

Well, Mom wanted us back, so we got on the Greyhound and back to St. Louis we went. We still lived in the same house, as Mom had been able to pay off all Dad's bills, and she had purchased an old car. Johnny and I were back in school with all of our friends and life was back to normal.

This only lasted six months. Mom, who was a waitress, took a fall in the restaurant she worked at.

"You will never walk again," her doctor told her. Mom had fractured her ankle in three places. She would be in a hip cast from her toes to the top of her hip for over a year. I don't think there was much in the way of workers' compensation in those days, especially for a waitress. So having lost her means of income, Mom was once again in financial straits.

Off Johnny and I went, back to Georgia on the Greyhound bus. Now, if it hadn't been for the circumstance of my mom getting hurt, I wouldn't have minded going back; I had really taken a liking to Georgia.

✳ ✳ ✳

During our first stay we'd had a TV, and the one and only program we ever watched was "Bonanza". Uncle Wilbur really liked Bonanza too, so when Saturday came around, I said, "Hey, 'Bonanza' is on." But the TV was gone. I never asked and never found out why. Uncle Wilbur and Aunt Edith were pretty religious, so maybe they'd decided TV was evil.

I never missed not having TV, though. There was so much to do and fun to have on the farm. I remember the Cuban missile crisis was going on about this time; people were building bomb shelters and hoarding food.

"Wilbur, you need to get some flashlights and batteries while you are in town and get a portable radio too. Those Russians could bomb Atlanta and we could get fallout and radiation."

Yes, these were some anxious times, and much prayer was offered. I never gave it much thought, as when you are young you have little fear.

✳ ✳ ✳

I didn't give a lot of thought to religion, either. Only as I got older did I come to realize the awe of life and the greatness of our Lord and maker. I still have little need for specific religions, as they are all like politics. I have chosen to try and lead a Christian life, but the different denominations of Christianity all have different pomp and pageantry.

In my younger years—and even now—I always wondered: if you were raised to be one religion or no religion and knew nothing of other religions, how could anyone say you have no chance to go to heaven unless you believe as he or she believes? I don't think God would hold salvation back for a good person just because he or she was raised in one religion or another, or for that matter never introduced to any religion.

I remember this song from my younger years written by Bob Dylan. I still have the album. The song went something like this:

> *God said, "Abraham give me your son"*
> *Abe said, "Man you must be puttin' me on"*
> *God said, "You can do what you want, but next time you*
> *see me coming you better run"*
> *Abe said "Where you want this killin' done"*
> *God said, ...*

Years later, when I actually listened to and understood what was being said in church, I would remember that song. It was basically about God telling Abraham that he would have to sacrifice his son, which Abraham did not want to do, but would have. I did some research on Abraham after reading a "TIME" magazine article on Abraham later in my life. From what I gathered from that research, Abraham was the father of the Jewish, Muslim, and Christian faiths; yes, the father of all three of those faiths! This research only fortified my belief that religion is good, believing in our Lord is good, and the politics of religion is stupid.

To go even further in my thinking, I have to believe that a good Buddhist or Hindu will also reap the same rewards of leading a meaningful and reverent life. I really think all religions have their own Ten Commandments, or paths to follow that are good and just. I actually think as long as you lead a caring, giving, and meaningful life you are basically leading a religious life, as these are the traits found in all religions.

I was raised Presbyterian but have worshiped in a Catholic church for many years, as that is my wife's religion. I figure if they can put up with my tripping them as they go to communion (as I am not allowed to take communion), then I can accept their rule that my not being Catholic precludes me from taking communion. We get along, and when I do attend, I enjoy it. The Catholic church is quite different from Protestant churches, yet they are all Christian. Praise to God is the largest part of all religions.

One funny incident during my indoctrination into the Catholic Church involved the way they say the Lord's Prayer. Now, I had been saying the Presbyterian version of the Lord's Prayer for 30 years before meeting my wife Sophia. In the Catholic Church, near the end of the Lord's Prayer, they stop after saying "but deliver us from evil". The priest then adds some words of advice or scripture, after which the congregation finishes the prayer. Everyone hits the right lines exactly on cue.

Well, you can imagine my first time; we got to the pause and all was completely quiet as I finished the prayer. I got more than a few looks—darn near the whole congregation turned to see who the heathen in their midst was. But it was funny and it took me a few years to not want to finish the prayer as I had grown up saying it.

❊ ❊ ❊

Almost every Saturday, Uncle Wilbur would take us up to what was called the corner store. It was near our school and was where people could purchase a few necessities without going into town. Saturday was our day to get a soda and a candy bar. I can still taste those Baby Ruths and grape sodas. I guess Uncle Wilbur and Aunt Edith were thinking of ways to make our stay seem as close to normal family life as possible.

One day, when Lynn and I were messing around in the field by the barn, Lynn said, "Monk, you can call Uncle Wilbur Dad if you want to."

I thought it over a bit and said, "Lynn, I think I will just call him Uncle Wilbur."

We then went to the barn, where Lynn grabbed ole Buttermilk's teat and squirted me with milk. The barn had a hayloft (where all the salted meat was hung), and it had a small door at one end to throw bales of hay out.

Now, this door was what looked to me like 20 feet off the ground. Lynn said, "Come on, let's jump out," and out he went. I looked down. There was no way I was going to jump.

"Come on, jump. It won't hurt," Lynn encouraged. Well, I slowly lowered myself till I slid out the door. Good thing kids are made of rubber; I was fine, but I think I only did that one more time.

* * *

Unk bought me a rifle with money Mom sent for my birthday. It was a great little rifle except that it only shot one bullet and then you had to eject the spent cartridge and reload. Everyone else had a weapon that would shoot more than one bullet before having to reload. I got to be a pretty good shot knowing I only had one chance.

Thinking back, it's a wonder we didn't kill anyone, as we pretty much shot in any direction we wanted to. We were careful around each other and used our safeties on the guns, but I never gave too much thought as to where the bullet would go. We knew that if there was a building in sight not to shoot in that direction; but still, when you are in the woods you can't see very far. A .22-caliber bullet can travel a mile.

There was this giant blue heron that frequently came to our lake. Lynn and I always dreamed of shooting him but could never get close enough to get a shot at him.

Well, one day, I was out at the lake by myself, with my single shot rifle. Right in front of me landed that heron. I raised my rifle, got him in my sights, and then started to shake. I froze and never got off a shot. I think that is what they call "buck fever", freezing at your first opportunity to shoot a deer. Well, I've never gone deer hunting—I prefer to fish—but that is what "buck fever" refers to. I am also glad I was not able to shoot that heron, although at the time I was devastated.

I basically gave up hunting years ago, as in getting older I lost the pleasure of killing something. I would, however, hunt and kill if I needed to eat or feed my family, as in my opinion there is nothing wrong with hunting as long as what you kill is eaten by someone. We almost always ate what we killed.

I think the turning point in my attitude toward hunting came while hunting rabbits one day. We were using a rabbit dog that, upon finding a rabbit, would chase it back to us for a shot. The last rabbit I ever killed was a very young rabbit the dog chased to me. I didn't realize how young the rabbit was because the land we were hunting had pretty thick vegetation. After I shot the rabbit, it started crying like a baby, as I hadn't killed it. I had heard that rabbits would sometimes cry when injured, but that was the first time I witnessed it.

Many years later I was working outside and saw a hawk swoop down and pick up a very young rabbit. I listened to that baby rabbit cry as it was carried away. That is a cry I will always remember.

❊ ❊ ❊

While we'd been back home, Unk had decided to raise shiners for bait fish. Shiners are like minnows that fishermen purchase when fishing for sport fish like largemouth bass. Unk figured he could make some money raising them, and had four small lakes dug out that were fed by the runoff from our big lake.

We had to put these fibrous mats out in the lake for the shiners to lay their eggs in to hatch more shiners. Man, there were millions of them at times. Mr. Brogden, a neighbor to the rear of our property, was over visiting when it was time to place the mats. The best way to place them was to wade out in the water, and the best people to do it, I was told, were Lynn and me.

Well, we stripped down to nothing, and out in the cold water we went. I still remember getting out of the water and ole Mr. Brogden mentioning my lack of manhood compared to Lynn. Lynn was hung like a damn elephant; I guess I was a bit lacking compared to him!

Anyway, Mr. Brogden, who was a nice enough man, came down with cancer a few years later. He sat down in his living room with his dog and double barrel shotgun and shot his head off. That's the way Unk told me it had gone down when I was visiting a few years later.

* * *

Lynn and I shared a bedroom with a large double bed, and Johnny and Will were in another room with twin beds. We hid our smoking paraphernalia under that bed. It was some kind of weed that grew in the fields. Lynn would dry it and we would smoke it out of a corn cob pipe.

"What do you call this stuff, Lynn?"

"Its rabbit tobacco. Let's smoke some."

It wasn't very good, and we eventually threw it away after trying it a few times. Life was never dull on the farm.

Johnny

Being brothers, Johnny and I would have fights occasionally—nothing big, and never while living with Aunt Edith and Uncle Wilbur. I, as the oldest, biggest, and strongest, had the advantage; but I never tried to hurt Johnny.

Johnny, on the other hand, knowing that I was bigger and stronger, would try and make up for his disadvantage. There were many times I had to duck as an object was thrown at me or outmaneuver Johnny's attack as he wielded some object as a weapon. I think that, while we were living with Mom, Johnny just wanted more attention; this was probably the cause of our bickering.

The breakup of our family was probably harder on Sis and Johnny than it was on Cheeks and me. Cheeks was very young when Dad left, so he did not fully understand what had happened. Johnny, being the middle child, might have felt the abandonment more than Cheeks and me, as middle children supposedly don't get much attention to begin with, so Dad's leaving meant even *less* attention. Sis was a young teenager, and losing her father figure as she entered the teenage years was surely a difficulty the rest of us couldn't relate to.

Johnny had this habit of vocally expressing his displeasure when mad or upset. Uncle Wilbur always said he sounded like a baby pig squealing, and he did not like that squealing one bit. But I can't really remember a time when Johnny and I fought when we were living with Aunt Edith and Uncle Wilbur.

That one time Johnny and I went to visit Sis and Cheeks in North Carolina, though, Johnny did manage to upset Aunt Dottie. Aunt

Dottie was rather prim and proper at times, and on this occasion Johnny decided to relieve himself behind a rose bush.

"Johnny, what are you doing?" demanded Aunt Dottie.

"I'm peeing."

"You can't do that out in the yard!"

"Why not? Uncle Wilbur does it all the time."

* * *

In the country, there is always something dead in the fields. Buzzards circle in the air, waiting to catch the smell of death.

Johnny would always ask, "What are those buzzards doing?"

Will explained that they could smell death in the air as far as two or three miles away. "Johnny, they will circle over a dead carcass and if all is right (there is no movement), they will come down and have a feast."

One day we saw Johnny lying out in the field. He lay there for a long time without moving. We ran out to see what was wrong, and Johnny chastised us: "Hey, they were just starting to come down! You scared them away."

He had seen the buzzards circling and thought if he lay still, they would come down to him. For years we laughed about that. Even after Johnny left this earth we still thought about that day and we always laughed.

* * *

I don't know why—maybe it is just a disconnect when you lose a family member—but other than a few vivid memories of Johnny, for the life of me I cannot remember much of him during the time we lived in Georgia, though he was there every day. He was a bright, cheerful, and at times somewhat mischievous brother, and it did hurt to lose him.

Country Life

Mark Johnston was my best friend. He lived pretty far away, so Aunt Edith would sometimes drive me to his house.

Uncle Wilbur had a car called a Kaiser, but they had stopped making them long before he'd gotten that one. I never saw a car like that before or since.

Mark and I would do everything together. We loved to hunt, especially birds. Meadowlarks and doves were usually our quarry. Mark would always clean them and we would eat them right out there in the field.

"Mark, these birds need a little salt."

"Monk, we ain't got no salt. Just spit on them."

"Why do that?"

"Don't you remember in school they told us our bodies are 90% water and it is kind of like a saline solution? Saline is salt; spit on them."

We ate a lot of doves and meadowlarks and always spit on them while cooking them.

* * *

Mark's home was a real country home. It had a big ole potbelly stove to heat the house, and Mrs. Johnston cooked on a wood stove.

And chickens were everywhere! If Mrs. Johnston wanted a chicken to cook, she would send Mark out to kill one.

"How you going to do that, Mark?"

"I'm gonna go grab one by the neck, spin it a couple of times, and then snap off its head. You know, Monk, after I do that the chicken will run around a bit before it drops dead."

"No!" I couldn't believe it.

"Watch!"

Yep, that chicken ran around with no head for a short time, then dropped dead. I guess that is where that expression came from, you know, "Don't go running around like a chicken with its head cut off." Everyone gets chickens all nicely cut and wrapped at the grocery store now so it's not too familiar a saying these days, but I heard it many times growing up.

"Monk, you want to see something really neat? I will show you how to hypnotize a chicken."

Mark grabbed this chicken (they are kind of like pets and allow you to handle them without much objection, unless you are wringing their necks). Well Mark held this chicken on its back in the palm of his hand and started moving his pointer finger toward the middle of the chicken's eyes. He kept this motion up for about eight or ten passes, right over its beak and between its eyes.

I'll be darned; the chicken kind of fell asleep like under a trance. Mark said, "Watch this," and gently set the chicken on a fence rail and balanced it, then let it go. The chicken started swaying back and forth, fell off the rail, and woke up squawking and fluttering. We laughed so hard. This is absolutely true!

❊ ❊ ❊

Across the road from Mark's house was another Mr. Ward (there were a lot of Wards). He was what a city slicker would call a shade tree barber. Mr. Ward cut everyone's hair for miles around. He had a shed with a small wood stove for the winter and just an old army tarp hung from trees to keep the sun off in the summer.

It was 50 cents for a good cut, 25 cents for a buzz. Aunt Edith liked the 50-cent cut, so that is what Uncle Wilbur always got us. Uncle Wilbur got the 25-cent cut for himself, as he didn't have much hair to cut. When we'd get back home Aunt Edith would always say, "Wilbur, your head looks like a snowball with that 25-cent cut." So we sometimes called him Uncle Snowball.

* * *

Mark and I were on the football team at McKeachon Jr. High. I was left tackle and he was right tackle on the defensive team.

Well, we weren't the best football players. But I do remember one of our bright moments. The other team had the ball on our five-yard line. Mark boasted, "They aren't coming over us!"

Well, he was partially right. They hiked the ball and the fullback came barreling in between us. We clobbered him, drove him into the ground, and got up smiling from ear to ear.

About that time we saw the guy who actually had the ball make an end-around run into the end zone. Touchdown. Still, we had clobbered that guy!

Later, the cheerleaders were outside the gym, and as we came out they asked to see my orange crate. I was pretty unaware of anything sexual at this time of my life, but I later found out they were talking about a jock strap, ergo orange crate... .

* * *

Jackie Hupstead had a crush on me and I had no idea. We went to the only party I ever attended in Georgia. It was Jerry Cudso's party; he was of questionable character, according to Aunt Edith, but she allowed Lynn and me to go.

We played a couple of games. Aunt Edith was right; this family was a bit different. For the first game, a couple of us kids were blindfolded and Jerry told us he was holding his dog in his arms. Each of us would have a turn to point to where we thought the dog's head, belly, and tail were. The one that got closest to the three would win. During my turn, I started pointing. When I was asked to point to the dog's tail, out went my finger and Jerry had an open jar of Vaseline which he thrust over it: "Oops! You missed, just a little low."

They had another game where you walked around the house with a girl that picked you. Jackie, a well-endowed, over-developed girl whom all the guys wanted, picked me.

Well, like I said, at this point in my life I was uneducated in sexual matters, so I walked her around the house. Jackie kept stopping, especially in the darker corners, but I kept on walking. Man, was I dumb; and believe me, Lynn and Mark reminded me of it for weeks. Jackie was embarrassed, thinking that I had spurned her, and never talked to me again.

✳ ✳ ✳

Oatmeal for breakfast always meant it was Sunday. I really did like going to church in Georgia. The preacher, Ted Allen, was a nice preacher and was never boring. And there was Andra Lovinggood—wow, what a knockout. Then there were Marilynn and Jenny Lemp, sexy little things (not that I knew anything about sex). I did like being around those girls. Andra, Marilynn, Jenny, and I were all in the choir; I was the only "monotone", or at least that is what our choir director always told me. Never knew what a monotone was till years later.

I always thought it was strange, but the Lemps would come to church in a pickup truck. Mr. and Mrs. Lemp rode in the front cab and Marilynn, Jenny, and Tommy rode in the back bed of the truck. The truck's bed had a canvas top over it and a wooden bench on each side. Rain, snow, or blazing heat, it didn't matter—that was how they came to church.

❊ ❊ ❊

Life was good in Georgia. There were a couple of little tough patches, like when I was being razzed at school about being a Yankee.

I said something like, "Well, at least we don't have no slaves." That brought on a little more conversation and Nan, a very nice girl, said something. I forget what she said and it wasn't bad, but I yelled something back at her that wasn't very nice. I have no idea why I said it. She was a beautiful girl, but it was a devastating thing to say to her in front of all the other students.

Well, it got back to Aunt Edith before I got home from school. She was waiting and after my explanation she merely in her most caring way said it was wrong to have said that, but that she understood. Lynn eventually ended up marrying Nan. I think that had been Aunt Edith's plan all along.

❊ ❊ ❊

Years later, when I would go through Georgia on my way to Florida, I would always stop at Uncle Wilbur's and Aunt Edith's. I went to Florida a lot, but I only saw Dad one time; I went for fun and sun, not to see him.

❊ ❊ ❊

Later in life, Lynn rented out Johnny On The Spots to construction sites, and then to the county and state too. I remember seeing, one time when I was visiting Nan and him, an open area behind the garden that was full of Johnny On The Spots, as that was where he stored them when they weren't being used.

He also had a funny-looking truck parked back there. I asked Lynn what it was for.

"Oh," he replied, "that's the honey wagon; it's what we use to suck out the Johnnies."

Later, Lynn started putting in water lines for the county and had his own construction company. He became very prosperous and successful, and had children and grandchildren. He was on the school board and ran for public office a few times.

I took my daughter and wife on a visit to Georgia once and we stayed at Lynn's and Nan's home. It was a very nice visit, and Lynn made us some of the best breakfast grits that I have ever eaten.

Home

Mom got better, nabbed a job as a bookkeeper, and brought Johnny and me back home once again. She was still in a cast, but she had rented a small house for us to live in. It was near the airport where her job was. She rented out our old house so she would not have to sell it. We would eventually move back into it.

The little house we now lived in had just three rooms: a kitchen, a front room, and a bedroom. There was also a small bathroom and a basement. The basement was dirt with an old ringer washing machine and a hose for filling it up. There was a door inside the house to go down to the basement but there were no steps; we had to go out the side door and walk outside around back to get in the basement.

The outside basement door was very hard to open, and once inside you had to walk to the middle of the room to get to the only light—a bulb with a pull string. Most of the time when the light came on you would see a mouse or rat scurry off. I never saw one inside the house, just in that dirt basement.

Mom would get home from work—still in a cast—and go down to that dirt basement to do the wash with that old ringer washer. My poor Mom; I didn't realize it so much then, but she had a hard life.

The year or so that we lived in that little house was not bad. It was a little close; I don't think my feet ever hit the bedroom floor. It was a very small bedroom and we had two double beds and two dressers that filled it up. I would crawl across Mom's and Johnny's bed to get to mine. To get dressed I would go to the foot of my bed, where there was just enough room to open the drawers. I would get my clothes out, get dressed on the bed, and crawl back across Mom's and Johnny's bed to get out of the room.

✳ ✳ ✳

It was 1962 or '63, I think. I remember some of the news stories of the day: Cassius Clay knocks out Sonny Liston, the Beatles hit America, and the Surgeon General declares cigarettes a health hazard.

Of course, this was also the time frame when John F. Kennedy was assassinated. I was at school when he was shot and I remember they let us go home early. It was pretty amazing to me that the President had been killed, but in a week or so things seemed to get back to normal in America.

✳ ✳ ✳

It was winter, it was snowing, and everyone had a sled except me. Mom said she was sorry but she couldn't afford one. She suggested I ask my father to send me money to purchase one. Of course, she was just kidding, as he never gave her one red cent or a single penny for any of his children.

Well, I wrote a letter and about the end of April I get a reply with $10 in it. A little late for a sled, but to my knowledge I am the only one who's ever gotten any money from dear old dad.

✳ ✳ ✳

"Mom, I hate powdered milk."

"Monk, I just got all the bills paid off and powdered milk is all I can afford."

"Well, Mom, as soon as you can afford real milk, please get some."

About this time was the first time I ever met Murill. He was a great guy in many ways, and eventually Mom married him. This first meeting, though, was a little rocky.

I was looking out the front window and saw a man pull up with an armful of grocery bags. He came to the side door; I don't think we ever used the front door—probably had furniture in front of it (I don't remember).

I opened the door and all hell broke loose. Here came this crazed woman, cursing and threatening. Murill put the bags down and went out in the front yard to meet his maker. The woman started whaling on him and cursing him. Murill only blocked her blows, never hit her back.

I did not see Murill for some time after that, but I did have real milk that week, as the grocery bags had a couple of gallons in them. Mom was at work, so she hadn't witnessed the incident, and I can't remember if I ever told her the whole story. I did find out that Murill was divorced and the crazy woman was his ex-wife.

❋ ❋ ❋

Things were getting better for Mom. We could finally afford to move back to our home in Glasgow Village (that was the strange name of our subdivision). Glasgow Village had street names like Caithness, Glen Gary, and Midlothian. We lived on Cameron.

Mom's best friend was named Velma. Velma was a one-of-a-kind woman; I liked her but always sensed that she lived on the edge.

Well, Velma helped us move back into our home. She and Mom rented a trailer for what little we had to move. They had no problem going forward with that trailer, but trying to back into the driveway... well, that took some time and many laughs.

Velma's husband John would have helped, but he was a truck driver and was on the road a lot. John was a big man, but had been born with one arm that had never fully developed. It was a bit crooked and much, much smaller than his good arm. To this day I have only seen one other person with an arm like that. John knew that the sight of his arm made me uneasy, and I knew that John knew it. He was a nice man though.

John and Velma had a small piece of land in Illinois, right across the river from where we lived. They also had a huge black German Shepherd named Satan. That dog scared me but I never told anyone.

I was out in the field with Satan one day and he just took off at blazing speed, grabbed the largest groundhog I've ever seen, shook it about three times, and threw it up in the air. By the time it hit the ground, it was dead.

Later that day John and I were taking target practice. After shooting, I ran to get the target. Satan was at my heels nipping at my ankles. John then told me not to run from Satan, as that tended to unleash his wild side. "He thinks you are prey," John said.

Well, I had seen what Satan could do to prey, so I stopped running.

❊ ❊ ❊

Velma loved Coca-Cola. Back then they sold bottles in two different sizes. One was a little tiny bottle (six to eight ounces).

Well, that was the only Coke Velma would drink, and she always had at least a case of them on hand. She said they were better and had different ingredients in them than the larger bottles did.

I have read that the original Coke contained a small amount of cocaine. Maybe these little bottles had some cocaine in them? I don't know, but it wasn't too many years later that Coca-Cola stopped making those little bottles. Velma wasn't happy about that.

*** *** ***

The grass at home was tall when we moved back in. Mom said, "Monk, I'm going to get you a new lawn mower."

I replied, "How are you going to afford that?"

"I don't know, but come this Friday I'm going to buy you a mower."

Well, Mom had a friend named Curt. Curt decided to take Mom to the horse races in Illinois and have dinner. Johnny was sleeping over at a friend's house, so Curt invited me to come too.

We had dinner at the track, and then went to the betting windows. Mom made her bet (with Curt's money) and I made a $1 bet with Curt's money. My horse came in third and I won $3. Mom's horse came in first and she won like $65.

She was so excited; by the time we left the track, nearly everyone in the place had heard that we were getting a new lawn mower. Sixty-five dollars bought you a real nice mower in 1964 (I think that was the year).

*** *** ***

Life was good. Johnny and I had many friends. Glasgow Village was a monstrous subdivision with a lot of kids.

Steve and Mike Ragan lived down the street. They were as big as the giant in "Jack and the Beanstalk". In fact, everyone in that family was a giant.

Sandy Carrington lived next door to us, and she was hot. She liked older guys and I sometimes saw her kissing them in between our homes. Still, I liked her.

One day, Steve decided it would be fun to get me on my back and sit on me. We were in Sandy's front yard and I was about to suffocate. Out the front door came Sandy; as soon as I saw her, I immediately became Hercules. Well, not really, but I did start tearing at Steve's shirt and ripping it to shreds.

All of a sudden this giant started crying and ran off to Mama. I found out later that the shirt was brand new and he'd been afraid his Mom would be very mad. She was upset with him and scolded him for sitting on me.

As for Sandy, I never hooked up with her, though I did run into her later in life.

❋ ❋ ❋

We were Presbyterian, but for some reason the Mothers of B'nai B'rith, a Jewish organization, decided to send Johnny and me to camp. I think Mom was on Aid to Dependant Children for a short time and the Mothers of B'nai B'rith, who would sponsor hardship families, chose us.

Johnny went to a different camp than I did, one for younger kids, so I can only tell you about my camp. We took a charter bus (kind of like a Greyhound bus) to Camp Hawthorne at the Lake of the Ozarks in south central Missouri. I was the only non-Jewish kid on the bus, but the trip down was fun. We sang Jewish songs, most of which I had never heard of, except for one: "Hava Nagila". So we were singing and going down the highway to the beat of that song; everybody was happy.

Camp Hawthorne was a little settlement of wood cabins with six double bunk beds in each one. There was Ira, David, Larry, Harvey, a few others, and a blonde Russian kid who did not speak much English. I thought if he was our age, then I never wanted to fight on the Russian front, as he was big, lean, and chiseled. I think his name was Ivan; he did not talk much but always participated in what we were doing and was a nice young man.

* * *

It was time for lunch, and Ira asked what I wanted; apparently we got a choice. I said, "How about a ham and cheese sandwich and a cold glass of milk?"

That got some looks…. . Jews don't eat ham and don't mix dairy with meat, apparently. I settled for a pastrami sandwich and Bug Juice—that was what they called Kool-Aid. I drank a lot of Bug Juice that week.

I remember maybe ten or so years later seeing Ira on channel 9 (a PBS TV station). The program was something about Jewish stuff. I had forgotten his last name, but I remembered it and him when I saw the program.

* * *

Now, David probably became a rabbi, as he would ask me questions and then correct my answers. But I was pretty smart too, and came up with more than one counterpoint.

"Hey, Monk, you know the Sabbath is the last day of the week, right?"

"Yeah, David, even a Christian knows that."

"Then why do you worship on Sunday?"

"'Cause that is the last day of the week!"

"Monk, here, look at the calendar; you can clearly see that Saturday is the last day of the week."

He had me for a second, but fortunately a Christian must have printed that calendar. "David, I don't know why Saturday is the last day of the week on the calendar, but if you will notice, Sunday is always printed in red, as are the holidays—the special days. Sunday is special. Maybe God started making mankind on a Sunday (the last day of the week)!"

David gave me a look and we then went off to have some fun.

* * *

One of the counselors at camp was a girl probably four or five years older than me named Renee. I had a crush on her, and would always try to make sure I was signed up for whatever activity she was heading.

One of the activities was sailing. We learned to sail in canoes that had small sails, and after a few classes we were to have a race. There were teams of two, as one person would man the sail and the other the rudder. Somehow I got Renee for my partner. It was a close race that we only won by hugging the buoy while making the turn at the midpoint. Renee hugged me and I was on cloud nine.

The next day I found out Renee had to leave camp for some family thing, and I never saw her again.

* * *

Years later, while Christmas shopping, I saw a wrapping table set up by the Mothers of B'nai B'rith in the mall. For years I would always go to that table, tell them my story of Camp Hawthorne, and have them wrap my gifts. They were excellent at wrapping Christmas gifts—it always brought a tear to my eye—and I always tipped then nicely. In retrospect I've always thought it rather strange, a Christmaswrapping table run by a Jewish organization.

* * *

I figured I needed to start making some money. It was 1964, I think; it was the last year the old Sportsman's Park was open. That is where the St. Louis Cardinals used to play ball.

Mom got my friend Gary and me jobs selling concessions at the games for a company called Sports Service. It was a good job, as I got to watch the game while hawking my Cracker Jacks.

We would get to the stadium, put on our little aprons, and get our goods. It worked like this: we paid a reduced price for a tray of whatever we sold, and then would sell it for the regular price. We got to keep the difference, plus the tips we got. We'd then go back and purchase more to sell.

But they hired about 50 more kids, vagrants, and the like than they needed to be concessionaires. That way they didn't have to worry about having enough bodies to fill their needs if someone didn't feel like coming in to work on a given day. So in order to work, we had to get in line. The front of the line worked; some at the back did not.

Now, Sportsman's Park was in a very bad part of town. Gary and I were white, and most of the other concessionaires were colored. Well one night we were at the front of the line waiting to get in. I noticed a little ruckus at the rear of the line. I saw a couple of young thugs wrapping leather belts around their fists. Back then, that was a common weapon.

I tapped Gary on the shoulder and said maybe we wouldn't work that night. Gary said, "Monk, we are at the head of the line. We are going to work."

I reassessed the situation but came to the same conclusion. "Gary, I'm pretty sure we are not going to work tonight."

"What are you talking about?"

I pointed toward the back of the line and Gary just shrugged it off.

"Gary, let me put it this way: I'm not working tonight. I will meet you across the street at the YMCA building." Gary said that was fine, but he was going to work.

As I left the line there was a bunch of hootin' and hollerin'; the natives were on the move. I saw them converging on Gary.

By then I was at the front of the stadium and saw a huge colored policeman directing traffic. I ran out into the street and yelled, "My buddy is getting mugged!"

Well, that cop ran around the corner with his nightstick and started flailing at the perpetrators. Gary made his way out of the mayhem and, to my surprise, only had a few scratches. I repeated, "I don't think we are going to work tonight!"

We crossed the street to the YMCA and waited for Mom to pick us up. Like I said, this was a bad neighborhood. Some white guy came up to me in the YMCA and somehow ripped me off for a dollar I had in my pocket. It was strange, as I knew he was no good, but somehow he enticed me into giving him that dollar.

That night served as a lesson that everyone should learn: desperate people do what they need to to get by, even if it is at your expense. Is it wrong? Hell yes! From the perspective of the young guys at the end of the line and the white vagrant, it may have been necessary for their survival; who knows? But the strong will survive. Use your wits if you are not the strongest; sometimes brains prevail and a lot of time luck is the deciding factor.

* * *

My sixteenth birthday was approaching and I knew I wanted a car. First, though, I needed money.

I decided to go up to Tetley's (a Sinclair gas station) to get a job. Tetley was the owner's last name, and he used to do all the work on Mom's car. She had a deal with him: her car always had used tires, and if she had a flat, she would leave the car at Tetley's lot and walk home. The next morning it would be waiting with a fresh used tire and off to work she would go.

You hardly ever see a Sinclair gas station anymore, but they used to be everywhere—you know, "Drive with care and buy Sinclair."

There were so many slogans like that back then: "See the USA in your Chevrolet", "Brill Cream a little dab will do you / Brill Cream the girls will all pursue you", "You'll wonder where the yellow went when you brush your teeth with Pepsodent". They all pretty much sounded the same. To this day I still use Pepsodent, but it is sometimes hard to find now. Everyone likes that damn gel crap.

Anyway, I went in and asked Mr. Tetley for a job. He asked if I knew how to work on cars and I told him no. He wrote a little note, handed it to me, and told me to go across the street to Bob's Standard station. I was to give Bob the note, as he was hiring.

Well, I handed Bob the note and he showed it to the other mechanics; they all started laughing. I then found out the note said, "Looking for a job, IQ of a piss ant." Needless to say, I wasn't hired.

❊ ❊ ❊

My friend Mike Tinson worked at Heidelberg Inn, a family restaurant. Mike was the fry guy; he cooked the fried chicken and wiener schnitzel. He got me a job as a dishwasher.

The owner of the restaurant was a little old lady from Germany that everyone called Mom. She ran the open flame grill and cooked all the steaks and chops. I can still see her in her cotton dress that looked like a nightgown, flames and smoke billowing as she flipped the meat. She always wore old white tennis shoes, never tied; I don't know if they even had shoestrings in them.

She told me, "I pay you $1.25 per hour but you only get $1 per hour on your check. The 25 cents is for your taxes. I take care of your taxes, you don't need to worry."

I never worried but I doubt she paid my taxes.

Heidelberg Inn was a real zoo. There were a number of characters working there. There was Ada, an older woman with huge knockers, as Mike described them. Mike was a cook, so when the waitresses came in, they would take the orders to him. Mike told me if he stood just in the right spot while Ada was going over the order with him, she would rub those knockers on him. I watched as he positioned himself. Yep, she rubbed them all over him. I don't really think it would have mattered where Mike stood; I think Ada just liked getting him all worked up.

Then there was Martha. She was as old as Mom and was the salad girl. Meanest woman I ever knew. She had fire in her eyes and a sharp tongue. I pretty much kept my distance from her.

Steve was scary; he helped get things ready prior to opening and also worked at the crazy house a couple of miles away. I pretty much stayed clear of Steve too.

Then there was Ritchie, a big bully who thought I would be his newest target. I was down in the cellar salting and peppering the raw chicken. Ritchie came down and started giving me trouble. He was very imposing, and I was a little afraid of what he was going to do.

Well, I started chucking thighs at him as hard as I could. He was holding up his hands to guard his face, as the thighs were coming fast and hard. He backed up the stairs and went back to the kitchen.

I gathered up the thighs; they had dirt all over them but it looked like pepper so I just brought them to the breading station. (To this day I kind of wonder about restaurants and what goes on with the food preparation.)

I went back up to the kitchen and Ritchie was mad. He was on one side of the cutting table and I was on the other. He reached across to grab me.

Well, they don't call it the cutting table for nothing; there was a selection of knives on it. I grabbed the longest, sharpest one and put it to Ritchie's neck. I told him I would stick him like the hog he was.

Steve grabbed me from behind and took the knife away from me. He then just walked outside to go to his job at the crazy house. Ritchie never bothered me again.

✳ ✳ ✳

I turned sixteen and got my first car. Murill was back in Mom's life, and the car was Murill's son's old car. It was a 1958 Chevy convertible 348, with a three-speed on the floor and a Hurst Mystery Shifter.

I was at work washing dishes when Mike came running into the kitchen and said, "It's hailing its ass off."

I thought about my car and the convertible top, which was down. Out I went to put the top up, figuring I would also park it under a large tree for shelter. As I started the car I looked to the gas station next door. They had U-Haul trailers. I saw two of the trailers lift off the ground and start a slow spin. I watched them go up about 20 feet and then drop to the ground across the street.

Later in life I was in another convertible (my 1966 Mustang) with some buddies and another tornado went over. Everything went black, mud and rain were squeezing in the sides of the top, and we were rocking back and forth. When it was all over there were many overturned vehicles but we were fine.

✳ ✳ ✳

After Heidelberg, I went to work at the airport for a company that serviced and loaded food for the different airlines. In fact, it was Sports Service, the same company that had managed the concessions at the ballpark.

Back in the day, passengers on airplanes would actually get full meals, plus chips and cookies. I mean they would serve steak dinners cooked to your specification, chicken entrees, potatoes, vegetables, salads, the whole works. People ordered their meals when purchasing their tickets.

I started out working in the storeroom from after school till about midnight. It was a good job, not much to do. I was actually the assistant to Dave, who ran the storeroom on the night shift. Dave was an assistant schoolteacher and was also still taking college classes.

Dave and I had a deal: I would help him grade papers late in the shift, and he would cover for me from 4 pm till I got back. You see, there was always a sandlot football game after school. I would drive to the airport, clock in, then race back to the game. (I think I was the only professional, paid sandlot football player!) I then had to get back to the airport to grade papers.

✳ ✳ ✳

Now, other than Dave and Gary (a different Gary, not my friend), I was about the only white boy working there. I never had any run-ins, but I was occasionally called a "cracker". I didn't know what "cracker" meant, but when everyone started laughing so did I. We had a good time.

I met many characters working that job. A big colored young man named Johnny was always nice to me. I would have never thought he was anything but nice.

Gary, though, didn't get along too well with him. Gary had apparently had sex with one of the colored girls in the parking lot. One day in the employee break room, Gary and Johnny got into it over that girl. Man, in the flash of light Johnny drew out a pretty big knife, thumbed it open like it was a switchblade, and had it on Gary's throat.

I grabbed Johnny—who could have brushed me aside like a flea—and said, "Johnny, don't, you'll go to jail!" He looked at me, then let Gary go.

✳ ✳ ✳

Well, someone got on to my sandlot game scheme, and it was decided that Dave did not need any help in the storeroom. I was promoted to servicing the planes.

We had this big box truck with a ramp over the cab that we would pull up to the plane. The storage part of the truck rose to the height of the kitchen access door of the plane. We would climb up a ladder on the side of the truck, walk out the ramp, and bingo: there was always a beautiful, young stewardess who opened the galley door of the plane for us.

Things were a lot more casual back then. I bet you would have to have an armed guard and a security check to get in the galley door of a plane these days.

I usually worked with either Willy or Eddie. They were twins and about 60 years old. They liked to smoke and drink.

Along with the food, we also loaded these little blue fiberglass suitcases onto the plane. They were filled with tiny bottles of booze to sell to the passengers. They had every type of booze you could imagine—whiskey, Scotch, gin, vodka—in all the brand names.

The accounting system was pretty much nonexistent, and Willy and Eddie always filled their pockets with the little bottles from the partially emptied cases. We would take the cases back to our building to be replenished. I figured if Willy and Eddie got all they wanted, that I should join in the harvest. After we got back I would get some of the partially empty cases and make one full case.

Now, I was a senior at high school, and seniors were allowed to drive their cars to school. There was a church right across from the school and that is where I parked. Every Friday morning was payday for me. I would open my trunk and be surrounded by kids with money wanting to purchase my little bottles. I was quite the guy on campus.

This went on for a couple of months, till someone told me I was going to get busted the next day. I knew I could get in big trouble so that night I drove out to the St. Charles Bridge and threw my case of goods in the Missouri River. My bootlegging days were over.

❊ ❊ ❊

While parked in front of our house, my mom's car got sideswiped by yet another a young guy named Gary. Gary had no insurance, and his family was connected to some underworld characters and was not about to give up any money. Gary probably didn't have any money either, as he too was from a broken home, but my mom did not know this. She contacted his mother to inform her of the situation.

Well, Gary's brother Jim was an enforcer for one of the powerful unions in St. Louis. Jim and a guy named Bonnie (from another racketeering family) came to our house and knocked on the door. I think they were just trying to scare Mom into letting her insurance pay for the damage and getting off Gary's back.

I was sitting in my room and heard arguing. I recognized one of the voices as my mom's. I looked out my bedroom window and saw these two thugs giving Mom a hard time.

Dad had left his 12 gauge shotgun when he abandoned us, and I went to Mom's closet and grabbed it.

"Get the hell out of here or I'll blow both of your heads off!" I pumped the action to chamber a shell and said, "Leave, now!"

There weren't even any shells in the gun, but I put on a pretty good performance and they skedaddled. Actually, I'm pretty sure they'd already been leaving when I arrived, as Mom never backed down from anything.

I was driving with the top down in my Mustang convertible one evening a few weeks later when another convertible pulled up next to me. It was Jim the enforcer, and he was yelling and waving his hand for me to pull over. I knew I didn't have a chance going toe to toe with him, but I pulled over and got out of my car.

I was leaning on the door when Jim came up, and he looked mad. He looked at me and saw that I was just a kid compared to him and said, "Kid, you've got some balls." He shook his head and then turned and left.

I didn't see him again till I got out of the Army. We actually become friends later in life, even though he is ten years older than me. My mother did not approve of it, but she rarely if ever tried to pick my friends.

※ ※ ※

I took what I thought would be pretty easy classes my senior year of high school, and typing was one. I was sitting in class the first day of school, and Mrs. Arb walked in.

"Young man, what are you doing in my class?"

I told her, "I'm here to learn to type."

"Well, I don't teach boys how to type; you will be disruptive to my class."

What could I say? I told Mom about what happened and she must have gone up to the school first thing in the morning and given them a good talking to, because at the end of the day, Mrs. Arb walked up to me and said, "As soon as you learn to type you are out of my class."

By the end of the first semester I could type 40 words per minute. I was kicked out of typing, which gave me a free period the rest of the year.

I never typed again for many years, but to this day I can type 40 words per minute. The computer age came and my typing skills were a blessing.

❊ ❊ ❊

I turned eighteen the January before I graduated high school. It was 1968, and my biology teacher mentioned that once we were eighteen years old, the boys had to register for the draft.

This involved going down to the Mart Building in St. Louis and getting classified. If you were ripe for the picking and in good health, you were classified 1A.

Well, about 200 of us guys were down there that day, and the first thing they told us was to strip down to nothing. We obeyed. They then said to squat down and walk like ducks. We obeyed. Next we lined up facing each other, still naked as jaybirds. We waited patiently while someone—I assume he was a doctor— came down the line. He checked our insteps to make sure we were not flat-footed and then grabbed our balls and rolled them around in his hand.

That was it. I was classified 1A and eligible for the draft.

❊ ❊ ❊

I wasn't a troublemaker, but I did occasionally get in trouble. Working 30 hours a week and going to school was not easy. I was late occasionally and missed a day here and there. One day I was called into the office after a few unexcused absences and was told to sit in a room till someone could talk to me.

A guy named Rosco, who was always in trouble, was in the room too. Rosco was a riot and an ingenious prankster.

He had found a receptacle for the phone in the room next to where he was sitting.

Now, in those days, there were many tricks you could do with the phone lines. For instance, there was a number you could dial on your own phone that would make it ring when you hung up.

My brother Johnny and I would both always want to sit shotgun (in the front passenger seat) when riding with Mom. After years of Johnny's and my arguing, Mom decided that whoever announced "I've got shotgun today" would get to ride shotgun the whole day. So that was the first thing we would do each morning when we woke up. Johnny would sometimes be standing by my room or me by his to see if the other was awake. I would always play like I was asleep, trying to get the jump on him. If he was asleep, I would dial that number and hang up the phone. I would let it ring till it woke up Johnny and then yell, "I've got shotgun all day today!"

Anyway, Rosco had figured out how to cross the wires in the phone box in the office, and I'll be damned if it didn't make the office phone ring. Man, did we have fun; the phone would ring and the girls in the office would answer, but there would be no one on the line. We could observe all of the action, as the door to our room was open. This went on for about 40 minutes and we would laugh every time.

Finally, one of the women came in and asked us what we were up to. "Us? We aren't doing nothing."

I finally got called into the office, and for not coming to school, I was told I could not come to school for three days. I don't know why, but the next day I went to school. I got called into the office and they asked what I was doing there. I said I'd just felt like coming to school.

❋ ❋ ❋

Riverview Gardens was just like any other high school; there were bullies and instigators.

One day, I was standing in the pit (an area we'd gather in before school started in the morning). There was always a lot of action in the pit. Finn was both an instigator and a bit of a bully. He got this girl to come up to me and slap me. I was caught completely off guard and instinctively slapped her back.

Finn then had Harley Thurwacker—a tall, lanky goon, not too bright, and who was afraid of Finn—come over and sucker-punch me in the face. Now, Harley should have knocked me out, but I just took a step back and shook my head. Harley left and I went to the bathroom to check out the damage. To my surprise, although he'd rocked my head, there was no visible damage.

We were all at a party a month later, and Finn and a couple of his goons surrounded me and told me I was to go across the room and punch Seth Redonovich. Seth was our quarterback, and I guess some of the guys felt he was not tough enough for the job.

I told Finn no.

"Okay, Monk, I guess I will just have my guys take you outside and kick your ass."

I was not friends with Seth, but he was the quarterback and a stud, so I figured the worst that could happen was he kicked my ass instead of the goons. I went over and instead of sucker-punching him I told him what the deal was, and that we had to fight. I then made sure I got the first punch in. I was holding my own when the parents whose house we were at came downstairs and broke us up.

Finn was an asshole. He was, however a great athlete. He was later drafted by the Cardinals as a catcher, but during a drinking binge soon after that, he got in a car crash, lost his legs, and was confined to a wheelchair. I heard later in life that he still tried starting shit even after losing his legs. Once an asshole, always an asshole, I guess. Still, that was a terrible thing to happen to anyone.

Finn was not the only bully, but back then one learned to handle the situation without the legal ramifications of bullying today.

This reminds me of a time when I was close to ten and Dad was still living with us. A guy named Tim Donovan used to pick on other kids. After my Boy Scout meeting one night, I was walking home when Tim approached me. He was doing a pretty good job of intimidating my friends and me when I noticed that my dad had just pulled up to give us a ride home.

Upon seeing Dad, I turned and punched Tim in the mouth, drawing blood. My friends and I headed for the car and jumped in.

Tim came to the window and said to Dad, "Look at what your son did to me."

"It looks like he did a pretty good job," my dad responded. Dad put the car in gear and drove off. I guess that was about the last thing I did to impress my dad before he left us.

Good Times

Frankie was—and remains to this day—a very good friend. He is Italian and good-looking; the girls have always loved him. When we were younger, every time I got a girlfriend, Frankie would end up with her. That was okay, as I could move on to the next.

At one point, I started taking out Peggy. I will always remember our first date. I had a '59 Plymouth piece of crap for a car. The front passenger seat was broken and I had to put a wooden wedge at the bottom of the seat to keep the back in an upright position. Every now and then, the wedge would slip out and the seat would fall back flat. (This was very convenient for making out.)

On our first date, Peggy's mom walked out with us to the car and Peggy and I got in. Peggy's mom was waving goodbye as I hit the gas. The wedge slipped out, and Peggy ended up flat on her back with her legs in the air and showing all. I didn't stop; Peggy gave me a look like "What the heck?"… I told her it just did that sometimes.

Well, Frankie stole Peggy from me, and I found Connie Z. Connie Z was, unlike me, very, very knowledgeable in the sexual area of life.

One night, Frankie, Peggy, Connie, and I went on a double date to the drive-in picture show. The drive-ins were basically places to park and make out. So Connie and I were putting on our own show, and Peggy got embarrassed or jealous (I don't know and don't care), as Connie was educating me quite well.

My mom met Connie and thought she was the perfect girl for me. Little did she know that this was one sexually active young lady. We were at my house and Connie wanted to go to my room for a little action.

"Hey, Monk, where are you two going?"

"Mom, we are just going to my room to talk."

We closed the door and were getting it on within five minutes. Mom and Sis knocked on the door and asked if everything was okay. I assured them it was, and in a few minutes Connie and I regained our composure and came out. Connie was a great actress. Mom still doesn't know I got some right under her nose (or at least that is what I will always assume—I will never know for sure!).

Connie and I had a great romance for a few months. Then she told me we should get married. There was no way I was getting married, so we stopped going out.

Later in life, after I got out of the service and had my own apartment, I got a phone call. It was Connie.

"Hi, Monk. I am married and living in a nice home very near to where you live. My husband is an airline pilot; he is in the air as we speak. You should come over, as I want to see you."

I thought about it and told her I would stop by. It all seemed rather covert and wrong, but I was in an adventurous mood. I knocked on the door and looked in her eyes when she answered. They were welcoming, and they brought back memories of our past romance. We went into her living room and talked for a bit, then embraced.

About this time I heard a baby cry in the next room.

"Yes, Monk, I have a baby and I am lonely much of the time," Connie said.

I got to thinking I'd better stop right then, as this was wrong. Connie sensed my feelings and we kissed goodbye for the last time. I never saw her again, but a couple of my buddies that went to a class reunion a few years later told me Connie was hot, divorced, and looking for me!

❉ ❉ ❉

The beginning of my senior year was when I met Bill. I forgot my gym shorts and the PE teacher instructed me to go sit in the bleachers till class was over. Bill got in trouble a bit more than most, and Coach had also sent him to the bleachers. We hit it off and were talking and having a good time.

Well, the PE teacher didn't like Bill and it looked like I did, so he decided he didn't like me either. Bill and I got kicked out of school for two days! For what, I had no idea. All I knew is I had two free days and that was just fine with me.

Bill and I went on to be best friends. "Beer" is what I called him later in life, and his wife Susan gave me the nickname of Michael, Michael, Motorcycle (Michael is my real name).

❉ ❉ ❉

It was time to graduate, and some of the boys and I decided to have some fun. We went up to the school campus. Riverview Gardens High was a brand new campus and was laid out like a college. Buildings were spread out, with large grassy areas between them.

Raymond, John, Frank, Ron, Jim, and I decided we should soap the school windows and TP some of the bushes for a senior prank.

Well, Raymond and Jim thought we should go a little bit further. They broke open a door and went to Mr. Sullivan's office. He was the assistant principal that no one liked. Raymond peed on Mr. Sullivan's desk while Jim ransacked the place.

Someone yelled, "Cops!" and we all skedaddled outside. Ron and I ended up together. I also had a dark green blanket (courtesy of some airline), which I was carrying because there had been a bonfire on the football field.

Well, the police had their spotlights on and were driving all over the grass between the buildings trying to catch us. I knew they were going to see us. I said to Ron, "Let's lie down and cover ourselves with my green blanket; maybe they won't see us!"

It worked, though I don't know how we avoided getting run over, as the cop cars came close many times.

The rest of the guys and a few innocent kids all ran to the broadcast tower on the football field and hid there. They got caught. All the students in that tower missed walking up to get their diplomas at graduation. They did graduate, but they had to sit in the audience at the ceremony.

※ ※ ※

We had such good times in high school. There was a club for teens called the Underground (or something like that). It was in the basement of a supermarket, and probably every city in the country had a club by that name.

Drugs were just creeping into St. Louis. My friends and I were not into them, but I remember certain things that, looking back, affirm that they were there.

Steve the Giant, I remember, was into music. Two albums I noticed in his room were definitely druggie music. Janis Joplin's group Big Brother and the Holding Company was one album, and the other was Ginger Baker's Air Force. The cover had some strange picture of an airplane with a face and tongue sticking out its mouth. Later in life I enjoyed Janis Joplin.

I also had an acquaintance who cut hair in his basement. (I heard he later became a barber and also cut hair when he was in the Army.) His parents were divorced and I guess he made spending money that way. He gave what was called a sculpture or razor cut. It was a popular cut prior to the hippie look that came into style a few years later. He used a straight razor, which kind of made your hair look liked it was sculptured.

I was one of the few kids in the class that had a sculpture cut. I would knock on this guy's door and we would go down in his basement for the cut. It was a weird basement; he had a blacklight with all kinds of fluorescent painted objects hanging from strings and such. He asked what I thought of it all. I had never seen a blacklight and just said, "Yeah, that's cool."

❊ ❊ ❊

One night a few of my friends and I were leaving the Underground after having seen some crazy band perform. It was real cool for the band members to smash their guitars at the end of the performance back then, and they hadn't let us down that time.

We hopped in my car, a 1960 Chevy, and down the road we drove. A car full of older guys pulled up next to us and wanted to fight us. I had this little wooden bat in the back seat, and Raymond grabbed it and leaned out the window, swinging away. Cars were really built back then; they could take a lot of punishment.

I decided to swerve into the side of the other guys' car while Raymond was putting little baseball bat dings in their car. We were yelling and screaming and no one could believe I'd crashed into the side of the other car.

The older guys decided they'd had enough and sped away; the car probably belonged to one of their dads. We, however, were in my own car, so I could do what I wanted as I had paid for it. But when we stopped to check out my car, there was virtually no damage.

Another night, same thing: a car full of older guys started following us and wanted us to pull over to fight. Well, a guy we called Clappy was passed out in my back seat. He came to and asked what was going on.

"Clappy, those guys behind us want a piece of our butts," I replied.

I don't remember why, but I had a ball-peen hammer on the floor of the back seat. Clappy picked it up and turned around, the other guys' headlights glaring in his face.

"You want something? Here, take this!" Clappy put that hammer right in the middle of their windshield. They swerved and come to a stop.

We laughed; life was good! Cars were everything back then; life revolved around them. Drive-in theaters, drive-in restaurants, drag racing on Hall Street, muscle cars,…

* * *

Steak 'n Shake drive-ins were the big hang-out places for almost everyone. Back then, they had both inside dining and curb service. A guy dressed all in white with a white paper hat would come to your car, take your order, and bring back your food on a tray. The tray would hang right from your window if you rolled it down.

Our Steak 'n Shake was located on a large circle intersection. It was the only intersection of its kind back then; they are referred to as roundabouts now. This intersection was at the end of Riverview Drive and intersected at the circle with four other major streets. "Circle Steak" is what we called our Steak 'n Shake.

Many a fight broke out at Steak 'n Shake. We were sitting there one night, eating our steakburgers and drinking our shakes. A '55 Chevy convertible was making the rounds. (That was all part of the glamour, driving through to see and be seen; and kids from all over St. Louis would come to Circle Steak, as not only could you cruise the lot, but we also had the circle.)

So this '55 Chevy convertible came cruising through with the top up, and all of a sudden some maniac jumped through the back plastic window and started choking the driver from behind. The Chevy ran into parked cars and food trays were flying, kids were jumping out of their cars—it was a glorious sight. You couldn't pay money and be more entertained.

✳ ✳ ✳

Hall Street was just down Riverview Drive. It was lined with trucking terminals and light industry. Being close to the river, it was a flat four-lane road with a pretty hard gravel median, and about two miles in length. It was a wild street. Any weekend from 11 pm to 3 am there would be 500 cars and 2000 kids drag racing. The cops would come to one end and start giving tickets; everyone would then go to the other end and start racing again.

There would be a flagman or girls flagging the cars that were to race. Down the flag would go; burning rubber, smoke, and a few fishtails that almost hit the flagman brought a huge adrenaline rush.

It got so popular that older guys would on occasion trailer their dragsters to Hall Street, unload them, and race!

Three o'clock in the morning, tires burning, smoke billowing from them, tractor trailers laying on their horns trying to exit their terminals, kids and cops everywhere… man, what a sight.

✳ ✳ ✳

At the end of Hall Street there was a granary where grain would be loaded on barges to be shipped down the Mississippi. This was a large operation that occupied a lot of land.

There were piles of rotting grain everywhere and there were rats all over—big rats, hundreds of them! It was eerie, as when you got out of your car you would be overwhelmed by the sound of squeaking.

We would then go rat stompin'. That is what we called it. We would take baseball bats or flashlights to hit them with—some guys would even wear boots called brogans and just stomp the rats. At the end of the night, a few guys would gather up their rats and tie them to the bumpers of their cars to show them off at Circle Steak.

* * *

One night while we were parked watching the drag racing action, a carload of girls pulled up next to us. The driver was a beautiful blonde and she struck up a conversation with me. I got out of my car and kneeled down by her driver's door to talk. About this time the cops came, and I had to get back in my car and leave, but not before she gave me her phone number and told me to call.

The next day I called her and we made plans to go out. I got to her house and knocked on the door.

Now, I had only talked with this girl for maybe ten minutes, and she had never gotten out of her car. The front door of her home was partially glass and I could see someone walking to the door to answer it. It looked kind of like her, but she was maybe five feet tall and probably 170 pounds. Her face was familiar so I thought it must be her sister.

She opened the door and said hello. I said hi, and told her I was there to see her sister.

"I don't have a sister," she said.

"Oh, I must have the wrong house." And I just turned around, without looking back, and left. What a rotten thing to do, but I was caught off guard and that is what I did.

Many years later I recounted the story and the guys at work were rolling on the ground laughing. For some time, whenever we would be taking lunch and see a short stubby blonde, a guy named Brian would turn to me and say, "Where's your sister?" We would all laugh, but I still think I was wrong to do that to her. I was just young and caught off guard.

* * *

Another night after racing, Bill Graff was driving a few of us around. Bill had a pretty fast GTO and we were making the rounds at Steak 'n Shake. I was sitting in back with a girl named Pam and someone else. Bill and his girlfriend Sharon were in front.

Suddenly, Sharon yelled, "Bill, slow down!"

Too late. We were headed for a light post, and there wasn't time to do anything but duck. When everything came to a stop my head was between Pam's bosom, and a nice bosom she had too.

Bill was the only one hurt. He'd had two teeth knocked out of his mouth. We actually found them and they were still in one piece. A dentist was able to put them back in his mouth and I think he still has them to this day.

* * *

I always had money, as I always had a job. It was nothing for me to have $100 or more in my wallet while in high school. In the late '60s, a hundred dollars was a lot of money for a high school guy.

I often participated in poker night; Rod, who was a stud in high school, always held it at his home. He had a great dad who made sure we didn't drink while playing so no one would get taken advantage of.

A couple of football studs and a few of us non-studs would gather at Rod's dining room table. It was a pretty professional affair and was always very organized. We played 5 card stud, 7 card stud, 5 card draw, and some more interesting games too.

In-between was a good game and we would play it for guts. Everyone would get two cards face up. We would ante sometimes as much as $5 apiece, which meant there would be 30 bucks in the pot to start. This was 1967-'68, and $30 was a lot for a high school kid to wager.

You could bet however much of the pot you wanted to that the next card you were dealt would fall between the cards you had on the table. If you won, you took that amount out of the pot; if you lost you put that much in the pot. You could go guts; that was when you would bet the whole pot. If you won, the whole pot was yours, but if you lost, you would have to put double the amount of the pot in. Thus it took guts to go the pot.

If you were dealt an ace on your first card you would have to declare if it was high (an ace) or low (a one). If you had a king and an ace that you declared a one, there could at best be only six cards in the deck that could make you lose, since your next card had to fall in between those two cards. If the card dealt was not in between or if it was the same as either card you had showing, you lost. I saw many a one/king and ace/two get beat.

The pot could grow to be quite large, and you could only go for the whole pot if you had the money to back it.

We would also occasionally lighten it up and play Indian. That was where everyone would get a card face down. We would all pick up our cards at the same time, without looking, and put them to our foreheads for the others to see. We would then decide whether we were in or out by the cards the others were showing, while still not knowing what our own card was. If we stayed and lost (you guessed it) we matched the pot. The highest card of whoever stayed in would win.

I learned a lot about life and people at those games and will always remember those nights.

✻ ✻ ✻

After graduating, Rod took a job at the brewery where his dad had been employed for 30 years. During his first week on the job, he somehow got his arm entangled in a conveyor system and lost the use of that arm completely. It was tragic, as Rod was a real he-man. I don't think his dad ever got over it.

Rod is still quite the athlete, though. He learned to play golf with one arm by constantly tweaking his swing till he could hit it straight. He then learned to hit for power and distance. I am only a marginal golfer at best and he beats me every outing.

Even now, Rod would still be a formidable foe. I doubt if I could take him in a fight.

At a recent guys' football and cards night, Rod told me he had just decided to live with the arm as it was, basically just hanging there uselessly, and to make the most out of life. I admire him for that.

More Work

"If no one can, Zycan!"

That was the slogan painted on my trash truck. I worked for Zycan Brothers Trash in the summer of 1967. It was a good-paying job—I made $9 an hour. Back then, if you wanted to work hard, you could actually get paid well as a teenager. The way the world is today you are lucky if you can even find a job.

I had a route to drive each day and I would stop at each house, get out, go to the other side of the truck, pick up each can, hoist it over my head, and dump it in the opening on the side of the truck; then I'd go back around and get back in the truck and drive to the next house. Just getting in and out of the truck 500 times a day was hard work.

I will never forget this one house. It always had cans that weighed 50 pounds when empty. There were three of them one day and they were all filled with wet grass; they had to weigh 200 pounds each. I gave it my best effort but couldn't get any of them over my head, so I got back in the truck and started to leave.

"Hey! Where in the hell do you think you're going? You haven't emptied my cans!" This burly, blonde Amazon lady was looking at me and she clearly wasn't happy.

I told her I had tried to empty them but that I wasn't strong enough. "Why do you have such heavy cans?" I asked.

"So you trash guys can't destroy them," she said. "I'll show you how to pick them up."

I'll be damned, she hoisted them right over her head and emptied them. I was glad I wasn't married to her; ouch!

✳ ✳ ✳

A lot of drivers had helpers that would ride on the side of the truck, holding on to a rail, as the truck went from house to house. That way the driver would not have to jump out of the truck at each house. The helper did not get paid as much and was usually a drunk.

I was forever getting my route finished before some guys with helpers, and damn if the supervisor didn't occasionally drive out to the end of my route to inform me I had to go help others finish theirs. I received no extra pay for this.

I got a little fed up one day and told the supervisor that if I was going to get shafted like that I should at least have a helper.

The next morning I got my helper—if you could even call him that! I don't know who he must have known to be able to land a job, but he must have been a drunken relative that Mr. Zycan didn't want to have to feed. This guy reeked of B.O., was filthy, smoked, and had no teeth.

Now, I always carried water to drink during the day. That particular day, it was hot and the humidity was stifling. By 10 am I was just about to take my first drink. Mr. Toothless B.O. jumped in the truck, grabbed my jug of water, and took a big slobbery swig. He wiped his mouth with his stinkin' shirt sleeve and offered me a drink. I declined and never touched that jug again.

The next morning I slept in until the phone rang. I picked it up and my supervisor started yelling, "Get your ass to work!" I hung up.

He called back and said I would be fired. I told him, "You can't fire me because I quit!"

I still have a nice toolbox that someone put out for trash and that I took home. That was 45 years ago! I wonder if it is worth anything, as it looked to be an antique even back when I took it.

＊ ＊ ＊

My friend Butch and I decided to take a trip to Florida after graduating. We took my 1966 Mustang convertible that burned oil pretty bad; but this was no problem as we bought a case of oil for the trip. We didn't have much money, and I came up with the idea of staying at my dad's house at least one night.

Now, I hadn't seen my dad but once in those preceding eight years, but I told Butch that I was sure he would let us stay. I had his address from the letter with the $10 he had sent for that sled, but I did not have his phone number; so we just showed up.

We found dear old dad's house—nothing fancy—and knocked on the door. Dad answered the door and asked what we wanted. I said, "I'm your son."

The house was not that big, and I could see into the kitchen from where I was standing at the front door. It was the first and last time I ever saw the redhead. She was sitting at the kitchen table smoking a cig and she didn't look none too happy! Dad looked back at her, then at me, and said, "You aren't my son."

Well Butch was almost in tears but I was too shocked to think much of anything. Dad then said, "Hold on. I'm going to take you to your Uncle Don's house to verify that you are my son."

Uncle Don had been a journeyman ironworker in St. Louis. He was Dad's brother and occasionally helped Mom with looking after us. But work was slow in St. Louis, so Unk had come down to Florida, as there was much work for ironworkers in Florida at that time.

I've used the term "Unk" many times, but Uncle Don was the original Unk! I really never started calling him that, nor had I ever called any of my other uncles that, till years later, after I became an ironworker. All of Don's nephews who became ironworkers, including me, always called him Unk. I kind of like that word, Unk.

We arrived at Uncle Don's home, and Dad said to Don, "This boy says he is my son."

Uncle Don was embarrassed for his brother and confirmed, "Yes, that is your son." After an awkward visit we went back to Dad's house.

There was a small foyer at the front door, about four feet by four feet. That is where Butch and I slept, where we got a beer before going to bed, and where we ate a bowl of Cheerios for breakfast. That was the only room we ever went in. We both peed on the side of the road after leaving Dad's.

I only saw Dad one more time before he died.

Butch and I went on to Ft. Lauderdale and did our best to pick up some chicks on the beach. We weren't too successful but we had a good time trying.

❊ ❊ ❊

I decided to try selling ice cream and Bomb Pops with the Bomb Pop Company. They would provide you a Jeep (no four-wheel drive, though) with a freezer in the back and an annoying bell to ring.

I did this for a couple of weeks but found it very frustrating. That bell was really the pits.

Over the years, on a couple of occasions, I have wondered how life might have played out if I had never driven that Bomb Pop Jeep. I will explain this later.

❊ ❊ ❊

I got a job at Consolidated Freightways, a trucking firm, on Hall Street. My mom's friend Velma's son Lee worked there as a fork truck driver. He was a quiet but imposing guy.

Growing up, I'd only known him as Sonny. But no one at the terminal called him Sonny and I guess that was how he liked it.

My first week on the job I happened to see Sonny in the break room. The place was packed, as it was right before starting time. I yelled out, "Hi, Sonny!" Everyone looked at me and then Sonny. Sonny was not one you wanted to mess with.

He winced, looked down at me, and said, "My name is Lee." So that was what I called him at work from then on. I did see him many years later at Velma's funeral and slipped and called him Sonny. He just grinned and said hello.

The pay on the trucking docks was good, but I had to work the third shift. It was winter, and the docks were cold.

My job was the same as everyone else's; we loaded and unloaded freight onto and off of truck trailers. There was a motorized chain line in the floor of the dock with a pull chain running the whole length and width of the dock. Trailers were backed into slots for either loading or unloading.

If we were unloading, we put freight going to the same city or region on the same dock carts. Each dock cart had a small chalkboard under the push handle, and we would note the destination, put the cart on the pull chain running in the floor, and off it would go.

When that cart got to a trailer that was being loaded for that particular destination, the person working that trailer would pull the cart off the line and load it in the trailer. This went on till the trailer was filled or emptied.

❊ ❊ ❊

I met Tim through this job. Tim was a Golden Gloves boxer, and he was crazy.

Tim and I were both usually running a little late for work. We'd hit Hall Street at the same time many nights and it was always the same: we'd be barreling down Riverview from opposite directions and make the turn onto Hall Street, spinning out, sending gravel flying, jumping curbs, and screaming our lungs out. Tim thought I was crazy; I knew he was crazier by far.

We both ended up in construction later in life. Tim's construction time was short, as everyone in his family was a policeman. So he ultimately became a cop and the bodyguard for the mayor of St. Louis. Later he became a narcotics officer and then joined the special task force.

I still see Tim from time to time, and we actually live about a half mile from each other in a nicer neighborhood than either of us would have ever imagined we'd live in one day. I know he's still crazy, as he has at times seen me in the front yard while driving by and will stop to talk. Just take my word for it; he is the last person you would ever want to tangle with.

A funny thing is that when we worked the docks together I always called him Timmy. Then later in life when we ran into each other at a function, I called him Timmy. Just like with Sonny, he asked (rather than told) me to call him Tim. I have on occasion slipped up and called him Timmy; he's just smiled.

The Army

Vietnam was going strong and my mom didn't want me in the service.

She had a friend named Tina from her early life. Tina was by then married to a U.S. Senator. Well, Mom got Tina to get her husband to talk to someone in the National Guard to make it possible for two of my friends and I to join the Guard. Some strings were pulled and Frankie, Ron, and I got in.

Some guys would have done anything to get in the Guard to keep from going to Vietnam; we didn't even have to try—Mom got us in and she was beaming!

This National Guard thing doesn't work in today's world, as there is no draft and Guard units now get sent overseas to fight. You are just as likely to get shot being a Guardsman as you are a Marine these days. But back then, it was a get-out-of-war card.

The National Guard was a six-year commitment—wow! But if you didn't serve the full six years, you didn't get in any trouble; you just got activated for two years into the regular Army.

* * *

It was 1969 and everyone had long hair and was kind of a hippie. News anchors, cops, teachers, and preachers all had long hair. If you were in the Guard, regulations stated that while at your monthly service periods (a couple of days every month), you had to have short hair.

"Hey, Monk—Ron and I are going to get our short hair wigs, do you want to come with us?"

Yeah, most guys in the Guard (at least the unit I was in) had short hair wigs! Pitiful! I told Frankie no and just cut my hair short.

✳ ✳ ✳

We were getting ready to go on a two-week training camp the Guard did every year, as we had joined just prior to it. After the camp we would eventually go to basic training for a few months, just like any other guy who joined or was drafted into the Army. We would then come home to our unit.

It was time to leave for our two-week camp. We got in the back of our troop carriers (I think they were "deuce and a half"s), and off we went to Fort Leonard Wood. A deuce and a half was like a large box truck with a canvas top and benches on each side.

I guess some of the drivers were smoking grass—it was 1969, after all—and one of the vehicles went off the road and killed two Guard members. It got me thinking, "What have I gotten myself into?"

✳ ✳ ✳

I have a heavy foot and have managed to lose my driver's license three times by getting too many points. The first time was just for 30 days and the second time was for 60 days.

Not too long after our little two-week maneuvers I got another ticket while driving. I was going to lose my license for a year!

That's it, I thought. *I'm going active.*

I told my commander I wasn't coming to any more meetings and asked him to activate me. He did. My mom was heartbroken.

It took a couple of months for the activation process to happen. Then, about two months after I activated, the government decided to have a lottery for the draft.

There are 365 days in a year, so they would pull out one number at a time from 1 through 365. When your birthday was drawn, the lower your number for that date, the more likely you would be drafted. I was already in boot camp when the lottery was conducted, so it didn't matter... but my birthday was picked on the 345th draw. I would have never been drafted!

Supposedly everyone back at home would sit down in front of the TV for the lottery to see what the number was. My buddy Butch wrote me of the results; his number was 358 and he was naturally never drafted.

❋ ❋ ❋

There were hundreds of us in the arrival barracks. Most had long hair, afros, or at least moderately long hair. The first few days, we had a great time getting to know each other. There were card sharks, county boys, city slickers, and blacks. ("Colored" was a word not used very much by that time.) We got to know each other by name and by sight.

It took about three or four days to get everything in order. First there was a general physical and our records were initiated.

Next we went to the dentist—or rather, we went to a bunch of guys who thought they were dentists. The guy working on me said I had five cavities and set to work drilling them out. To this day I wonder if I had cavities or if those bozos were just learning the trade and using us for practice, figuring half of us would be dead in a year or so. Years later, more than one of my dentists would remark on the size of those five fillings are and say I must have had terrible teeth. I never had a toothache in my life! FTA... if you don't know what that stands for, keep reading.

The next day was a real trip; we headed off to get haircuts, or should I say, scalpings. These barbers were worse than the dentists. I have a smooth head, but woe be to the guy with a bump or rise of any type on his head. At least 15% of the guys came out bleeding profusely from the scalping.

We got back to the barracks and all the friends we had made were now strangers. We all looked like eggheads and no one recognized anyone; it was funny.

❊ ❊ ❊

I don't know what the criteria was, but during the first week of boot camp a few of the recruits had the opportunity to go to officer training.

I was offered that chance, but I had heard that a rookie Lieutenant, upon getting a command in Vietmam, was often not very respected. Let's face it, a combat-ready unit isn't about to take orders from some First Lieutenant that knows nothing about war. Also, I'm pretty sure that to be an officer you had to do at least a four-, maybe six-year enlistment. I turned the offer down.

❊ ❊ ❊

I will say one thing for the Army at that time: they definitely made a man out of you. If you went in skinny, they beefed you up. If you went in fat, they slimmed you down. At the end you were a fit, chiseled he-man who could run circles around most any civilian.

There were also some neat weapons we learned to shoot. My favorite was the M79 grenade launcher. It looks like a short, fat single-shot shotgun. You load what looks like a huge bullet; it's a little fatter than a baby bottle. You see your target out in the distance and must judge the angle and trajectory your projectile will travel. The shell is slow enough that you can actually see it travel to the target.

I was shooting at an old tank used for a target and on my first shot I hit it. *Bam! Boom!* A big cloud of smoke! What a neat weapon.

* * *

Basic training was over and most of the guys in my troop were National Guardsmen, as that is what I originally was. Well, they were all going home. My sergeant—a real asshole—made a point to the other guys that I would be in hell's way real soon. I guess he was trying to scare me or something. I had never even given Vietnam a thought when I had activated, nor at any point up to this time. Youth has no fear or realization.

About the time I'd started basic training, it had seemed the politicians wanted us to go into Cambodia. When I was getting out of basic training, they decided they now wanted our troops out of Cambodia. Orders were given for our troops to leave with our tails between our legs—or at least, that is how it looked.

There were many little slogans in the Army at that time. FTA ("Fuck the Army") was one of them. My favorite went something like this: "We the unwilling, led by the unknowing, sent by the uncaring, to do the impossible, for the ungrateful." Politicians and wars haven't changed much.

* * *

The imbecile politicians gave me orders to report to Germany, as with all the troops coming back into Vietnam from Cambodia there was little space or need for new troops over there.

Skinny Frazee was the other guy in our troop that was not a Guardsman. Skinny Frazee was one of the few whom the Army could not beef up too much. He was in excellent shape though, and off to Germany we went.

We were sent to the 3rd Armored 12th Calvary in a little town called Buedegan. It was a neat little town and was probably very old, as it had a small castle with a stone wall. There was also a clear stream running through town that was full of trout. We could guard their country, but were not allowed near the stream, and fishing was definitely not allowed.

The town also had royalty, and a few times a year the prince and princess would ride through town with all their pageantry. Germany was a real vacation, and I am glad I had the privilege of seeing it on Uncle Sam's dollar.

Skinny and I, upon landing in Germany, commenced drinking beer (the national pastime of Germans). Skinny said we also needed to find some stuff called hash (hashish). Well, we found some—it was everywhere, as this was now 1970, and damn near the whole Army was either high, drunk, or both.

We walked around our new home, fucked up and laughing our heads off (I guess that is why it's called dope). Everything was funny and we laughed for days. Skinny went to the PX (post exchange) and bought a battery-operated record player and a Three Dog Night album, which we played till the batteries ran down.

The next day, I was sent to Alpha Company and Skinny was sent to Charlie Company. We did not see much of each other after that, but I know he got into trouble more than once.

Skinny volunteered for a transfer to Vietnam and said I should do the same. I went to my First Sergeant and made the request. He denied me and said to take it up with the CO (commanding officer). The next day I went to see Captain Kotrus. He said he could not send me as I might not make it back.

I looked at his chest and saw his Combat Arms medal, so I knew he had been there. I said, "You made it back." But he still said he wouldn't send me and that I had to ask the base commander.

By this time, Skinny had already been shipped out and there would be no way for us to be together. I decided Germany wasn't so bad and never went to the base commander.

Skinny and I wrote to each other occasionally. A couple of times I mailed him a little hash, and a few times he sent me some Thai Stick (pot from Thailand). We were stupid, as if we had been caught we would probably have been put in the brig and drummed out of the Army. But then, damn near the whole army was smoking either pot or hash in those days.

A few years later Skinny and his girlfriend were in St. Louis and looked me up. They stayed at my place for a couple of days. He had become like, oh I don't know, maybe a person that lived in a commune. He and his girlfriend were very quiet and like docile hippies. We enjoyed our time together, but I never saw Skinny again after that.

❈ ❈ ❈

I ended up working in the mailroom and training room, which was a choice job. I mainly got the position because I knew how to type—thanks, Mrs. Arb

I would make out schedules for the week; no one ever really followed them, but we were required to have them.

Another requirement was that the training room be inspected every so often. I remember one time the NCO (non-commissioned officer) who inspected my training room asked me some questions about what I thought of the Army. I told him it was okay but not what I had expected. I could tell he thought the Army was going to pot. He wasn't far off… .

✳ ✳ ✳

My unit was an armored unit, and I was also a driver for an APC (armored personnel carrier), which is kind of like a small tank that can transport half a dozen troops. Chuck was my APC commander, which means he got to sit on top; I was in the front driving with my shoulders and head sticking out.

APCs have a gas pedal, but to steer it there are two sticks you can pull and push. Each stick controls one of the APC's tracks, so if you pull back the stick on the right it will stop that track and the other track will still be turning, which makes you go the right.

Now, Chuck had been in the Army for fifteen years and was still only a Buck Sergeant. He was from, as he called it, West by God Virginia. Chuck was pretty country and not very well educated, but he wanted to have the fastest APC on base.

Ours was already pretty speedy but I asked the guys in the motor pool about making it faster. I found out there is a plate between the carburetor and manifold that has holes in it to allow fuel to enter; it's called a governor, and it keeps the track (what we usually called our APCs) from going too fast.

We were in Germany with no war anywhere near, so there was no need for our tracks to go all-out. If we removed the plate it would be obvious and we could get in trouble. So Chuck and I decided to drill bigger holes in the plate to allow more fuel to get to the motor. It worked; we had the fastest track on base and just the right guy to drive it—me.

We headed out on maneuvers and our Lieutenant was leading the way in his track. I gunned it and pulled up next to it. He looked down and told his driver the race was on: to the top of a distant hill.

There is no padding and little comfort in a track. We were hitting ravines and bumps and jostling all over. Chuck looked like he was riding a bull in a rodeo as he was thrown from side to side, his head bobbing like one of those little dogs you see in the back windows of cars, but he was in heaven. The Lieutenant's track was pretty fast but we beat his to the top. Chuck was delirious.

* * *

Germany (and Europe in general) doesn't have anywhere near the open space the U.S. does, but it does have some wildlife areas. We were in one of them, in a region bordering the Black Forest. We were heading back down the hill after the race, and I saw the biggest rabbit I've ever seen in my life—I was thinking I must have smoked too much hash the night before. Chuck said that it was some certain type of hare and that they get huge.

We went a little farther and then I stopped the track. Again, I thought I must have been hallucinating, as I was seeing this little tiny deer! It was no baby deer, as it had antlers; but it was about the same size at that hare.

"Yep," Chuck said, "that is as big as that deer will get."

We emerged from the open area and continued back to base on cobblestone roads. All along the way we saw Germans with pads and pens. I asked Chuck, "What's up with them?"

He replied that they would take down our track number and claim we tore up some cobblestones—even if we hadn't hurt any—and charge Uncle Sam. Just another way Americans pay for most everything. I saw a German writing down my track's number as we passed. I gunned the motor, pulled back on the stick, and did a 360-degree turn. Cobblestones flew everywhere, and Chuck was laughing his head off. I figured they would earn their reward that time!

Cobblestone roads are rampant in Europe, as they are extremely durable. I don't know how all Europeans construct and repair them, but I know how they do it in Buedegan.

There is a crew of four rascals, who have wheelbarrows full of cobblestones and sand, and this tool that looks like an elephant's front foot from the knee down. I almost forgot—at the time, they also had a milk carton full of "flippies". Flippies was beer—I don't know if it was a brand name or what, I just know that is what the soldiers called them. They had a porcelain cap with a rubber washer that sealed the top. There was a wire hinge with a thumb bar you would press to open the bottle.

German beer can be pretty potent. I think a Budweiser has 5% alcohol and comes in twelve-ounce cans or bottles; flippies were 17% alcohol and came by the liter. I guess that is why the cap could be opened and then resealed, as you couldn't drink it all at once.

I have seen cobblestones in St. Louis, at the riverfront. They look kind of like bricks but are made of granite (I think). In Germany, the cobblestones are only a three-inch by three-inch square at the top and are about ten inches long or in height, depending on your perspective. They also get smaller at the bottom and come to a point, kind of like an upside-down pyramid but skinnier.

In Buedegan, the base of the streets is sand, and the workers place a few cobblestones into that base, with the pointed end down. They then sprinkle some sand around the stones and take the tool that looks like an elephant's foot, place it over the stones they just put in place, hit a trigger, and *bam*; whatever that tool is, it drives the stones into the ground.

You have to actually witness the process to fully appreciate it. Here is how it actually went: the four rascals would show up with their tools and materials and, let's not forget, the milk carton of flippies. Everyone would grab a flippie and take a drink, then close it back up with the porcelain cap. Next they would get the cobblestones in place and sprinkle the sand. It was then time for another drink. Next the elephant's foot, and *bam*. They would all step back and say "Ja!", lean over, and take another drink. This would go on till the job was finished.

What a job… . That's what I wanna do when I grow up!

✳ ✳ ✳

This was a time of racial strife in the U.S., and the Army was not excluded. For some reason there were many more blacks and Puerto Ricans than whites on our base, so I got a taste of being a minority. Usually I got along just fine but there were a few dicey moments.

I had a part-time job as a bartender after hours at the NCO club, and I had two bosses. I worked with Jim and learned the basics of making drinks and using the cash register. At these training sessions we always counted our cash drawer before starting.

The first day I was on my own, I relieved Jim. I started to count the drawer and Jim said it was not necessary, as he had counted it for me. I told him I thought I should count it, but he said I should just get to work. At the end of the shift I locked my cash box, put in my receipts, and went back to the barracks.

The next night, Jim and the boss called me into the office. The boss said, "Boy, you came up $50 short on your shift." He said that happened sometimes when learning the ropes, but it would be no problem as he would just take it out of my salary.

Jim was sitting to the side and said something that ticked me off. I said to the boss, "I ain't your 'boy', and Jim refused to let me count the drawer when I took over after his shift." I told him he could take the short out of Jim's pay because he was going to pay me. The boss looked over at Jim and I kind of got the feeling that they'd been in cahoots to get this white boy. I got paid and then promptly quit.

Another time, we were on a forced march to keep us in shape, but it was a pretty laid-back affair with little procedure. Everyone was talking during the march, and I said something to the guy next to me. Sergeant Reggie Wilkes, one of the NCOs in charge of the march, ran up to me, put his face to mine, and said, "Boy, you got a problem?"

Now, Reggie had been carrying on during the whole march. I put my face real close to his and said, "I ain't your boy and you's the one with the problem!" He informed me that I would be reported.

We assembled after the march, and Reggie informed Staff Sergeant Clyde Boone of my disrespect. I explained to him that Reggie was full of himself and that I hadn't done anything wrong. Lucky for me, Sergeant Clyde Boone was a redneck; and I wouldn't doubt if his relatives were members of the Ku Klux Klan. He told Reggie he was out of line.

Reggie and I eventually came to respect each other. I ended up buying his stereo when his time was up and he was heading home. Everyone always sold their stuff when it was time to go home.

※ ※ ※

Jimbo, a white guy from the New York City area, hated the Army and couldn't wait to get out. He was not too fond of being in the minority on base, either.

We hung out together from time to time. One day, we were on the way to the mess hall. To get to the mess hall you had to climb this long, steep, narrow staircase. The line wasn't moving; I still wonder if the line was stopped because the mess hall was full or if it was stopped to show some white boys who was boss.

There were five or six white boys at the top of the staircase, and everyone else was black or Puerto Rican. We looked down at the bottom and saw some Puerto Ricans with metal bedposts working their way up the line.

Jimbo, who was pretty white in color to begin with, turned even whiter. He was a big guy and said, "Monk, we are going to have to stand our ground and fight."

The stairs were very narrow, so we knew only one or two of them could get to us at once. They were about three-quarters of the way up the stairs, beating their metal bedposts on the rail.

About this time four MPs (Military Police) and the base Commander busted through the closed door to the mess hall. The Commander demanded to know just what the hell was going on. No one said anything, he mumbled something, and all went back to normal.

I never much cared for MPs, but I sure appreciated seeing them that day.

❊ ❊ ❊

We were in formation and Sergeant Boone asked for a volunteer. One never wanted to volunteer, but he looked at me and gave me something of a high sign; so I conceded.

It seemed the German Army or the equivalent of our National Guard was having a military Olympic-type thing. I got to fly to the event in a helicopter; I hadn't known until then how noisy and rough a ride in a chopper was.

After I got to the venue and signed in, we Americans mingled with the Germans and I couldn't understand a damn thing they were saying. They were doing their best to get us drunk, though, as the competition was starting the next day, and the Germans were mostly middle-aged and somewhat out of shape, as they were not regular Army. We were all young recruits so their plan to get us drunk was a good one. We traded badges and belt buckles and drank a lot of beer.

The next day it was us—the Americans—versus the Germans. I was to compete on the obstacle course and a forced 20-kilometer march. The obstacle course wasn't supposed to start till the afternoon and the march would be the next day.

This 40-year old fat German Army guy told me there was food for us. He suggested this green soup (pea soup or something), which was actually pretty good. I was almost finished with my second bowl when we were informed that the obstacle course would start in ten minutes instead of a couple of hours. The fat old German was smiling from ear to ear.

Well I was about midway through the course and all of a sudden it hit me. I bent over and puked my guts and a bowl and a half of whatever was in that soup out. I managed to finish the course but my time was pitiful.

I was fine for the forced march event the next day, though. It was timed and staggered—everyone started at different times. The course was laid out over fields and through woods and towns. There were markers so the participants would know which way to go.

I got to a point in a little hamlet where all the residents were watching as we came through. The marker indicating which way to go was lying on the ground, so I wasn't sure which direction to take. My Lieutenant had told me at an earlier checkpoint that I had the best time so far.

The residents all had innocent faces and pointed down a road to direct me. I headed that way. About two minutes later, my Lieutenant came by in a Jeep and told me to turn around as I should have gone the other way in town. He handed me a pole with a banner on it and said to get going because I could still win.

I was young and just out of basic training, so I was in good shape. The end was in sight and I'll be damned—right in front of me was the fat old German, carrying his rifle. He must have gotten blisters, as his boots were slung around his neck and he was running through the gravel with only socks on his feet.

Even though he was in front of me, I knew his time was not going to be the best since we had all started the race at different times; but nonetheless, I was not about to let him beat me to the finish line. We were coming down the last 200 or so yards, my banner was flying, the crowd was screaming, and I passed his fat ass. I had the best time in the event, but I'm pretty sure my obstacle course time is what kept us just out of first for the whole Olympics.

Later, Fatty and I had a flippie and talked a lot; I didn't understand a damn thing he was saying but we were happy.

✳ ✳ ✳

There was a club in Frankfort called Crazee Sexies. Sandy—a surfer from California—and I decided we needed to find it and get some. However, Frankfurt is a huge city and we had trouble locating it.

But Sandy did know where there was a pub with private tables in the rear, so we went there. He warned me, "Monk, be careful when we go back. They will try to rip you off if you let them."

We went to separate private tables and a beautiful blonde came to mine. She closed the curtain and unzipped my drawers. I was standing at attention, anxiously awaiting her next move. She informed me she needed a drink; the curtain opened and the head gal told me she only drank cognac and it was $20. I felt that was a little expensive and passed.

Out the blonde went and in came an equally gorgeous redhead. I still wasn't buying it. The redhead left and a brunette emerged, but I was turned off by then and went out to the bar to have a beer while waiting for Sandy. He came out all smiles and sweaty.

As we walked out, Sandy asked, "Didn't you bring any money?"

I said of course I had.

Sandy told me the head gal had told him I'd had no money and that he would have to pay double for each drink. Seems it took about three drinks to finally get what you were paying for (six for Sandy).

I burst out laughing and reminded him of what he had told me—to be careful because they would try and rip you off.

✳ ✳ ✳

We headed off to the bahnhof (railroad station) to go back to base. You could—and still can—go almost anywhere on the train in Germany. (You could also get a cab with some crazy back seats; they were kind of like bicycle seats with a back, and they swiveled. The cabs were all Mercedes Benzes.)

Germany was crazy. The men's bathroom in the train station was a round room with a trough along the bottom of the wall. You just stood facing the wall and did your thing. Meanwhile, a lady would mop up the floor behind you. The toilet paper was unique in that it had what appeared to be small flakes of wood embedded in the paper. At a very nice hotel in Frankfort where we stayed one New Year's Eve, everyone on our floor shared a common bathroom. It is things like that which make Germany very interesting and different.

That New Year's Eve was a wild night; people were throwing these huge firecrackers that sounded like hand grenades going off. We would walk down the street and these hooker-like girls would be sitting in the window sills beckoning us to come in. There was this little nightclub with some strippers out front who seduced us into entering the club. It was actually very entertaining, as they performed a little play. It was a cross between vaudeville and a strip show. All the while and throughout the night, those damn hand grenades were going off. Crazy!

Germany was a real experience. Everything seemed smaller and packed more tightly. Many of the buildings even in large cities seemed medieval. For sure, the smaller towns and hamlets were like a fairy tale.

I saw my first ever two-man-on-one-three-wheel-motorcycle race in Germany. One guy drove the bike while the other leaned; if the track was curving right, he would lean left, and vice versa. They were both inches off the ground while reaching some pretty high speeds. Germans seem to love life.

I marveled at how commercial goods were transported there, with all its narrow cobblestone streets. Apartment and business doors on some streets actually opened just a couple of inches short of the curb. There were large round mirrors mounted on posts at some tight street corners, which allowed drivers to see approaching traffic at these cramped intersections. Many of the large trucks had two or three short jointed trailers, which allowed them to more easily maneuver around the narrow streets. It was all so different.

* * *

You couldn't get by without having to pull guard duty in the Army. You were issued a .45-caliber pistol and one damn bullet, which the commander of the guard detail told you not to fire under any circumstance.

My area to guard was the motor pool, just a bunch of tracks, tanks, and trucks. It was three in the morning and I heard a noise in the back of a line of APCs.

On the base, there was a weird guy—I forget his name—with little blemishes and wart-like things all over his face. I had seen him around a couple of times, and he had few friends. He was rather imposing, large, lanky, and kind of scary like the bizarre character in "The DaVinci Code" or Gollum in "The Lord of the Rings". I will call him Gollum.

So I was guarding the motor pool and kept hearing this rustling. It was dark and I couldn't see a thing, as we were not furnished with flashlights. I pulled my .45 and went to investigate the noise. I saw a shadow and turned; nothing. I looked up to the tops of the tanks and saw someone with a pipe raised over his head. I fired my weapon into the ground and said, "Halt!"

It was Gollum, and he was stealing C-rations to sell to the Rads. (Each vehicle had boxes of C-rations in them; they contained food, candy bars, and cigarettes—yes, the Army furnished troops with cigarettes. And "Rads" was slang the soldiers used when talking about Germans.)

Well, Gollum knew I only had one bullet, and I knew he knew. I also knew the guard commander had probably heard the shot. Gollum said I was lucky he hadn't hit me with the pipe. I told him he was lucky I had fired into the ground and he better get the fuck out of there before someone came.

He left and the whole guardhouse arrived. I explained what had happened and said there was proof that the APCs had been broken into. I felt sorry for Gollum so I told the Commander I hadn't been able to make out who it was because it was dark, and that he had run away after I'd fired my weapon.

I never told anyone the whole truth, and from time to time I'd see Gollum on base. I'm not sure if he made out my face that night and knew that it was me. I guess I'll never know.

❊ ❊ ❊

I had a room to myself in the barracks until Archie Blackman got assigned to our company. Archie, who was from somewhere in southern Missouri, had been a door gunner on a chopper in 'Nam and was in no mood to play Army in Germany.

He decided he would take his frustrations out on me. He was ornery, and if I ever see him again I'm gonna thump him on the head.

He got much pleasure in screwing with me, and I let him for the most part. After all, he had been in 'Nam fighting and risking his life, and all I had done was drink flippies and smoke a little hashish here in Germany.

One day I came back to the room after showering and Archie was drunk as a skunk! He said he was going to show me what combat was like. I just had a towel on and was not really prepared for a tussle, but Archie grabbed me and we started wrestling.

We were creating quite a ruckus but I was in control; remember, Archie was drunk and I was at a disadvantage (I had to be extra concerned with my private parts, as I was naked), so I felt I had to take control immediately. I felt like I was in combat, so Archie was accomplishing that goal.

A bunch of guys burst into the room to see what was going on; I told them everything was okay and not to worry. They looked curiously at me naked and on top of poor ole drunken Archie, and then left.

Well, this was 1971 (I think), and the Army decided that if you were drafted or enlisted for two years you could get discharged after 18 months. I guess the government figured that if you made it through a one-year tour of duty in Vietnam you need not hang around for a few more months. Apparently Archie fell into this category, as he was soon gone.

I thought, *Great—I'm out of here in a month or so!*

But it was not to be; I had been neither drafted nor enlisted for two years. I was an activated National Guardsman and was not allowed the early out.

The good thing about having been in the Guard, though, was that the eight months between when I had enlisted and the time I actually went active counted as time in the service. So after only one year and four months in the regular Army I started receiving over-two pay. It was a considerable pay increase.

❊ ❊ ❊

There is always some job to do in the Army—usually one that requires virtually nothing on your part, still the Army is based on structure and procedure. I was assigned to go to a warehouse that was filled to the ceiling with extra mattresses. But there was nothing to do, so I climbed up on top of a stack to take a nap.

Just as I was getting comfortable, a soldier came in yelling my name. I was to report to the First Sergeant pronto.

I got to his office and the orderly, Tim, looked kind of worried. Now, Tim was someone I kind of knew, and I knew he was aware of why I had been summoned; so I asked him what was up. Tim looked down at his desk and just said I needed to talk to Top ("Top" is a nickname for First Sergeant).

I went into Top's office and he had the same concerned look on his face that Tim had had.

"Monk," he said, "I regret to inform you that your brother has died."

I started bawling and then asked, "Which one?"

Top told me my brother Johnny had been killed in an auto accident. I bawled some more.

Arrangements were made for me to leave immediately to attend Johnny's funeral. A Lieutenant was summoned to personally drive me to the airport. He was a nice guy and tried to make some conversation on the way. The Autobahn in Germany has no speed limit, and he was in his personal car—a Porsche. We were flying.

I remember the flight attendants on the plane were extremely nice to me. I don't know if they knew my situation, but servicemen were not always treated nicely in the Vietnam era. There was much anger about perceived wrongdoing toward our enemies. Hippies and candle burners would routinely harass servicemen at the airports during that time. Many hippies and candle burners got their asses kicked.

Damn, no one wanted the war except the politicians. Even Jane Fonda thought the soldiers were wrong for fighting the enemy. I have no respect for her to this day, as she acted like a traitor to our POWs, and her actions most likely caused many of them to be further tortured. Who the hell was she to judge what happens in war?! I won't go so far as to call her Hanoi Jane, as I guess in her small mind she was doing the right thing. But she should have gone after the politicians, not our boys in the POW camps.

If her last name weren't Fonda she would just be some average girl, as she is only an average actress at best. I did like the movie "On Golden Pond", in which she co-starred with her dad and Katharine Hepburn. I managed to look past her ignorance as the movie was very good, though that was thanks to her dad and Katharine. I always thought Peter Fonda was a better actor than his sister. I mean, "Easy Rider" and "Ulee's Gold", not to mention "Dirty Mary, Crazy Larry"... those were great movies!

Anyway, my flight to St. Louis had a changeover in Philadelphia, and I needed to use the bathroom in the terminal. But if you didn't have 50 cents in change, you couldn't get in the stall. I went to climb over and there were sharp points along the top to keep people from doing that. The City of Brotherly Love sucked!

I figured I would crawl under the door. A nicely-dressed man saw what I was doing, put the money in the door for me, saluted me, and left. I will always remember that and I always salute our men in uniform.

Mom, Sis, and Cheeks all greeted me. I hadn't seen Sis for years, and we embraced. Sis and Cheeks had moved back to St. Louis while I was in the service. Mom was a mess, but she is strong and proceeded with all that was required for such a sad occasion.

Dad had been supposed to come, but thank God he had the decency not to make it. Or he might have just been too big of a wimp to face the music.

Connie Z was at the funeral with her parents and gave me a big hug. There were a lot of people but it is all kind of a haze.

Two days after the funeral, my Aunt Sue called and said Dad was at her house and wanted to see me and visit the gravesite. My Aunt Sue was my dad's sister. Her husband, Uncle Joe, had taken me fishing a few times after Dad had left, so I figured I should appease her.

I went to Sue's home, and after a little awkward conversation, Dad and I left for the cemetery. I found the site, pointed to the grave, and said, "There he is." That's all that was said (at least, that I can remember), and I took Dad back to Sue's. That was the last time I ever saw him.

He did call me many years later, after the redhead died. He was in St. Louis for the family reunion. (All the years he was gone, he had never made a family reunion, and I myself only went occasionally.)

"Hello, Monk, do you know who this is?"

Well, it sounded just like Uncle Don (Unk), so I said, "Yeah, Unk, how are you doing?"

"This is your Dad."

"Oh… . What's up?"

"Well, I'm in town and will be at the family reunion tomorrow and just wanted to let you know I am anxious to see you."

I thought about that and said, "You know, if you are going to be there, I will probably not attend."

"Oh, come on, come see your old man… . "

I didn't go and that was the last time I ever talked to him.

Apparently Johnny had decided to drive a Bomb Pop truck like I had, and that was what he'd been doing when the accident had happened. There is a big downhill curve on Interstate 44 coming into St. Louis County. Those Jeeps had a freezer on the back, which made them kind of top-heavy. Not too good for fast curves. The Jeep had tipped and rolled a few times in the grass median. A passerby had stopped and run to Johnny; he later told my mom that Johnny's last words had been, "Tell my mom I love her."

There was some controversy as to who had actually been driving the Jeep, as there had been another employee, who survived, in the truck with Johnny. The Bomb Pop Company also told my mom that they didn't have insurance for such a situation, and that she would be responsible for any expenses from the hospital where

Johnny had been pronounced dead. She would also have to bear the financial burden of the funeral.

Now, Mom had not been on her feet for very long, and just providing a home and food for us had left her with very little discretionary money. Butch and I went to the Bomb Pop office to talk to the head guy. He wasn't in but a supervisor was; he was a nice man and apologized for the company's actions. I think he was sincere, as he started crying and said he would use whatever influence he had to make things right. I'm not really sure if they ever helped, and Mom was not the suing type.

I hated to leave Mom, but I was required to return to Germany.

✳ ✳ ✳

"Where are you headed?" the fellow serviceman next to me on the plane asked.

"I'm headed back to Germany; I was only back in the States for my brother's funeral."

As we were preparing to land, the serviceman informed me that I could request a hardship discharge or at least a reassignment to the States. I did not really care about getting out early, but it would have been nice for Mom; so I figured, what the heck, and upon landing at Fort Dix, New Jersey for my connecting flight I made the request.

It seemed like I was going to get discharged, and I ended up getting transferred to the Granite City Army Depot to wait for the decision. It was about fifteen miles from our home in Glasgow Village, right across the river in Illinois.

The Army was silly; here they were giving early outs to plenty of other servicemen, but I had to wait to see if I qualified.

My assignment was equally silly. I worked Mondays, Wednesdays, and Fridays from 11 am to 3 pm as the guard at the officers' liquor store. My job was to sit in a chair by the register for four hours, three days a week; that was it. I was allowed to live at home, and the Army actually gave me something like an extra $250 a month for off-base living expenses. Two hundred and fifty extra dollars a month was pretty nice back then, especially since I was living at home anyway.

This lasted for two months, as my early exit was denied. So I still had two more months of service left and was transferred to Fort Leonard Wood in Missouri.

❋ ❋ ❋

Joe, our neighbor across the street, had been a St. Louis Police Officer. He'd been in an accident which had messed up one of his legs. He received some type of pension, but to supplement it he had a bait shop.

Joe had asked another neighbor not to sell an old car he had because he wanted me to have transportation when I got home from the service. Well, Joe and I went to the man's house, and I think he actually gave me the car for free.

It wouldn't start and hadn't been driven for some time, but Joe told me that he was sure I could get it running. I got my buddy Mike Tinson to give me a hand, as he was good with cars. We decided to drain all the old gas and put in a new battery, and he told me he would pull my car with his till it started.

"Monk," he said, "just put it in second gear and turn on the ignition, and when we get up to about 20 miles per hour, let the clutch out slowly."

I did; Mike tied a rope to his car and pulled that old green Chevy around the neighborhood for about fifteen minutes. It finally came to life. It was smoking, sputtering, and shaking, but it was running! I took it to Fort Leonard Wood and actually kept it for about another two years. I also ended up giving it away.

* * *

At Fort Leonard Wood I actually had a real job: I was a stockade guard. It was a great job, as I was on duty for four days and then off for three. Fort Leonard Wood is only 150 miles from St. Louis so I came home every time I was off.

To be a guard you were required to be at least a Buck Sergeant. I was a Specialist Fifth Class, which was the same pay grade as a Buck Sergeant, so the Army gave me three stripes and bingo, I was a guard.

The guys I was guarding were basically losers, potheads, and undesirables that could not make it in the Army. I had my own little barracks to look after with about 25 guys. They had little jobs to do during the day while waiting to get discharged. We were required to have formations and such and to march to the mess hall. I felt a little silly belting out "Attention" and calling cadence while marching. That just isn't my thing.

Jonesy was a black guy and was kind of funny. I would always have Jonesy march us and call cadence. Jonesy and the guys came up with kind of a version of the stockade shuffle. They would take three steps and then drag a foot; all the while Jonesy would be yelling out some nonsense. We had a good time.

Most of the prisoners had pretty long hair, and a lot of the blacks in the regular Army had afros. Regulation stated that your hair could not come down over your ears. The brothers had their afros which did not come down over their ears, but their hats would sit precariously on top. Sometimes it would be hilarious-looking, but it met regulations.

The hair thing was always a big issue in the early '70s. Later, when women became more prevalent in the combat part of the services, I wondered about that. You see, we were always told the reasons for a short hair regulation were that long hair was dangerous in combat situations and that short hair was more sanitary. I am not against racial or women's rights, but damn it, if a male soldier has to have short hair for those reasons, then a female soldier should also have to adhere to the hair regulation.

For that matter, I really don't think a woman should be in actual combat with men, but like I always tell my wife Sophia, I'm a dinosaur.

Anyway, I was about 30 days from getting out of the Army and I let my hair get just a little long in preparation for my return to civilian life. Naturally, some damn First Lieutenant saw me and told me to get a haircut and to report back to him the next day. I was a little ticked, as my hair really wasn't that long, but I gave myself a light trim and went back to the Lieutenant.

He was a butthole and screamed, "Soldier, I told you to get a haircut!"

I said, "Sir, I did."

He said, "Which one?"

"This one right here, sir." I grabbed a strand. I then looked at the clerk sitting across the room, who happened to be one of my prisoners. "Sir, take a look at that guy at the desk. His hair is almost hippie-looking."

"But he is getting kicked out," said the Lieutenant.

Just then, in walked a regular soldier with an afro that looked like the Leaning Tower of Pisa with his hat (which was, I guess, glued to his hair).

"Sir, do you see what just walked in? I have nineteen days till I get out. You can bust me a rank if you want, you can take some of my pay, you can write me up for an Article 15, but I did cut my hair and I am not a disgrace to the uniform like those two bozos."

He couldn't bust me because I had to be a Buck Sergeant to do my job, but he did give me an Article 15, a minor blemish on one's record.

✳ ✳ ✳

Two and a half weeks later, I was a free man. I got one of my Army fatigue shirts, drew a pretty good rendition of the guy on a pack of Z rolling papers, and printed "I'm Free" on the back of the shoulder area. I think I still have that shirt.

I drove out of the base and into a new life. I did enjoy my time in the service and I do believe that everyone should serve his or her country in some way for two years. It would be a growing-up time and an opportunity to learn responsibility and structure. It would make our country very strong and unite us all, as all would serve.

I'm Free

The first thing I did was buy a motorcycle. I could afford it because I'd had the Army send some of my pay home during the whole two years I was in. It was a combination street and off-road bike.

It was a blast! I took it to a hill climb; I had never done a hill climb before, but I had seen it done on TV. Off-road biking was pretty new back then and was very popular. There was even a movie documentary on motorcycle racing, "On Any Sunday". Even though I wasn't too religious, I always thought it should have been called "On Any Saturday", as Sunday is a holy day.

There was a program on the local rock radio station at that time that was sponsored by the Church of Scientology. It was an interesting program, and they sucked me into attending one of their services. What a joke—it was just some asshole preaching some off-the-wall bull while some bozos were checking me out and sizing up my wallet potential. I never went back and stopped listening to their program.

Okay, it was my turn to conquer the hill. Some guy told me my bike wasn't a hill climber. I hit the gas anyway and up the hill I went.

Now, in hill climbing, when you get to the top it is best if you kind of pull back on the handlebars a bit and let off the gas. I did neither; up in the air and then nose-down into the ground I went. My knees dug into the gas tank and I actually put a dent in each side, but I kept the bike upright and didn't crash.

On the way home I got pulled over by the Highway Patrol for a brake light issue. I showed him my Army ID by mistake but then pulled out my driver's license. He ran a check on me and informed me that I had eight points on my license (at that time, you did not lose your license till you hit ten points).

"Officer, you must be mistaken, as I have been in the service for two years."

"Son, you must have had one heavy foot, because two years ago you had twelve points." He told me it took quite a while to get those points to vanish and advised me to slow down for at least another year. I went quite some time before I got another ticket—not that I wouldn't have deserved a few more... .

I later bought a larger bike, a 650 Triumph. There were a couple of nights I had to outrun the police, turn off my lights, and drop my bike on its side and slide into the nearest yard to wait for the cops to pass. I could also do many stunts on that bike. I could pull a second-gear wheelie at 40 mph and go for an eighth of a mile on my rear wheel. I would go down the highway doing 70 and get up and stand on top of my seat, hands folded across my chest.

* * *

At that time, I also had a Buick Regal with a sunroof and cruise control. Those were features not a lot of cars had back then. I would get on the highway, put the car on cruise, climb out the sunroof, and steer with my feet. Once while performing this feat, a Highway Patrol car was traveling in the opposite direction. Luckily there was a barrier so he could not turn around to catch me, but it scared the heck out of me. I jumped back in the driver's seat and my knee hit the steering wheel. I almost lost it but got control and got off the highway.

I was the best backwards racer too. There was this abandoned parking lot that we would race in. It was too small to go much faster than 45 or 50. I would race in reverse while my opponent went forward. Many times I would win.

I loved driving in reverse, and once while at a picnic at a local union labor complex I showed off my skill. There was a pavilion next to a lake where a group of us would gather. I showed up at the pavilion and unloaded my car.

"Hey, Monk, do you have one of those pin joints?" someone asked.

I always had around a dozen joints rolled. They were very thin and perfect for one person. I never liked passing a joint around, as not everyone was sanitary in how they mouthed a joint. I remember a time in the Army when we were passing around a pipe of hash; one of the guys took a really strong drag off the pipe and a bunch of black tar came out of the stem onto his tongue. Man, that was nasty looking.

Getting back to the joint thing… the song goes, "Don't Bogart that joint, my friend." I mean, who wants to take a hit off a joint that some fool has just slobbered all over? So I decided to take a spin around the lake in reverse. Everyone was egging me on so I took off.

I made the trip around the lake and slid into the pull-off area by the pavilion. This was a huge gathering, as the grounds were over 200 acres with an Olympic-size swimming pool and a nice complex with a restaurant and bar. The place was packed, and there was little space to park as the lots were all full.

As I started to get out of my car, a police colonel walked toward me with his gun drawn and pointing at me. The St. Louis Police had been hired to help with crowd control, and I guess this guy was going to arrest me. I knew if I didn't leave my day would be ruined, and he was on foot; so I hopped in my car and gunned it up a hill to the parking lots.

I could see the police colonel in my rearview mirror, still pointing his revolver at me. I hadn't really done anything wrong except drive around the lake backwards, so I figured he would not shoot. I was real sure I would have been in handcuffs and off to jail had I not fled.

There were no empty spaces in the parking lot, but I saw a dumpster with a small space next to it. I slid into that spot, dust flying, and jumped out of the car. Phew—no one was around; so I put on a baseball cap and walked back down to the pavilion. Everyone gave me a standing ovation and we had a good time. We did notice some action up on the hill at the parking lots; I'm sure the police were looking for me.

I knew a few policemen during those years; I did not hang out with them much, but we knew each other. Once I was on my Triumph doing a wheelie through a red light at about 50 mph (there were no cars anywhere in sight). I did not see a patrol car parked by a building. The patrol cars lights came on, the siren was blaring. I was thinking, "Great; I'm going to get a ticket."

Out of the patrol car casually stepped Tom. He was a real bruiser and the brother of Tim, with whom I used to work on the trucking docks. Like I said, he knew who I was and I knew who he was. He was smiling from ear to ear; nothing was said but I gave a little wave and got back on my bike and hit it.

It's a wonder I never killed myself. I am forever thankful I never hurt anyone, as I later came to realize what could have happened to ruin my or someone else's life.

* * *

When I had entered the Army I had been working for Consolidated Freightways, and it was the law that you got your job back when you returned from the service.

Well, I had only worked a little over 90 days prior to joining the Army. Becoming a regular employee and joining the union required 90 days of work. I hadn't known this when I'd taken the job, but I'd figured I would keep quiet about my impending activation.

On my 93rd day, I had informed my supervisor that I would be leaving for the Army. He'd blown up.

"You knew this when you were hired, and now you expect me to be okay with it?! You're fired."

But I knew he couldn't fire me; I had met the 90-day trial period for the company and was now in the union. So upon returning to civilian life I showed up to work. The same guy was my boss and he still didn't like me much. He told me he would get rid of me if it was the last thing he did.

I worked there a few months but hated the third shift. I was late a few nights and my boss got his wish; I was fired. I could have had the union save my job, as I was a good worker and his threats to get rid of me were common knowledge on the dock. But I decided not to fight it as I didn't really like the hours and it would have taken many years to earn enough seniority to get on the day shift.

※ ※ ※

Joe, our neighbor in Glasgow Village, told me that until I found another job I could dig worms for his bait store.

"Monk, all you do is go down by the river with a garden fork and turn the dirt over, and there will be more worms than you can count."

He was right—once you got past the mosquito issue, the gathering of worms was pretty easy.

My buddy Beer was part owner of a Shell station. At that time oil was sold in cans instead of the plastic containers used today. The cans had been all metal till recently; they were now cardboard with a tin top and bottom. They were perfect worm cans—you could just remove the top and add worms and dirt.

Well, Beer would give me all the empty cans I wanted, and Joe would give me $1 for every can with 25 worms inside. Joe would then sell them for a $1.50. What a deal! I always made a couple of hundred dollars a week, in cash! I did that for the remainder of the summer.

Joe and his wife were always extremely nice to my mom and us kids, especially me. I will always remember their kindness and I sometimes think I gave little back to them. Hopefully they felt fulfilled knowing their actions were good and appreciated. They were the best neighbors anyone could have. I kept in touch with them off and on for a year or two after getting out of the Army, but I should have done more to show my thanks.

Wayward Son

I had moved out of Mom's place and rented a small house by myself. The trucking dock had paid me plenty and I'd had no problem moneywise. Now, without a good job, I figured I better get a roommate or two.

Much to my mom's dismay, I had Jim the enforcer and a character we called Rickerts move in with me. Rickerts's last name was Richards, but we called him Rickerts. I'm pretty sure "Rickerts" was an alias, as he was of questionable character at times.

The house had two bedrooms and a dining room that we ended up using for a third bedroom. Jim took the dining room for his room, Rickerts the back bedroom, and I the master bedroom.

My landlady lived next door, and for some reason she really liked us; I guess because we paid the rent on time and kept the grass cut. We tried many ways to cut the grass as it was a large lot. Jim got an old self-propelled mower, drove a stake in the ground, and tied the mower to the stake with a long rope. The idea was that as the mower went around the pole the rope would wind up and get shorter till it got tight to the stake. This did not work too well. We all had motorcycles, so we tried pulling the mower around the yard, and that didn't work too well either. But we always kept the yard cut.

* * *

We had many a party at that house, and there was always such diversity of guests. Ron the county police chopper pilot; Phil the car salesman (who would on occasion just get naked right in the middle of the party); businessmen; construction characters; Playboy Bunnies; and many girls in general.

I was kind of dating Lois at the time; she was wild and crazy and liked to display her boobs (in the raw). They were some nice boobs and I wasn't in love with her so it never really bothered me.

I remember Cheeks came over one day when Lois was there. "Lois," I said, "my little brother is coming over; would you give him a show?"

Cheeks came in and sat down on the couch and we talked a bit. Lois came in from the kitchen, sat down next to him, and started taking off her top. Cheeks was turning redder by the minute and I was biting my tongue trying not to laugh; it was hilarious.

This was the early '70s and free love was the national motto. The world was crazy back then; but then, the world is always crazy—it just has different phases. The early '70s were all about grass (pot) and free love.

Lois wasn't too big on pot and really didn't drink that much either, but she was big on the free love thing. She and I decided to leave our party one night and stay at her apartment.

When I get back home the next day those damn construction characters had placed all the furniture from the house up on the roof. They must have worked their butts off, as each piece of furniture was sitting exactly above where it had been sitting in the house—the living room furniture was above the living room, the kitchen table and chairs above the kitchen, and so on. I still have photos of that incident.

That was the only time my landlady called to voice a complaint.

"Monk, you know that is a brand new roof, don't you?"

"Yes, ma'am." I assured her that we would take everything down and that there would be no harm done to the roof.

She was a great landlady and must have once been just as crazy as we were, to put up with us. There were always girls, girls, and more girls. There were also motorcycles, motorcycles, and more motorcycles.

It was a neat little house with a one-acre lot and a fancy metal ornamental light standard in the front yard; kind of like ones you would see in New Orleans. That light post was the land mark which allowed all the girls (and everyone else) to find our house.

❊ ❊ ❊

Along with the parties and good times, we would take our motorcycles to a place called Flat River. There were many trails and paths leading through small creek beds and up and down some chat (loose rock) hills. It was a great place to let it all hang out.

I somehow managed to flip my brand new Triumph end for end without hurting myself. I did, however, crack the frame. I ended up having to get an older frame from a wrecked Triumph and take my bike apart to reassemble it on this older frame. It worked out and I actually liked the older style frame better.

❊ ❊ ❊

Mom was not happy with my choice of roommates, as she considered Jim a hood. Though she did have him over to dinner one night, much to my surprise.

I guess she wasn't too far off the mark about Jim, but for the most part we just had fun and did exciting things. Yeah, we drank too much sometimes, but we were not really drinkers. We did smoke a little pot; at that time, who didn't? Triumph Motorcycles and Jeeps—those were our toys.

We gave our bikes names; Jim's was "Ole Yellow", mine was "Trump", and Rickerts didn't have a bike but he always rode

Walsh's bike, "Wolf Tickets". I'm not sure what the name referred to, but the bike had a real nice professionally painted wolf head on each side of the gas tank.

Walsh was an electrician but rarely worked; his dad was a state politician of some sort. Walsh was too large to ride Wolf Tickets, but he liked having a bike.

If you saw "Star Wars" then you know who Jabba the Hut is. That is what Walsh looked like. He was huge and always lived on the floor. I only went to his apartment once, and he stayed on the floor the whole time. He moved around like an elephant seal.

He also had a big Caddy convertible, and Lois and I went somewhere with him once. Naturally Lois plus convertible equaled time to show boobs. Walsh loved it and we drove around all night, Lois flashing from time to time.

Walsh didn't live a long life, as he was a mess and had a very unhealthy lifestyle. He had a pleasant personality and just lived to have fun.

❊ ❊ ❊

One day we went to a hill climb at a time when my bike wasn't running. Rickerts wasn't much at riding bikes, so I used Wolf Tickets. I didn't know it, but Rickerts had loosened the handlebars on Wolf Tickets and hadn't re-tightened them; he wasn't much of a mechanic either.

There were probably three or four hundred spectators at the climb and they were all sitting on the side of the hill. The announcer spoke into the microphone: "Ladies and gentlemen, give a round of applause for our contestants!"

We would have three runs to determine the four finalists: two semifinals and then the final run for the all-out winner. There were twelve riders overall. We were supposed to form two lines, and whoever was next to us was the person we would race up the hill. We decided to all get in the same line for the first run so we wouldn't have to race each other.

This climb had a small hump about 20 yards from the starting line which made it hard to go all out till after getting past it. Beer, who had made it to the semis with me, and I were trying to figure out how we were going to handle that hump. Jim said, "I'm just going to go all out as fast as I can."

The starting light flashed and Jim took off, way ahead of the other bike.

"Wow! Folks, give Jim a hand," the announcer blared. Jim had hit that hump going all out, crashed front wheel and head first into the hill, lost his front wheel, and gotten up waving to the crowd.

Beer and I looked at each other and said, "I guess we won't try that."

It was my turn—we were off! I let up a bit, hit the hump, and then hit the gas. It worked; instead of going head first into the hill I made the jump and landed on my back tire.

Boom! The front tire came down and the next thing I knew my chin was on the gas tank. The handle bars, being loose, turned downward on impact. I regained my composure with my hands now down below the gas tank but still gripping the handles.

I hit the gas with my chin resting on the gas tank; the crowd was cheering and I just barely beat the other guy. The announcer was going crazy and so was the crowd.

I headed back down the hill looking for a wrench to tighten the handlebars. Either no one had one or maybe the other guys didn't want me to win, but a wrench was not to be found. Beer was up next and he won his climb too.

Next I was up against a guy with a bike that was designed strictly for hill climbing. I figured I didn't have much of a chance as my handlebars were really loose by then. I did make it up the hill again, but was eating his dust. Beer won his next climb and went on to race the guy that had beaten me for the championship. Beer lost that final run and came in second overall.

* * *

Beer decided he and I needed to take a road trip on our bikes to Daytona Beach, Florida.

We left right after Thanksgiving and it was cold! Beer bought us both some leather shoes that were ankle high with a zipper on the inside, and leather gloves with no lining. That was over 35 years ago and I still have both the shoes and the gloves.

Going through the mountains of Tennessee at night was brutal. My hands felt like they were frozen, but we kept going. Sometimes we would get right behind a semi truck so it could break the wind and we would get a bit of relief. I remember that one of us would ride in front of the other, and the headlight of the rider in back would cast the leader's shadow on the back of the truck. Sometimes whoever was in front would make shadow puppets on the back of the truck. I'm sure the truckers loved us doing this.... .

Naturally we stopped at Uncle Wilbur's and Aunt Edith's for a short visit and to warm up. Aunt Edith always made pickled peaches each year. Beer had never had one. He loved them. If you have never had a pickled peach you should definitely try one!

I found out later that Uncle Wilbur offered Beer some money, as we had little, and definitely not more than we needed for the trip. Beer thanked him but told him we would be just fine; yeah, right.

We hit one hell of a rainstorm in southern Georgia, but it at least was getting warmer by the mile. Doing 70 mph in a driving rainstorm on a motorcycle is crazy. I remember we wore these little wire-framed sunglasses which kept the raindrops from blinding us. I can still visualize passing people in cars who were looking out at us as we drove by them in that blinding rainstorm; I wonder what they were thinking.

Ah! The sun finally came back out and we were in warm, humid surroundings. We made it to Daytona and stayed at the Redbird Motel (we were—are—St. Louis Cardinal fans). The bikes were parked and we were happy to be off of them. Amazingly, for a day or two our hands felt like they were still vibrating from the ride down.

I remember we only ate at two places the whole time we were there: a breakfast diner and a McDonald's across from our motel. We had breakfast at the diner every morning and went to McDonald's for the rest of our meals. That was the only McDonald's I ever ate at that had sweet yellow buns for the burgers. Those buns were the best I ever had anywhere.

The beach was great, and at that time it was legal to drive vehicles on the beach. Daytona has hard, wide beaches, and I think the world motorcycle land speed record had been broken there some years prior to our trip. It was broken by a Triumph motorcycle, later to be produced as a Daytona 500cc Triumph.

We decided to get back on the bikes and try out the beach. It was pretty neat; as we went through the gears the rear wheel would break loose and we'd do a little fishtail till we got to the higher gears.

"Oh man, Monk, here come the cops."

It seemed that the room adjacent to ours at the motel had been broken into and the guests had told the police they thought we were the culprits. The officer requested that we follow him to headquarters, which we did. I figured they were just going to ask us some questions and let us go. We gave them permission to search our room and told them we had nothing to hide or anything to do with it.

The next thing we knew they were escorting us to the cells!

"Monk, what are they doing?"

"Beer, it looks to me like we are going to get locked up."

"No way!".... *Clink* .... "Yep, they are definitely locking us up."

We were put in a large holding cell with a bunch of losers. I found an empty metal bunk, grabbed a Bible for a pillow, and took a nap. Beer couldn't take it; he had to get out pronto. But it seemed we needed $100 apiece for bail till the cops could sort things out (guess we should have taken Uncle Wilbur up on that offer of extra money).

We had met two guys at a bar the day before, and Beer, always the great communicator, had made friends with them. He got the cops to let him make a phone call, as he remembered their names and where they were staying. They only had about $300 between them but Beer talked them into bailing us out. I couldn't believe it but I was very happy to be free.

These guys kept a pretty close eye on us till the next morning, when we get some money wired to us from Mom. We paid our newfound friends back, and as we were packing our bikes to go home I saw our motel neighbor. I wanted to give it to him good, but I just glared at him and bit my tongue.

It was time to head back home and we hit the highway. We were about 50 miles past Jacksonville, Florida, and my bike started acting up. I lost my headlight first and then my bike just sputtered to a stop. It was 1:30 am and pitch black in the middle of the Osceola Forest. I figured it had something to do with the battery, so I hopped on the back of Beer's bike and off we went to this little town to see if we could find a battery.

There was absolutely nothing in the town, and we headed back toward my motorcycle. Along the highway we noticed a car broken down not far from my bike.

"Beer, that car has a battery, and it is a 12-volt that will work in my bike. Let's take the battery out of the car and hook it up to my bike."

"Monk, that battery will be too large to put in the bike."

"I will just ride with it on top of the gas tank between my legs till we get my bike somewhere to see what is wrong with it."

We walked across the highway, lifted the hood of the car, and started to take the battery out.

"Monk, there are some headlights… it looks like they are pulling over."

Damn, it appeared the owner of the car was coming back (he had probably just run out of gas). This was Florida, and the sides of all the highways had tall grass. Off we went to hide in the grass. We overheard the two guys talking.

"Damn, it looks like someone was trying to steal my battery. I wonder where they went."

We waited in the tall grass while they put the battery back in, and all the while mosquitoes were killing me. One guy decided to relieve himself and walked out into the grass not five feet from me. He did his thing and they left.

I can't remember where we got it, but we found a rope and tied my bike to the rear of Beer's and he towed me to Macon, Georgia. That was as far as we could stand to go, riding in that manner. We found a Shell station and Beer told the owner he was part owner of a Shell station in St. Louis. I was allowed to leave my bike at this station till I returned with my car to pick it up.

Off we went, taking turns riding on the back of Beer's bike. We were going through those mountains of Tennessee again, but this time in the daylight with the sun on our backs. I always found it amazing how a motorcycle can travel virtually on the edge of its tires, leaning into a tight curve, with your knee a few inches from the road, and not lose its traction. That is exactly how we took on the mountains with both of us on Beer's bike.

We made it back home and I had to go retrieve my bike, so it was time to head back to Macon. Cars were bigger back then than they are now; I was actually able to take the front wheel off my bike and put the bike in my back seat and the wheel in the trunk.

After getting home again I inspected my bike and discovered the only thing that was wrong with it was the wire from the battery had somehow gotten squeezed between the seat and the frame. All that trouble for a bare wire!

Of course, on the way back home again I stopped to see Aunt Edith and Uncle Wilbur.

Beer and I were—and still are—best buddies.

* * *

While Beer and I were on this trip, he and his wife Susan were expecting their second child.

He and Susan have been married since high school. Susan was always very understanding of Beer's need to be a little wild, as they did get married quite young. Who would have thought the marriage would last?—but it did. I think it's called love!

I have three best friends who got married just out of high school and another who married just a few years after. They are all still married and are grandparents.

* * *

On another road trip to Florida, Wiz came with us. Wiz had served his country in Vietnam and had been Beer's friend before I knew Beer. We headed out—this time in warm weather.

Well, Triumphs are excellent handling bikes but are known to break down occasionally. We didn't get out of southern Illinois before one of our bikes threw a chain. We fixed it and had no breakdowns the rest of the trip till we got back to southern Illinois on our return home.

Our destination was Daytona again, and we discovered the Wreck Bar on this trip. It was a neat place with a lit dance floor that had alternating panels that would light up to the beat of the music. I remember "Smoke on the Water" by Deep Purple was popular at that time and was played often at the Wreck Bar.

The next day we decided to go to the dog races. None of us had ever been to a dog race, and we figured any dog could win any race, so our strategy was to not bet on the same dog.

"Here… comes… Lucky!" That was what the announcer would say at the beginning of each race.

There was a little puppet-like rabbit mounted on an arm that was attached to a device that traveled around the whole inside of the track. It would go just fast enough to stay ahead of the dogs. The dogs were intent on catching that rabbit, or at least that was how I saw it.

Wiz's dog came in first and he won a couple hundred dollars, then another couple hundred on another dog. Our strategy had worked, and Wiz shared his winnings; we spent it all before the trip was over.

On the way home, Wiz's bike broke down in southern Illinois again. We went to a farmhouse owned by a really nice old man and his wife. We asked if we could leave the bike there. The owner seemed tickled pink to oblige us; maybe he'd never had the opportunity to make a trip across country. Whatever the reason, we were allowed to leave the bike there. Wiz tied his belongings to Beer's handlebars and off we went.

Illinois had a law that riders had to have their headlights on at all times if they were on a motorcycle. (They did not require a helmet, just a headlight. Crazy law!)

We were crossing the Mississippi River—so close to home—on the Eads Bridge. There was much traffic and little room to pull over. I can still see it: I was following Beer with Wiz on back and saw smoke. Then I saw a flame coming off the front of Beer's bike and wrapped around the bundle Wiz had tied to the handlebars. The headlight must have ignited his belongings.

There was no place for them to go except to finish crossing the bridge. Looking back, it was hilarious, but at the time it was rather scary. Somehow Beer was able to untie the burning bundle while he was driving and threw it on the road. We didn't hear anything about it on the news that night so I guess we hadn't caused an accident.

※ ※ ※

A year or so later I decided to go to Florida by myself, just to get away for a few days. I figured I would drive my car instead of my bike. I stayed at the Redbird Motel again and decided to get a little sun and rest before going on the prowl later.

The beach was not crowded but I parked my car up by the sand dunes, away from everyone. I didn't have a swimming suit so I just stripped down to my tighty whities, spread out a towel, and enjoyed the peace and sun.

"Hello. I see by your plates that you are from Missouri."

This matronly old lady was standing over me, eyeing my undies, and it seemed like she wanted to get acquainted. After a lengthy chat she finally left me to my quiet and peacefulness.

Naturally, that evening I went to the Wreck Bar for a little action. The place was just as it had been before—full of women and good music.

At one point there was a break in the music, so I went outside to get some fresh air. I noticed two guys—a big one and a small one—kind of going at it. I took a wide berth, not wanting get involved.

I heard this girl yell, "Look out!" and then a guy's voice: "Hey, you, we're gonna kick your ass." I looked around and these two dudes were coming towards me. I squared off, preparing to defend myself.

The big guy was definitely drunk on his ass, but he was tall and looked very healthy. I could tell by his accent he was from the South, and I told him I used to live on a pig farm in Georgia and that he smelled like a pig. I then gave my best hog call (I'm a pretty good hog caller) and egged him on.

He took a big swing and just missed my head. I ducked, but wasn't able to make my own punch, so I kicked him in the balls. He went down and I kicked him in the face with my Jesus Christ sandals. (Everyone wore sandals in the '70s and they were sometimes referred to as Jesus Christ sandals.)

In the meantime, the little guy had vanished, but not for long. He reappeared and at first it looked like he had a big knife. Wrong—he had a huge pistol and was pointing it at me.

A large crowd had gathered around by this time, and we had managed to move the ruckus from the parking lot out to the street. Cars were honking and people were screaming when the gun went off.

Thank God the twerp was either a lousy shot or was just trying to scare me. I saw the blast from the barrel and a spark from the street between my feet as the bullet ricocheted. He missed, but my toe was bleeding; there was more screaming from the crowd. The guy grabbed his buddy and they headed toward their pickup truck.

I was pretty pumped and for some stupid reason I chased them to their truck and started banging on it as they drove off. I turned around and there was a huge crowd of people with their mouths ajar.

Years later, while on a huge construction project, my foot started bothering me. I went to the doctor to get it checked out. He took an X-ray and asked me if I had ever been in the service; I told him I had. He said, "Well, it looks like you have a piece of shrapnel in your toe." I told him I hadn't seen any action in the service, but then it hit me—Florida, the twerp, and the shot between my feet. I told the doctor my story, which he thoroughly enjoyed. He said that wasn't what was causing my foot pain and that it would be best to just leave the bullet fragment in my toe. To this day that toe always feels funny, kind of numb.

With a gun having been fired and the big crowd of gawkers hanging around, I figured it was time to exit stage right before the cops arrived. It was late but I got to my car, went back to the motel, checked out, and headed home.

At three o'clock in the morning in southern Georgia, I figured I could speed a little, as I was out of Florida. I believe at that time the government had made 55 mph the speed limit on all interstates. This was to conserve gas due to an oil shortage from the Middle East.

It was pitch dark, I was doing about 80, and all of a sudden headlights came on two feet behind me—I mean right on my ass. Next came the the red lights and siren. A big ole boy bruiser of a cop walked up to my door and said in a very southern drawl, "What's your herry, son?"

"What?"

He repeated himself. "I said, what's your herry, son?"

"What did you say?—Oh, *hurry*! I'm not in a hurry; I'm just trying to get back to St. Louis so I can go to church with my girlfriend tomorrow." I don't know why that came out of my mouth, but that is what I said.

You guessed it; I had to follow him to the station. Nowadays following a cop to the station would never happen, but back then that is what they did. I had about a hundred dollars on me and figured they would take it all. As I was following him, I hid all but $25 between my seats.

He put me in a cell and told me that when the Lieutenant came in they would figure out what to do with me. I told them all I had was a bag of Florida oranges and $25. They told me to keep the oranges and that they would take the $25.

Of course, I stopped at Uncle Wilbur's and Aunt Edith's on the way back. We had dinner and I told them my story. Aunt Edith said, "Lordy, Lordy, Monk, that is quite a story." Will and Lynn were a bit skeptical, even after I showed them my toe. But the story is true and I have the X-ray to prove it!

* * *

Paula was a girl who used to hang out with us, and though she was pretty straight-laced, she did enjoy our mischief and fun. At different times Paula and I kind of liked each other, but never at the same time for more than a couple of days.

One morning Paula taught me how to make French toast. I had always thought I knew how to make French toast, but she instructed me on the correct procedure.

"Monk, you must make sure to get that little white embryo-like thing off the yolk." She did not like it at all and I must admit I never much cared to bite into it either.

Paula's French toast was superb.

She also liked motorcycles, and one day she wanted me to take her for a ride to a county park. I had my bike set up for off-road travel, with knobby tires and geared pretty low, but I agreed.

We were almost at the park and making a pretty sharp turn. Knobby tires are good for dirt and mud but not so good on slick asphalt, especially if someone is riding on the back. The bike came out from under us and suddenly Paula was rolling across the pavement with me on top of her.

She and I ended up on the side of the road and my bike was in the middle of the road. I saw a car coming, so I got up and ran to get my bike off the road so the car wouldn't hit it. Paula thought I was pretty uncaring, ignoring her to save my bike. Damn, I had seen that she was out of harm's way and didn't want anyone else getting hurt!

It turned out that Paula only had minor scrapes and bruises. There was a small chunk of skin taken off her elbow which resulted in a small scar. But it was in a place that couldn't easily be seen, and she now had a battle scar to show off.

Paula was, and is still to this day, a good friend. I don't see her very often, but on rare occasions we either see or write each other. Sophia and I did go to her wedding after we were married. It was a very nice reception at a swanky place in Clayton, a ritzy neighborhood near St. Louis. They had a nice little band and I asked them to play "Hey Paula". They acted like they didn't know the song and made me sing a few lines. I remember Sophia and I got drunk as skunks that night. Sophia rarely if ever gets drunk.

Paula and Don, her husband, have homes in Utah and Florida and they both visit St. Louis on occasion. They have been to our house and I am happy for them as Don is a very nice guy.

There was a night after we were both married that we met at a friend's semi-retirement party. We both had a few too many drinks and ended up walking out together. Somehow we ended up in one of our cars to talk. We embraced for the last time and told each other we still loved each other.

Out of the corner of my eye I noticed two young black men eyeing us. The club where the party was held was in a part of town known for violence.

"Paula, we better leave right now!" I said, and we did. As we drove off we blew each other a kiss. I went home to my beautiful wife.

* * *

One time, Wiz and his first wife, Beer and Susan, and my Cousin Dennis and I went out for dinner and drinks. We were at a new complex in St. Louis called Westport, which had some pretty nice establishments and some high rollers.

Upon leaving, we spotted a brand new, bright white Cadillac Eldorado. Inside was a pure white dog—I think it was a spitz but it looked like a small husky. It was hot out and the dog was going crazy and needed water.

Dennis decided the owner should not have a dog, opened the door, and took the dog. Wiz was driving that night (cars were bigger then, so all six of us could ride together); we all got in with the dog and went home.

I decided to take the dog to my apartment, as it was a neat dog. The next day was Mother's Day and Wiz's mother-in-law was visiting. The police came to his door to arrest him and the owner wanted his dog back. Wiz called me and thankfully I still had the dog. The owner didn't press charges so Wiz wasn't arrested. His mother-in-law was not impressed… .

The marriage didn't last too much longer, but not because of the dog incident. Wiz decided to get married again. Funny thing about his second marriage: he got married in the same church as his first wedding. He even had the same preacher! Upon reciting the "'till death do us part" line, they both started laughing.

His second marriage did not last too long either, but his third wife, Alyssa, is a keeper and they have stayed together now for around 25 years.

⁂ ⁂ ⁂

My lease was up and I decided to get an apartment by myself, as I had a new job. There were many girls in the apartment complex, plus a nice swimming pool and tennis courts. Jim and his brother rented a house not far from my apartment and we remained friends. I haven't seen Jim for some time but he is still alive.

Right before I moved into my apartment, I was driving down the road and for some reason this doofus hit me from behind with his bright lights. I couldn't figure out why he was flashing me and I was getting annoyed. I finally pulled over and got out of my car as he was getting out of his. He didn't say a word, but picked up a short 2x4 piece of wood that was on the side of the road and started coming at me.

I told him, "I'm going to stuff that up your ass," and just like that he dropped it. I walked over and hit him once for being such an idiot and told him to get back in his car and leave. I never did find out why he was flashing me.

The next day I moved into my new apartment and wouldn't you know it, doofus and his new bride were living in the unit above mine. I lived there for a year and I don't think I saw him more than five times… though I will say that I heard him often as his bedroom was above mine, and he had a very squeaky bed. Like I said, he was a newlywed.

❋ ❋ ❋

Sis and Ed, who had just gotten married, also lived in the complex.

I had first met Ed a few months after I had been discharged from the service. Here came this guy that kind of reminded me of a Beatnik (I guess he couldn't figure out this was the early '70s, not early '60s). He'd been, however, dressed for the '70s, as he'd had on polyester bellbottoms, a wild polyester shirt, and a sport jacket.

Ed always wore a sport jacket, as that way he had two pockets for carrying a tumbler or two of Scotch; Ed loved his Scotch, his cigs, and my sister. When he and Sis would go grocery shopping, they needed a place for their drinks; they would keep them in Ed's jacket pockets. I would occasionally wear a jacket when out drinking and I must admit a tumbler of whiskey on the rocks fit nicely in the pocket without spilling. This was a handy way to leave the establishment with a fresh drink.

Ed drove a 1960ish powder blue Dodge Dart (you guessed it, convertible). I looked inside the car and it was a mess—the ashtray was overflowing, and empty glasses and trash were strewn about. He had a little goatee and a friendly grin.

It turns out that Ed is very talented and also a genius. He played piano bar and sang at a night spot for the uppity crowd for fun and tips. He can play the piano and organ as well as anyone I've ever heard, though his singing is a little better than average.

Ed is very smart and holds a degree in Engineering, plus a couple of Masters from Washington University in St. Louis. Washington University is a very prestigious school—one of the top ten universities in the country. Ed works in the aerospace industry and one of his many projects was to help design the heat tiles for the space shuttles way back in the beginning of the shuttle program.

Then he married Sis and has always been a dedicated husband and a very good father. They moved to California a few years later.

Just recently Ed visited us in St. Louis while on a business trip. Ed and I are both getting old, and Ed has had some health issues for many years. We had a discussion on life and death. Ed told me something that used to bother him when he was just a boy in Cleveland.

"Monk, I remember sitting on the porch with my dad and a car would drive by. I would always think, I don't know who is in that car and I never will." That, he told me, really used to bug him.

I told him that one of my youthful thoughts was about Jesse James. I had always thought it was weird that Jesse James did not know me and never would or could, and vice versa.

This was our analogy, of sorts, of death; no one really knows what it fully is all about. It is what it is… .

We told each other that we thought when the time came that we would accept it as part of life. Time will tell.

I don't remember if Ed told me what his thoughts on heaven, but I did tell him mine: I may end up in hell in my thinking, but my idea of heaven will be realized at the moment of death. I really can't imagine floating around in the clouds with the angels and other souls that have made it to heaven. My thinking is that no matter how you die—be it in your sleep tucked in your own bed or in a fiery crash—if you are at peace with your life and how you lived it, then that is heaven. Your soul will also be at peace wherever it may end up. Peace is a big part of all religions, and that is what I base my thought on. I am usually at peace with the world and can only hope I am at peace with myself when the time comes.

More Fun

Dirty Nellie's Roadhouse was an action-packed night spot in North St. Louis County. It had great music, hot cocktail waitresses, and a game room (no electronics like today), and was quite roomy with a bar area, many tables, and a dance floor.

The game room had one pool table and one foosball table. I had learned to play foosball while in Germany. I think—but am not sure—that it originated in Europe, as it is a soccer-type game. I was really good at it and Beer became pretty good too.

At Nellie's, the winner of each game continued playing till someone beat him. The new opponents would put money in the coin slot to start each new game. Beer and I would play till we got tired of winning on most nights.

There was a small window right behind the table just large enough for someone to slip through, and we would open it for fresh air. Now, Dirty Nellie's had some of the biggest and meanest bouncers. Beer and I knew them and were on somewhat friendly terms, but being bouncers they were a bit too masculine and pushy at times. I guess when you are the enforcer you have to be that way.

One night Beer and I were at the foosball table kicking butt and some guy took issue with us being at the table so long.

"Hey, pal, it's the house rule that the winner keeps possession of the table," Beer told him.

I'm not sure what happened next, as some pretty little thing had caught my attention. All I know is all hell broke loose, and Beer had thrown his beer bottle and hit the head bouncer with it. He was a brute (I think his name was Nick), and I knew this was not good.

About this time, a friend of the bouncer—who was a couple of years younger than me and not quite as experienced in life and confrontations—grabbed me. We locked into a struggle for dominance and I broke free, grabbed him, looked right into his eyes, and said, "You don't want any part of me" (a classic line that John Wayne would have been proud to say). I saw Beer heading for that small window above the foosball table, and out he went. I gave my guy a little push back and, with an "Adios", followed Beer.

By the time the bouncers got outside, we had mounted our bikes and were gone. But this incident created a predicament, as Dirty Nellie's was our favorite night spot.

"Monk, I'm just going to have to go back tomorrow night and face the music. If Nick beats me up, so be it; but I've gotta smooth this over."

Beer told me later that Nick was real impressed that he'd had the balls to come see him. Nick evidently gave Beer a scary grin and forgave him. We were back at our favorite night spot.

✳ ✳ ✳

It was wet T-shirt night at Nellie's, and there were some real beauties. The winner was a doll and was sitting at a table with her friend, who was also a doll. I went over to their table and said, "My buddy over there and I would like to take you to the East Side for some drinks."

To my surprise they accepted. Off in my car we went, with Beer driving. The sun roof was open and doll number one said she wanted me to climb out and sit on the hood while we were driving down the road.

I told her, "Sure, if you show me those winning wet T-shirt tits."

She did; I climbed out the roof, sat on the hood (cars were stronger then), and grasped the lip of the hood where the wiper blades were.

We hit the East Side and didn't know where to go, as we weren't real familiar with the area. We just knew places there stayed open three hours later.

"Beer, there's a night spot over there. The street in front is all lit up with cars and there's a wide sidewalk."

There were no parking spots, so Beer just drove up on the sidewalk and parked right in front of the entrance. We hopped out of the car, entered the establishment, and were kind of blinded by the light.

Upon reaching the bar, we noticed that we were the only white folks in the place. There were some pretty manly-looking brothers eyeing us and probably thinking we had to be cops or something to be that stupid.

Well, I had worked at a place called Maloney Electric for a year or so prior to joining the Army. It was in the city, and many of the employees were blacks. A big burly guy we called Bubba had worked in the same area of the plant that I had. We'd gotten to know each other a bit, and thank God for that. Someone tapped me on the shoulder and I turned to see Bubba.

"Monk, is that you? I think you and your friends should leave… right now."

I told Bubba I was pretty sure that was a good idea. Beer and I gathered up our two dolls, hopped back in the car, Beer did a 180 in the middle of the street—tires squealing and smoking—and we headed back to St. Louis. I never saw Bubba again, but I pray that he has been as fortunate in life as he made our lives that night!

Dolls number one and two were not too impressed with us, and we took them home; they lived in the Mansion House in downtown St. Louis, where many high-class hookers lived (I guess the dolls were probably hookers). We never saw them again.

✷ ✷ ✷

I went to Nellie's alone many times, as Beer was married. I'll never forget the housewife (that is all I knew her by), though I only knew her for one night.

I walked in about closing time and the housewife grabbed me and said, "You'll do just fine."

I looked at her and said, "What?"

She asked if I had my own place. I said I did.

"Good. Get in my car; we are going to your place for fun."

She was pretty nice looking and just a few years older than me. She got out these crazy white pointy 1950s glasses and asked if I was okay with them because she couldn't see to drive without them.

"Oookay," I said, and off we went.

When we got to my place, she gave me me one hell of a ride and was extremely vocal while doing so. (I hope doofus and his bride living above me enjoyed the rodeo.) The housewife had her fun and drove me back to my car. I never saw her again.

✷ ✷ ✷

Nellie's was a great place if you were single, as this was the time of free love, and there was a lot of free love given to me in those days. I can't remember all the one-night stands I had there, but I do remember a couple of doozies!

Coyote Girl was one of those. I was a little too inebriated to notice that Coyote was a less than stellar choice. Back then, as now, "Coyote Ugly" was the term used if you woke up with your arm under a girl who was a bit less good-looking than you had thought she was the night before. Hence, like a coyote caught in a trap, it was better to chew your arm off rather than wake her.

Well, Coyote Girl wasn't that bad, but when she woke up I was looking for a way out.

"I'll make us some breakfast while you get dressed," she said.

"That sounds great!" I replied.

What a butthole I was; as soon as she left the room I went out the balcony door, climbed down the post, and started running. Luckily I caught a ride home before she came looking for me.

Another night I was at Nellie's with Jim. We went to the bar and there was Sandy (who had been my neighbor in Glasgow Village). She had just been hired as a barmaid. I hadn't seen her in years, and she was still beautiful.

Now, Jim liked to throw a knife; he was very accurate and could make it stick on every throw. Nellie's had these large rough wooden posts around the bar area. He was throwing his knife and sticking it every time. (We knew the owner, and he was okay with the knife act.)

Well, Sandy bet a drink that he couldn't hit a certain small area on the post.

"Make it a double and I'll have Monk put his hand there and spread his fingers around that spot, and I will stick my knife right between his fingers," Jim offered.

I had seen Jim do this many times with other people, so I know he could do it. I put my hand up, spread my fingers, and—*boink!*—suddenly the knife was quivering back and forth between my fingers. Sandy gave us a double on the house.

I went back a day or so later, but she had quit and I never saw her again. I also never let Jim use my hand in his act again. That had been stupid... .

✳ ✳ ✳

One time, my cousin Dennis and I went to a large hangout called the Granary in southern Illinois. It was a large, out-of-service granary that had been converted to a huge venue for live music and drinks.

We went our separate ways once inside the club, as there was much to see and do and we had different personalities. I was standing on a staircase going to a balcony that overlooked the band and dance floor, minding my own business, when someone passed me a lit joint. I thought, *What the heck?* I took a hit off it and passed it on.

Up came a bouncer and told me I had to leave. I really didn't feel like leaving, and I didn't know where Dennis was. The bouncer told me again that I had to leave, and I repeated that I didn't feel like leaving. He grabbed me and we went down on the floor.

I was getting the best of him, but realized there were quite a few bouncers in there, so I let him go and was just about to make myself scarce. The next thing I knew there were two other bouncers on me and now the first one joined them.

"Let's give this guy a lesson," one of them said. I was just shielding myself and backing out across the dance floor to the rear door. I was getting a pretty good working over, but I knew I mustn't go down. We got to the door and they pushed me out.

I needed to find Dennis, as he had no idea what had happened, as he was on another floor of the club. So I sat on a handrail next to the door and glanced through a porthole in the door. Suddenly I saw one of the bouncers walking toward the door with the biggest, meanest head bouncer.

I don't think they knew I was sitting on the rail, and I did not realize the door would hit the rail if it were opened all the way. *Bam!* The monster bouncer about tore the door off the hinge as he came out. It missed me by a couple of inches. Had it hit me, I probably would have had two broken legs.

I jumped off the rail and the bouncer told me to leave. I told him I needed to find my cousin; he told me to leave right then. I was backing up and repeating that I needed to find my cousin. I don't know why he didn't hit me; he just kept coming and I kept backing out—all the way to the parking lot, where I got in my car.

The bouncer left and I waited there till Dennis came out an hour or so later.

"Monk, what the hell happened to you? You look like you've been in a fight and it looks like you lost."

I told him that was basically what had happened.

The next day I called up Big Al (my boss) and told him I couldn't make it in to work, as I looked pretty bad. He didn't believe me until one of the girls who worked in the store told him she had also been there the night before and seen the whole thing. And he definitely believed me the next day when I showed up with a shiner, cuts, and bruises. Ouch!

✳ ✳ ✳

Uncle Lee was my cousin Dennis's dad and was a lot like my father (his brother). Lee also abandoned his family, but unlike Dad, he chose to stay in the St. Louis area with his new bride. Like dear ole Dad, he also did not support his first family. (I don't know how he got away with that, since he was living in the same state.)

When we were growing up, Uncle Lee always had big BBQs in the summer, while his first family was living in squalor.

Lee's son from his second marriage, Sammy, was a bit of a bully, but I never really got to know him too well. It was shortly after I got out of the service that Dennis and Sammy were in Dennis's car and had an accident. Sammy died in that crash, but Dennis came away from it unscathed. In a way, one could say it served Uncle Lee right; but it was a sad, sad situation.

Uncle Lee and his wife Connie moved to the country after Sammy's death. One time, Dennis asked if I wanted to join him to go visit his dad. I agreed.

We were on a gravel road near Uncle Lee's house when we came up on another car. It was Uncle Lee and Connie. Dennis gunned the car and pulled up next to Lee.

"What are you doing, Dennis?"

"I'm just going to scare him a bit, Monk."

Lee looked a bit nervous and yelled out his window, "If you want to come to dinner we have food in the oven and will be home in 20 minutes."

We passed them and headed to Lee's house.

"Come on in, Monk, we will see what's cookin'," Dennis said.

There were some huge butterfly pork chops and dressing in the oven with the heat turned down. It did all look good.

"Monk, I'm hungry; let's eat."

We demolished all the food and were walking out the door when Lee and Connie pulled up. Dennis said, "Thanks for the meal, Dad," and off we went. I guess Lee had that coming to him for sure.

※ ※ ※

Dennis had some friends who lived on the edge. One of them was Gregg, whom we actually just called by his last name, Binaker. Binaker was quite the hustler. I only knew him for a few months, as he and Dennis moved to Colorado after that summer.

There was a night when Binaker and I went to an outdoor concert.

"Hey, Monk, let's go to the SIU campus tonight." SIU (Southern Illinois University) had outdoor music fests during the summer months.

"Who's performing tonight?"

"Monk, I don't know and I don't care, but if you come with me we will make some big money."

"How's that?"

"Well, there will be a lot of potheads and druggies there, and I am going to sell them acid (LSD)."

I said, "I don't know if I want to be a part of that."

"Oh, don't worry, I won't be selling them any real drugs; they will just think that is what they are buying."

Back in the day—and maybe now, I'm not sure—they sold this candy called Dots. Now, Dots came on a roll of thin paper like a very small roll of paper towels. The rolls were only two or three inches wide, and when completely unrolled they were maybe a foot or so long. The Dots—little round pieces of sugar candy—would be attached to the paper rolls. They were spaced just so, it was very orderly. You would just put a little pressure on the Dot and it would dislodge from the paper, leaving a perfect little grease spot.

Binaker had about 20 rolls of Dots with the candy removed, so nothing was on the paper except those perfectly spaced little grease spots.

This was still the early '70s and acid was somewhat popular with some potheads. There were many types of acid and they had crazy names—purple barrels, orange sunshine, windowpane, blotter. Blotter was a liquid form of acid that would be applied as a drop to a substance, like paper.

This was what Binaker would tell the hippies he was selling.

He needed someone to keep an eye on him and the action while he was selling. We walked the crowd, found some druggies, and before you knew it there was a small crowd around Binaker.

This feeding frenzy was quite a sight, Binaker sitting in the grass cutting those little grease spots off the roll and exchanging them for money. He gathered up the money and off we went to another part of the crowd.

This went on for an hour or so until one of the first buyers found us and told Binaker that he wasn't getting off.

"Well, maybe you got a weak dose," Binaker told him, and then offered him a couple more Dots for free. "Here, take these for free. They will get you off. Monk, it's time to go!"

"Yeah, let's get out of here."

Binaker gave me $100 and kept the rest. I have no idea how much he made, but he had a bundle of cash.

The next time I saw Binaker, he and Dennis were heading off to Colorado. They were in Dennis's Mustang convertible that had no top, and it was raining. They both had plastic trash bags over them (with their heads sticking out) and were smiling from ear to ear.

Dennis got married a year or two later and then had a massive stroke while on vacation with his wife a couple of years after that. I have called Dennis a few times since the stroke, but I don't think he knows who I am. It was a very sad thing, but I believe his wife will stick it out with him. I never saw or heard of Binaker again.

Boys and Their Toys

Jeeps were our other toys; Jim was the first to buy one. There are few places on Earth that a Jeep can't go.

We went on a Jeep run; that was an event where people tried to destroy their new Jeeps and/or get them stuck. It was sponsored by Reuther Jeep, a family-run dealership in the St. Louis area.

The run consisted of a trail with many mud and water obstacles in the beginning. The run then dropped off into a ravine, or should I say, an abyss. Once you got to the bottom of the abyss, you had to climb a steep, muddy, tree-infested hill to get out.

Tim, one of the dealership family members, had a brand spanking new Jeep Wrangler, which at that time was more like a big station wagon. Tim took that new Jeep and headed up the hill, bouncing off trees, mud flying everywhere; he didn't make it. In fact, don't think anyone made it up that hill. Reuthers must have known it was impossible, as they had a small bulldozer on hand to pull everyone up the hill once they could go no further.

Jim and I were among the last to go, and after witnessing the previous participants' futile efforts, Jim decided not to try. I was dumbfounded, as that was the only time I had ever seen Jim not try something.

When we got back to the staging area, we saw Tim. He was a huge man and rather imposing. He was standing there looking at the damage to his vehicle, and I think he'd had a few too many beers. There was a honey locust tree (I think) behind him, with long, sharp spines along its limbs and trunk. Tim turned and punched the tree. Wow—I saw one of those spines go through his knuckle and out the back of his hand! He grimaced and let out a howl, then a growl. He took it like a man.

* * *

I decided to check out a used Jeep and picked Beer up for the test drive. We headed for some open ground. I don't think Beer had ever been off road in a Jeep before.

A couple of days later, Beer had a brand new Jeep. I guess he had been impressed by the test drive!

I decided to buy a brand new 1979 Golden Eagle CJ7 V8 from Reuther's. It had ugly gold wheels. I made the deal with the stipulation that the gold wheels had to go. I wish I still had that Jeep, as it was a very neat vehicle.

* * *

Jim and Beer were a bit reckless in their driving. It was nothing for Beer to be going down the road and just suddenly veer off.

One day we were in Beer's Jeep and passed a cornfield. Beer whipped off the road into that cornfield, ears of corn hitting the windshield, and I was gripping the bar on the dashboard. The only things I could see were stalks of corn. Then suddenly we popped out of the field, jumped a drainage ditch, and were back on the road.

Another night we were tooling down the highway while it was snowing. Beer veered off the highway onto the shoulder; we traveled next to the highway for a bit and finally whipped back on to the highway, snow and ice flying.

Once I was following Jim and his brother Gary up a Jeep trail. We were going up this hill through the woods at about 40 mph, and Jim's rear tire hit a tree stump. I still can't believe it, but his Jeep actually went end over end, up the hill, and landed upside down.

Now, Jim's Jeep had a full roll cage and professional racing seat belts. Jim and Gary were hanging upside down in those belts with their cooler, ice, and beer scattered about. We rolled the Jeep back over and I'll be darned, there was no damage, though the Jeep did smoke for the next few miles. I guess some of the oil had drained to the top of the engine while it was upside down.

We had much fun with the motorcycles and Jeeps.

✳ ✳ ✳

Jim had a powder blue Ford Falcon convertible that we used as a hunting car. One time, we were all loaded up, sitting in and on the car as we talked to Beer, who was on his Triumph bike. He was under a huge tree near our driveway and the sky was clear blue, without a cloud in sight.

Crack! Bam! A flash of light followed. Out of nowhere, a bolt of lightening hit a branch right above Beer. We all jumped out of our shoes. I've never seen anything like it; maybe God was trying to tell us something?

✳ ✳ ✳

We were out and about one night—Jim, Bonnie, Doug, and me. We had been drinking a little when some guy ran a light and we darn near ran into him.

Doug was a tough guy and liked to fight; he also liked to win, so he always sized up the competition first. He got out of the car and decided that the bozo driving the other car didn't look like much competition. Doug started whaling on him and another car stopped behind us. I always referred to this guy as the innocent bystander. He objected to Doug beating up this guy and Doug knocked him for a loop too. We drove off.

The next day Doug was arrested; the innocent bystander must have gotten our license plate number.

Now, Doug's dad was kind of a political wannabe and also owned a small construction company. He called me up and asked that I come down to Clayton to talk with his and Doug's attorney. I agreed.

Watergate was going down about this time, and as I entered the building—home to many law offices—everyone was talking about that. Even as I got in the elevator, the talk was only of Watergate. I guess Doug's and his dad's attorney thought he was prepping for a seat on the Watergate defense team, as he was totally full of himself.

I found out that Doug and his dad wanted me to say in court that Jim, not Doug, was the guy that had hit the innocent bystander. Well, Jim was my friend, and I told them no.

I'm not sure what this lawyer had been smoking, but he said to me, "Son, I will subpoena you, and when I get you on that stand, you will say whatever I want you to say. I will have you squirming in your chair." He was so full of himself; pathetic, is all I can say.

I put my face in his face and said, "You piece of crap, I'll tell you exactly how it will go down. I'm going to tell that judge we were all drunk and smoking pot, and that I can't really remember a damn thing. That is what I'm going to say; and you, my friend, are going to look real stupid!"

He got real indignant and pitiful-looking. I was sure Doug and his dad were not happy with me, and I left.

I always thought it was pretty low that they wanted to pin it on Jim. Jim and Doug didn't seem to have any hard feelings toward each other later, so who knows what had really been going down. I just knew I wasn't going to be a part of it.

✳ ✳ ✳

I guess I should have parted ways with Jim and Rickerts, but we did have some good times and for the most part stayed out of trouble.

Rickerts had been some sort of traveling salesman, and he'd had a company credit card and a company car. It was a big Buick, a real nice travel car. He had quit his job just before moving in with Jim and me. But what I didn't know was that he had quit his job without turning in the car or returning his credit card.

We took a trip to Wichita, Kansas for a motorcycle race. I had never been to Kansas in the daytime and was not really paying much attention to the scenery as we went along. We got out of the car to stretch, and wow—Kansas hit me. It was so flat, and there was nothing for as far as we could see.

We got to Wichita and checked into a nice motel, ordered room service, and had a case of cold beer sent to us at the pool. The whole trip was on Rickerts's credit card.

While we were leaving the motorcycle race, Rickerts's transmission went out. Rickerts called a repair shop and told them he was a salesman staying at the motel. He asked if they would come get the car and repair it ASAP, as he needed to get back on the road. They came to pick up the car and told Rickerts they would call his room the next day when the repair was completed.

The bill was going to be expensive, and Rickerts was fearful that the charge would not go through. So he devised a plan. When the guy from the shop called, Rickerts told him to meet him in the lounge, where he would pay him. We then checked out of the motel and waited across the street for the car to be delivered. It pulled up and out came the mechanic. As soon as he entered the motel, we ran across the street, hopped in the car, and took off, thanks to the extra set of keys Rickerts had.

I kept thinking the shop would call the police and we would get caught. We decided to get some beer and go to a park for the day, till things quieted down. Nobody ever came after us.

After the trip, Rickerts's company caught up with him and got its car and credit card back.

A New Day

It was time for me to get serious and get a good job, as I wasn't getting any younger.

My friend Frankie was working as a manager for a retail outfit in St. Louis that had about 20 stores scattered around the metropolitan area. He told me they were going to be hiring a new assistant manager for one of their stores and that I should apply.

Sal Simons—the owner—and I hit it off on the interview. He hired me and I must say, he was probably the best person I have ever worked for. If nothing else, he taught me a sense of urgency and that you must make your money work for you. A sense of urgency is something one can use in any job setting.

All of the 20 stores in town had different names; I went to work at Sportique Fashions, and Big Al was my manager. Big Al was a nice guy but he was like a dog in heat. He would only hire pretty, sexy girls to work the store. I was in heaven, as these stores were very popular at the time, and along with the girls working in them, there was no one but females shopping in them.

Tweety Bird came in and applied for a job. She was blonde, thin, and very voluptuous, and dressed in this little short skirt and bobby socks! She had the facial expression of the little bird in the cartoon (Tweety Bird); hence that was what I called her.

"Big Al, are you going to hire her?" I asked him after she left.

"Damn right I am," he said.

Well, Big Al never made it with her, but I did for a short time.

* * *

Our stores were always crammed to the roof with merchandise and were also always very crowded. We had an issue with theft; nothing too big, but it was an ongoing problem. Tweety Bird was real good at catching shoplifters. Sal, when he found out that she had caught quite a few, gave her a bonus.

Our stores also had a problem with inventory shortage from time to time, which likely meant that employees were stealing. One time we got a letter with our paychecks saying that all employees were to take a polygraph or lie detector test to see how honest we were.

What an uproar! Sandy, our best employee, came to me and said, "Monk, I can't take that test. What should I do?"

"Have you been stealing?"

"No, not really, but I have probably given myself a discount on a couple of occasions, plus it just makes me nervous to think about it."

"Sandy, just take the test and be truthful. Tell them you have done a very small amount of pilfering; all will be fine." She did, and as I had told her would happen, nothing came of it.

It was my turn, and I remembered I had taken some special hangers (different and more expensive than normal pant hangers) for my pants. I had also given my cousin my store discount a couple of times. I wondered if I was going to get fired! I told the truth and nothing happened.

It was Tweety Bird's turn a couple of days later, and she came up to me to tell me she was quitting.

"Why are you quitting?" I asked.

"Monk, I can't take that test."

"Sure you can. Probably every girl here has done a little minor pilfering. Don't worry, just take the test."

Now, no one would have ever thought little Tweety Bird could be a real thief, but she assured me that she was and that there was no way she was going to take the test. Sal asked me about her a few days later, and I explained why she had quit. Needless to say, no one ever got another bonus for catching shoplifters.

※ ※ ※

We had a system for the dressing room to help with the shortage problem. When a customer went into the fitting room, she would get a card indicating how many articles of clothing she had taken in. When she left, the number of pieces brought out had to match the card. No one—customers or employees—liked the system.

One afternoon a middle-aged black woman was having a heated discussion with the girl running the fitting room. She was accusing the girl of racial prejudice. I went over to smooth things out and she got in my face with the same crap. I told her my name and politely explained the rules of the dressing room, and said that if she couldn't adhere to them she should probably shop somewhere else.

Wow! Right before closing this monster St. Louis Police detective came barging up to the checkout counter and asked if my name was Mike. I said yes. He pulled out his badge and started giving me hell, saying I had abused his wife. I was pretty sure he was going to get physical, but I wasn't backing down and told him his wife was lying. This really got him going; his eyes were bugging out, his neck veins were bulging, and spit was coming out his mouth.

Just then, Ray—the local policeman that would sometimes work security for us on big sale days—walked in. I'm sure Ray saved the day for me; that detective was sure hot around the collar!

※ ※ ※

Beer called the store one evening to tell me that he, Jim, and a guy we called Moon were meeting at Gildersleeves's (a bar down by the Brewery in St. Louis), and that I should meet them there. It was a nice bar where some of the single local newsgirls would hang out.

Well, prior to my arrival at the bar, someone had slipped a Mickey in one of the newsgirls' drink. This caused some discussion among the patrons as to who was responsible and words were exchanged. Naturally, Jim and Beer were in on the discussion, as they had been talking to the girl.

I walked in and everything seemed just fine. I sat down at the bar and ordered a beer. In walked one of the meanest guys I've ever seen. He had what was clearly an old scar from his eye down to his chin, and he took the stool right next to me. We looked each other over. (Many years later I recognized him on the news; he was a detective for the East St. Louis Police Department. At the time, I'd figured he was some gangster and he may well have been, knowing how the East St. Louis Police were back then.)

The bar had two sets of doors at the front entrance with a foyer between them large enough to hold ten to fifteen people. I was keeping my eye on the monster next to me when I heard a commotion in the foyer. The partitions were glass, so I could easily see what was happening: Beer and Jim were in the foyer with about eight other guys and everyone was fighting.

I looked over at Mr. Meanie, finished my beer, and said I had to go. As I entered the foyer, more guys followed me, and I saw a hand reach over and grab Jim by the head. Jim has a shaved head and it looked like the hand was gripping a white bowling ball. There was much punching and pushing going on, and all of a sudden Beer came crawling out of the crowd with Jim right behind him.

The police had been called, and they started breaking up the fight. For some stupid reason, Beer said something to the cops and they didn't like it. They handcuffed him and put him in the paddy wagon. I saw a policeman that I kind of knew, and asked if he could help with Beer. He said he couldn't but that Beer would be okay. Well, Beer about this time kicked one of the police in the paddy wagon and all I could hear was a bunch of screaming and rustling going on. Beer spent the night in a cell.

Moon was, in my opinion, a nice guy, but he had gotten in trouble with the law a few years earlier. He'd spent some time in a state prison and I was told he was never the same after getting out. He was married to a very nice girl who was an operating room nurse. Moon had gotten cancer after getting out of prison, and had lost a leg. He was at the bar that night just discussing things about his life.

After the police left with Beer, Jim, Moon, and I hopped in our cars and went home. Moon never made it home. They called it an accident but people who had witnessed it said it appeared Moon had intentionally run into a concrete divider in the middle of the road.

I saw his wife, Sherry, a couple of months later. She was such a nice person. I talked with her for a bit and she cried. I took my hand and wiped the tears off her face, and for some reason while we were eye to eye I licked the last tear from her cheek off my finger. She seemed to like that gesture. I would have asked her out had she never been married to Moon; I figured it would have been in bad taste to ask her out so soon after Moon's death. I rarely saw her after that.

＊ ＊ ＊

I got promoted to manager of Tempo Fashions. It was the smallest of the 20 stores and in a poorer part of town. The previous manager had been let go as the sales were down, payroll was up, and a pretty big inventory shortage had just been discovered.

At first the girls and Tony, the assistant manager, didn't like me, as they were mad that the previous manager had been fired.

"Okay, everybody, let's all get together and talk this out," I told them. "The old manager is out and I am in; it's as simple as that. I was not responsible for his termination. Anyone who does not want to work for me should just quit. I will be fair, but will run a tight ship. I will not ask you to do anything that I cannot do and I will pitch in and help along with my management duties." That was how I laid it out.

Tony told me he would quit, which I said was just fine. Arnetta was the girl who had been there the longest, so I made her the assistant manager.

All seemed to be going well, and after the next inventory our CFO called me to discuss the outcome. I had no idea if it had come out good or bad; he told me we had come up $142 short on inventory.

"Is that bad?" I asked.

"No, Monk, that is very, very good. How did you manage to turn things around?"

"I don't know, other than that my girls seem like good employees."

We figured Tony and the old manager had had something going, but we'd never know. As the old saying goes, it's hard to catch a thief.

* * *

Sal Symons, the store's owner, gave us money to have a store picnic every year. Once, the girls wanted to go to Johnson's Shut-Ins, a state park with a neat, clear little river that had a stretch of granite boulders in the main channel. It was like a water slide except it was natural and pristine, and the boulders were all smooth and slick. There was also a high point that you could jump off of into a deep, clear pool. I have never heard of anyone getting hurt jumping off that point, but I doubt it's still allowed in this day and age, as it was probably a 40- or 50-foot plunge.

I was probably 24 and the girls, except for Arnetta, were 16 to 18. They all thought I was cool and a couple had a crush on me. It was a situation where I had to be careful, and I knew I shouldn't dabble with dating.

I had a purple Triumph Roadster, a tiny two-seater convertible. I asked Sue, one of the girls, if she wanted to ride with me. She was ecstatic and we had a nice ride to the park.

I had invited my cousin Andy, whose nickname was Adrian Skywalker, to come with us and take some of the girls in his car.

Andy had gotten his nickname from being an ironworker. He'd lost his balance once while connecting iron on a high-rise building and managed to grab hold of a piece of iron on the way down. When his partner had come to his rescue and was looking down at Andy with his legs flailing in the air, he'd found it rather funny and given him the name "Adrian Skywalker". (This was probably around the time the first Star Wars movie came out, hence the name Skywalker.)

Andy was a crazy, fun-loving guy, but he was kind of different; he would do things on the edge but usually in a safe way (that seems contradictory but is true).

Andy had four of the girls in his car, and we were almost to the park. He was a couple of miles ahead of me on this little two-lane road. As I came around a bend, I saw Andy's car on its side, with the girls and him looking at it. It seemed Andy had deliberately made a slow roll off the side of the road and perfectly balanced the car on two of its wheels and the bottom side of the car. Andy and the girls had all precariously climbed out and were giggling with glee. We tipped his car back onto all four wheels and continued on to the park.

Andy was always doing stuff like that. He has now retired from ironworking and is an auxiliary policeman at the Lake of the Ozarks. We tease him that he is allowed only one bullet in his gun and refer to him as Barney Fife.

✳ ✳ ✳

On the way home from the picnic, I asked Sue if she would like to go to my apartment and help me unload the pots and pans we had used. She said yes.

We ended up on the couch and embraced a bit, but she was only 17, and I was 24 and her boss. I sensed she was a little nervous. I took her home and she was probably heartbroken. I did like her and also was a bit sad, but I am sure I made the right decision. She was always one of my best employees and we continued to work well together.

Funny, but about 30 years later, Sophia and I were attending the wedding of a friend of mine. I kept seeing this woman walk past our table and she kept looking at us when she went by. I knew I vaguely recognized her and asked Derek (the groom) who she was. He said it was his Aunt Sue! Who she was finally hit me; I walked over to her and we had a nice little talk and gave each other a hug.

✳ ✳ ✳

I was transferred to our warehouse store, which was called, naturally, the Warehouse of Fashions. The store was connected to our warehouse and corporate office. It was a high-profile store for the manager and, like the Tempo Fashions store, had an inventory shortage problem.

The first thing I noticed was an unlocked door that led from the corporate office into our store. Our back storage room, where inventory was stored and tagged, was basically a huge cage. It was connected to the warehouse area, so a regular wall was

145

never needed. This storage room also had a door leading to the warehouse, which was also never locked.

I figured I'd found the source of the inventory shortage problem. I had new locks installed on both doors without telling anyone in the warehouse or corporate office, and instructed my employees (girls) to keep them locked at all times—we could get out in an emergency, but no one could get in from the outside.

But I never gave a thought to how this might look from the perspective of the people on the other side of the door. Larry, the number two guy in the company, always used to come through those doors, as he liked to check in and see how things were going. The number one guy in the warehouse, who was pretty young, used to come through the caged area to chew the fat with my girls—as did all the other guys in the warehouse.

I got a phone call telling me to report to Sal Symons. I obeyed.

"Monk, what the hell is going on with you and the locked doors?"

"Sal, you have an inventory shortage problem, right?"

"Yes."

"Well, this store is going to be just like all of your other stores; the back doors will always be locked from the inside."

Sal rubbed his chin and said, "Monk, we will do it your way, but Larry needs a key to both doors."

That was fine with me, as I liked Larry very much and he was the number two guy in the company. Of course, the warehouse guy was miffed that he didn't get a key, and his boys didn't like the fact that they could no longer come in and flirt with my girls.

My first inventory a few months later indicated that my decision had probably been a good one, as the results were much improved.

We did have a shoplifting problem from time to time, as this store was in the city and surrounded by all types of communities— good, bad, rich, and poor, depending on which direction you went.

On some days, I had a security guard named Glenn. Glenn was a huge black man with a pleasant personality.

One day, I had just put out a new round of rabbit fur coats. (A "round" was our lingo for a certain type of rack.) Glenn came to my office and told me there were some shady characters in the store.

The warehouse store was pretty big, so Glenn went to the back of the store and I stayed in the front. There were three suspicious folks, and I was watching a young man who was definitely up to no good. He kept moving about the store, and I was not far behind him. I kept my eye on him and I knew there was no way he was going to get out with anything.

This went on for a bit and then they left.

Within minutes I got a phone call from someone in the corporate office telling me there were three people running down the street with rabbit coats.

Impossible! I asked Glenn to come with me and we headed out the door. We saw the shoplifters running across the campus of Forest Park Community College on the other side of the street, and took off after them.

We were not gaining on them, so we left the sidewalk and started cutting across the lawn. There were these black iron posts with black chains hung between them. They were about knee-high and we jumped them as we came to another sidewalk.

I heard a thud and someone yelled, "Monk!"

I looked back, and there was Glenn, sprawled out on the sidewalk.

"Hey," I said. "I thought black boys could jump!" Glenn cracked up and so did I.

Needless to say, we didn't catch those thieves.

Life is strange, as years later I meet up with Glenn. It turned out that both he and I eventually became ironworkers.

❋ ❋ ❋

There was another evening when three young black guys came into the store. I found out later they had been taking Judo classes at the community college across the street. Well, this one guy—he was a real hothead—came to the checkout counter and demanded I give him $40 because something his girlfriend had bought at our store had fallen apart.

"Do you have her receipt and the article of clothing?" I asked. "If you do, or if you bring them in later, I will gladly refund you."

"No, you are going to give me the money now," the guy said, and then he took a swing at me.

I pushed the silent alarm to summon the police and came out from around the counter. I noticed one of the warehouse workers was in the store with his wife, but I guess he was still pissed about my locking the back door, as he never offered any help.

I stepped out to confront this guy, and he must have kicked me fifteen times before I knew what was happening. I was amazed, as all the kicks were short and just barely grazed me, but there were black marks all over me as he was wearing black patent leather shoes.

I got in one punch and told him I had activated the silent alarm and the police were on the way.

This guy kicking me turned and left, but there was another very tall, thin guy still there. I tried to get in his face but he was a good foot taller than me. I told him to get the hell out immediately.

The store was fairly busy, which is probably the only reason they left. I followed them out the front door. There was an elderly black lady named Shirley who worked for me, and she followed us out.

Two of the guys were in the car, but the guy that had kicked me was standing by the car and I guess he wanted my ass. We were standing there and about that time Shirley said in a loud voice, "Monk, you get back in here; those boys will hurt you."

Well, that distracted the guy, and as he looked to her, I kicked him right in the balls. It was a good solid kick, and he went down holding his goods. He stumbled into the car and they pulled out just as the cops were arriving.

The cops asked me what was up; I said, "Nothing now! What took you so long?!"

* * *

I always tried to get the girls something for Christmas, but with 15 to 20 employees it was not an easy task to find something affordable. I bought Christmas toe socks one year, which the girls all liked.

Another year, I bought little cactus plants that had colorful cactus bulb-like grafts on top.

Rosalyn was a very light-skinned African American girl who worked for me. Her skin was a pretty, creamy, mocha color. She was a nice girl and pleasant to work with, but she often seemed depressed.

Well, one and only one of the cacti at the nursery had a piece grafted to it in a color very similar to that of her skin. I thought it would be nice to get her that one. When the girls gathered round and I was handing out all the brightly colored cacti, I handed Rosalyn her brown one. I could see she was disappointed with my choice for her, and I realized I had been an idiot to get her the brown one.

Later, I talked with Rosalyn to explain my choice for her. She said it was okay, but I know I had hurt her feelings with it looking like a racial thing. Man, how dumb could I be?

I had also bought a special cactus for Mary. Mary worked in the corporate office and would shop in the store from time to time. I kind of took a liking to her but we were totally opposite types of people.

There was a managers and office help meeting, after which a few of us went to a neighborhood bar for some drinks. Mary and I were getting along fabulously, but we both probably had a drink or two more than necessary. As everyone was leaving, I picked Mary up and carried her out the door. She said something—I forget exactly what, but it doesn't matter, because the liquor was probably doing the talking for her.

There was a round trash can out on the sidewalk and for some reason I walked over and played like I was going to put her in it. That was the wrong thing to do. Immediately she wanted me to put her down, which I did, and she went home. We dabbled a bit at getting together for a month or so after, that but never really hit it off.

Anyway, when purchasing the cacti for the girls, I had noticed a larger one that had what looked like a white beard grafted to it. I had asked the saleslady about it, and she'd said it was called an Old Man Cactus. I figured Mary needed a man in her life, so I'd said I'd take it.

After giving the girls their cacti, I went to Mary's office and gave it to her.

"Monk, this is very interesting; what kind of a cactus is it?"

"It is called an Old Man cactus; I thought you should have an old man."

We laughed, but still never got together. She was a strange bird—but then, look who's talking.

✳ ✳ ✳

Lori was the assistant manager when I took over the warehouse store, and I kept her on because she was a very good worker. She was my age and had a boyfriend she was always fighting with.

I didn't know it, but evidently she wanted to date me. Marge, an older lady that worked for me, came in my office one day.

"Monk, you know Lori has a crush on you."

"No, Marge, I did not know that, but in any case, it is probably better not to date someone I work with every day. Not to mention she has a boyfriend."

"Well, Monk, just try not to hurt her feelings."

"I will be thoughtful, Marge," I assured her.

Twenty minutes later, in walked Lori with a blouse that was showing everything—she might as well not have had a top on. It was hard not to stare, and she got the vibe that I wasn't biting. Marge came in and saw Lori wearing this revealing blouse. She put her arm around Lori and they walked out of the office together.

Later that night I heard a knock on my apartment door; it was Lori, and she had the same top on. She didn't say a word, just reached down, undid my pants, and pulled out Li'l Monk.

Naturally, we ended up in bed, having sex. I guess she thought I was going to fall madly in love with her, as the whole time she was asking me to hold her close and wanted to know if I loved her. I thought to myself, *I can't hold you much closer, and no, I'm not in love!*

Lori was also a smoker, and I never dated smokers. But smoking was much more prevalent back then than it is now, and even I on a rare occasion would have a cigarette. We both lit one up. I gently asked her about her boyfriend.

That didn't go over too well.

"Monk, I thought we could become boyfriend and girlfriend."

"Lori, that is probably not a good idea, since we work together every day."

Lori lay there for a while, and we decided over those cigarettes that we would accept what had just happened as a good experience and a fun thing, but nothing more.

✳ ✳ ✳

I was promoted and became manager of Sportique Fashions, the banner store of the 20 stores in town. I also became the training manager for new hires; corporate would send me new people on a consistent basis and I had to decide if they would make it or break it. This was one thing I did not like doing, as occasionally I would have to make the decision that some were not up to snuff.

We always had some type of promotion going on, and since it was fall, a coat sale was upon us.

Estelle was a 40ish, sharp-dressing black lady. I had hired her because she was more mature, as well as always perfect in appearance. She was also a very good salesperson.

Sal was impressed with our coat sale's success, as our store sold the most week after week. I told Sal about Estelle, and he told me to bring her to the next managers' meeting.

"Okay, everyone, this is Estelle. Monk has told me that she is one of the main reasons Sportique is outselling all the other stores. Feel free to ask her questions and for advice."

Estelle really held her own answering questions from the upper-echelon management and corporate people. Then one of the corporate higher-ups asked her how she cared for her own coats.

"Well, I just keep them in plastic bags and put them in the trunk of my car for safekeeping," Estelle said, in all seriousness.

You can imagine the silence in the room! It was all I could do to keep from falling on the floor laughing, but I bit my tongue, put my arm around Estelle, and explained to everyone that Estelle had just moved out of her apartment, was staying with a friend for a short time, and had to keep some of her clothes in the car. That wasn't true, though; Estelle lived in a bad part of town, and that was actually how she cared for her nice coats.

After the meeting, Sal came up to me and said Estelle had been great and he had really gotten a kick out of her. I'm sure some of the hoity-toity managers had been taken aback, but they just didn't realize how lucky they were to be able to live in nice and safe neighborhoods.

* * *

My new position required me to travel to other cities on occasion to help open new stores that were either corporate stores or franchises. The company was also having growing pains and many new people were coming and going in all departments—managerial, merchandising, corporate—the whole organization was changing. Traveling for work was not really my thing, but I accepted the challenge.

I was told there were some franchise cities that needed my expertise, and corporate asked me to consider making a move. I knew I wasn't about to leave St. Louis, but I said if someone wanted to interview me, I would listen.

A Korean group with eight stores in Minnesota wanted to interview me. I flew up to Minnesota and three of the owners picked me up at the airport. They spoke in Korean almost the whole time we were in the car, which I felt was a little rude. Finally they asked me about my aspirations or something and I just said I liked to ski, as we had just passed a sign advertising a ski resort. I don't think they wanted to know anything about my personal interests, because their conversation shifted back to Korean.

It was really cold in Minnesota, and I also noticed all the street signs were about three feet taller than they were in St. Louis. I figured I needed to break the ice, so I asked why the signs were so tall.

"Oh, very much snow, yes," someone replied. Wow—if they got that much snow, I knew I wasn't going to leave St. Louis for Minnesota!

"Monk, this is our main store; what do you think of it?"

Well, it looked only okay, but I wanted to be polite.

"Ah, very nice," I said, "and I like the displays on the wall."

The whole experience was uncomfortable, though I will say they took me out to a nice restaurant and we had a good meal. They made me an offer and I told them I would think it over and get back with them in a day or two.

The offer was only a bit more than I was already making in St. Louis, and I had the feeling their enthusiasm for work would be too extreme for me. I believe in doing a good job and taking pride in my work, but my work is not my whole life! I could see they were concerned that I was not totally gung-ho about the prospect of running their stores.

After getting back to St. Louis, I called Sal and set up a meeting with him.

"Sal, I'm never going to move to Minnesota, nor am I planning to ever leave St. Louis," I said frankly.

"That is fine, Monk, but it means your chances of moving up any further with the company are limited."

I figured my days were numbered, as Sal was basically handing over more power and decisions to the new people coming into corporate. About a month later, I met with Sal again and told him I would be leaving, and thanked him for providing me a good living for those four years. We shook hands and that was the last time I ever saw Sal.

Within two or three years, most of the managers and owner-managers that I had started out with either left or sold out their interest in the company. I guess I had made the right move, just a little early.

❊ ❊ ❊

I was not sure what direction my life would take, as I had just given up a fairly lucrative job. I applied for managerial positions at a couple of retail operations, but I knew the end game would be the same.

Fortunately, the country was different then, as there were always jobs to be had. One of the guys I used to play sandlot football with told me that the company he had just started working for was hiring in their PortaFab building sector, and that he would put in a good word for me if I applied.

I got the job, and it was a decent one, but I could see that the future was very limited. I did learn a good deal about working with tools and my hands, which would, in the not-too-distant future, be very helpful.

World Wide Willy

Mom, as always, was there to help out. She and Murill had a Dairy Queen franchise but they were always looking for ways to make more money.

"Monk, Murill and I have been speaking with a company out of Texas that is opening up some franchises here in St. Louis. Why don't you go down to Dallas and participate in their six-week franchise school? We will put up the front money, and you can run the franchise."

The franchise was called World Wide Stereo and Sewing Centers. I thought it rather strange to combine sewing machines with stereo systems, but I figured I had nothing to lose by attending the franchise school. The company even provided housing during those six weeks.

The school was very well organized and plenty informative. I also spent time in some of the Dallas stores, which seemed to have a fair amount of business. I really liked their mantra, "KISS"—which stood for "Keep it simple, stupid"!

There was one thing I did not like about this franchise: the number two guy did not seem on the up and up. At one point, the company took us to a Dallas Cowboys vs. St. Louis Cardinals football game. (The Cardinals eventually became the Arizona Cardinals and the Los Angeles Rams became the St. Louis Rams.)

At that time the Cowboys were supposedly America's team, and the Cardinals—surprisingly—had a very good record against them. The Cowboys were favored by six, and I made a bet with the number two guy that the Cardinals would win if he gave me those six points. The Cardinals did lose, but a last-minute safety by the Cardinals made it a five-point game. I won the bet!

So on the charter bus back to corporate office, I asked the number two guy to pay up.

"Monk, you lost the bet; the Cardinals lost."

"Yeah, but you gave me six points, so you lose. You owe me."

"I'll have to think about that."

Well Joe, the company's number one guy, was listening in, and I turned to him and said, "Is this what I am to expect from your company?"

I got paid, but the incident gave me some doubts.

✳ ✳ ✳

When I arrived back at home, Mom, Murill, and I found a location for our store. There were two units side by side, and we rented them both. I figured if we cut out a large opening in the wall between the two units, we could have the sewing section on one side and the stereo section on the other. It was a good design and the store looked nice.

We placed ads in the newspapers, and all the new owners—there were five other franchisee openings in St. Louis at the same time—volunteered to work the phone banks for the local PBS station in St. Louis. In exchange, we got to talk about our new stores on TV. We got Cheeks to wear the World Wide Willy costume as we were being interviewed.

There were probably 200 people working the phone banks, and they all put their coats on a large table. I was wearing my Army fatigue jacket, which I really liked. I put it on the table and that was the last time I ever saw it. Man, was I pissed; I was sure someone had seen me put it down and decided they wanted an Army jacket. I looked through every coat on that table and went all around the building looking for it. I even went down in the basement and asked some workers there if they had seen anyone with an Army jacket; they hadn't.

Aside from the matter of my jacket, things were looking pretty good—until all the papers in town went on strike. (Newspapers were the best way to advertise back then, as there was no Internet.) To top it all off, two of the franchises that were already in business in town filcd for bankruptcy.

But we knew our location was a great one, and we decided to go ahead with the grand opening anyway. The Dallas corporate office let us keep the World Wide Willy costume for a week. Cheeks got the honors of wearing it again and walked up and down the street in front of the store. Thankfully for him, it was winter, and the costume kept him nice and warm.

All of the other new owners wanted to have Playboy Bunnies at their grand openings. World Wide's corporate office was in the same building as the Dallas Cowboys' office as well as the Dallas Playboy Club. Well, I was dead against hiring Bunnies, as I felt it was a waste of money. But all the new stores were sharing the grand opening expenses, and I was outvoted by the other owners.

I guess it was a good thing I was outvoted, though, because the Bunny that came to our store was Bunny Sophia. She was HOT, and I even managed to sell her a stereo a couple of days later. It came with a free setup by none other than me. Mom really liked her.

* * *

We found out that the Dallas corporation was basically in business to sell equipment to its franchises at a profit to itself, and that we were pretty much left on our own.

Business wasn't terrible, and the sewing machines actually sold almost as well as the stereo equipment.

Unk bought a new sewing machine for his wife, Aunt Pat, and he also bought a turntable for his home system.

A big-time labor guy that I knew from my days with Jim and Rickerts came in and bought a complete top-of-the-line stereo system. He had been a victim of a car bomb (mob stuff) years earlier and had lost both legs. But in he came with his wheelchair and entourage. He just said "Hi, Monk", wheeled around pointing at items, paid in cash, and left with a big smile on his face. Those mob and labor guys always remembered people they liked.

Ed (Sis's husband) was also good at selling. He and Sis would come in after getting off work and help out.

I had learned to repair sewing machines while in Dallas, so that was my main personal income; the money from these repairs was mine to keep, and the rest of the sales kept our store in business.

A couple of the other new stores were having trouble, which naturally impacted our store too. Though we had had a decent start, business got pretty slow. I decided to work as an ironworker at a new nuclear power plant in outstate Missouri. Unk got me a permit to work till I could join the union if the store did not work out.

I worked the third shift, which was a seven-hour-per-night gig for eight hours' worth of pay. I would leave the store, drive 95 miles to the power plant, work, and then come home and open the store around noon. I remember one morning I actually fell asleep while driving through an intersection in a small town. I woke up just barely rolling through, with horns blaring and people screaming at me.

Working in both places became quite a chore, and the store's business still wasn't picking up because of all the trouble the other franchises were having.

* * *

During this time, I was also trying to impress the foxiest rabbit in town, Bunny Sophia! I took the stereo she had purchased to her apartment and set it up for her. We put on a couple of records and she sang a couple of songs for me; one was "You Belong to Me".

Sophia was and still is an excellent singer. She belongs to the Missouri Choral Society, perform in plays occasionally, is the main Cantor in church, and sings for weddings and funerals. Sophia's voice has brought a tear to my eye on many occasions.

She would sometimes come to the store to say hi, and we had a few dates. I was madly in love and remember sitting at my repair desk writing "Sophia" and then adding my last name to it. Yeah, that sounded good!

✳ ✳ ✳

We decided to close the store and moved our entire inventory to Mom's garage. It took a few months, but in time we sold the entire inventory, and in the end I do not believe Mom and Murill lost much money in the venture. We definitely fared better than the other franchises in town.

It was a learning experience, and not once did anyone in our family ever have bitter words over what I guess could be termed a failure. That is one thing about our family; we have always loved each other and never have the kinds of petty fights that are prevalent in many families.

Callaway

Callaway Nuclear Power Plant was my salvation. I was in need of money to keep living on my own, and Callaway provided income. It also gave a whole new meaning to my life. It was my indoctrination into working as a journeyman ironworker.

The construction industry was a bit slow in the late 1970s, so the new Callaway plant was a Godsend for many construction workers. It required more men than the labor unions could provide. This was great, as I—along with many other young men—were given permits to work alongside union craftsmen.

The plant was located in the middle of Missouri, so the employees needed to either commute a long way or rent a place out there. Many guys shared trailers and rooms in run-down motels. Some who worked the day shift took an old school bus to work each day; about 20 or 30 guys would pile in and basically party, fight, or gamble to and from work. I heard many a story about that bus, but I never traveled on it myself.

I decided that since the third shift was only a seven-hour shift, it would be like cutting the commute in half (timewise). My cousin Tommy, a guy named Skip, and I decided we would take turns driving our own cars, with the driver paying for gas. This would keep the miles down on our vehicles and everyone would be contributing equally.

The first night, Skip drove. He pointed out that if I looked at the moon coming up over the horizon, I could see the top of the cooling tower for the main reactor. The job had been going on for about a year prior to my getting hired, and the cooling tower had been the first structure built. We would be working on the reactor building.

Third shift wasn't known for being a hard shift, since we mainly just got projects ready for the day shift to complete. And many nights there was nothing to do, so we would find a dark corner and catch a few Zs. It was really a perfect job to have while still trying to keep the stereo store going.

＊ ＊ ＊

There were people from all over the country working at Callaway. There were boomers from Canada, New York, Chicago, Kansas City, and everywhere in between.

"Boomer" is ironworker slang for someone coming from out of town to work a large project. The huge cranes and rigs used in setting steel girders and beams had booms to enable the rigs to reach out for some distance. This enabled workers to set a lot of steel without having to move the rig too often. Therefore, if you traveled a great distance to get a job, you were referred to as a boomer.

Most boomers were very good hands as well as colorful individuals.

There were many men of questionable character at Callaway, and the third shift had its fair share. There was this guy who looked like Sasquatch and went by the name of Razor. Razor was rather dirty most of the time; he looked like he hadn't shaved or had a haircut in years.

Razor was, however, quite the thief. Hardly a night went by that he didn't walk out without having stolen something.

Third shift was always cooler than the other shifts, and it was getting close to fall. Razor would wrap two full lengths of welding lead around his body and put on a huge full-length coat like you would see cowboys wearing in the winter on a cattle drive. I think they are called dusters. Razor would walk past the guard office, turn in his brass, and waddle out the gate to the parking lot.

("Brass" was how our time was kept. Instead of a timecard, everyone had a piece of brass with a unique number etched into it. We would pick up our brass at the beginning of our shift and turn it in at the end.)

Now, a full length of welding lead would weigh at least 80 pounds, and Razor would always take at least two leads. He never said much, and no one ever said much to him either, but I'll bet he stole at least $15,000 worth of welding lead and tools in the short time I worked with him.

* * *

We had a foreman, Jerry, who insisted we always be busy doing something, even if there wasn't really anything to be done. Now, as I said earlier, third shift was known as an easy shift as often there would be nothing to do. But Jerry would sometimes have us take things down or apart and then have us put them back together just to keep us looking busy.

Many of us were permit hands, so we just did what he said so we could keep our jobs.

Curly, however, was a real character, and one day he decided he'd had enough of Jerry's bull. Jerry always had a monster thermos full of coffee to keep him awake. Curly started putting downers (like sleeping pills) in Jerry's thermos.

It was funny; Jerry would be yawning and getting sleepy, so he would go to that thermos and drink some more coffee. By break time, he would sit down and fall asleep.

The rest of the night would be ours and we would find a dark corner and styrofoam or something to use as pillows, and get some sleep. The sun would rise and Jerry would look around wondering what the hell had happened!

❊ ❊ ❊

Tommy and Skip would have made excellent boomers, as they too were quite the characters.

Skip lived on the edge of life and was fairly trustworthy; he did have a soft heart. One morning as we were driving home, he slammed on the brakes. Sitting out in the middle of the road was the puniest, sickliest puppy I've ever seen. Skip said, "I'm taking him home."

And he did. He loved that little dog, and we would always greet him when we got back to Skip's apartment after work.

Occasionally we would get rained out after having traveled all the way to work (a hard rain made it impossible to work safely). On those nights, we would usually hit one of the local bars, which were in business solely for the tradesmen. Skip and Tommy were both married, but they were also hound dogs, and they would jump at the chance to hook up with most any free-spirited woman.

The Robbers' Roost was a favorite hangout, and a certain barmaid with fabulous knockers who worked there was on Skip's list of conquests. We referred to her as Horse Face because she had a long face and kind of buck teeth. Other than that, though, she was gorgeous. Horse Face also had a girlfriend I nicknamed the Baby Whale.

"Monk, we are going to Horse Face's trailer when she gets off work."

Skip was driving so I had no choice and little else to do anyway. As soon as we got there, Skip and Horse Face headed off to the bedroom. That left Tommy, the Baby Whale, and me in the living room. I figured I would just lie back in the chair and catch a nap. When I woke up I saw Tommy crawling back and forth over the Baby Whale, trying to figure out what to do with her. I just chuckled to myself and closed my eyes.

"Hey, Monk, wake up! We're going home."

Skip had a brand new Jeep that he drove on his nights to drive. He had taken the top off, as that was how he preferred it. It was still raining cats and dogs out. We got three plastic trash bags from Horse Face and put them over our heads, and off we went.

I was sitting in the back as we went barreling down the two-lane blacktop road.

"Skip, are you awake?... Skip, there is a bad curve coming up and it is pretty slick out!"

Too late—we went off the road and rolled over. I saw Tommy get flung out of the Jeep as Skip's face hit the windshield before he too was tossed out. None of us had been wearing our seat belts.

I just went straight up in the air and ended up in the ditch with the Jeep right above me. I remember in kind of slow motion seeing the Jeep start to roll back toward me. I scrambled to get out of the way, but my leg was pinned under the spare tire attached to the back of the Jeep. Luckily for me, the spare for some reason had very little air in it so it wasn't hard enough to break my leg, but I was still trapped.

Tommy saw me and he and Skip lifted the Jeep, which was on its side in the ditch, just enough for me to slip my leg out. Skip's jaw was the size of a watermelon, but we were all okay for the most part.

I gathered up our lunchboxes, which were scattered all over the road.

"Hey, Skip, your wife has made you some butterfly pork chop sandwiches. They sure look good," I observed.

"Go ahead and eat them. I won't be eating anything solid for quite some time," Skip said.

We climbed up and sat down on the side of the Jeep—with the rain pouring down on the trash bags we were wearing—and waited; we know that sooner or later some construction workers would drive by. The pork chop sandwiches were delicious.

Skip and Tommy both ended up taking some time off work to recuperate. I decided I would just drive by myself to work every night, as I knew I wanted to get into the union and get on a job in town.

✳ ✳ ✳

Around that time, I decided to change my lifestyle. Hippies and the laid-back persona had gone out of style. The new thing was disco and go, go, go.

It was also a time when cocaine was becoming the drug of choice. I had a couple of close friends who were pretty impressed with its effects.

Cocaine was a bit expensive, and definitely not good for one's health. It could also get you in big trouble with the law. I tried it out on a couple of occasions and decided that was not what I wanted out of life.

This decision created a good deal of tension between a couple of my closest friends and me. You see, it was expected that people would join in with friends when they were getting high, that all would bear the burden of the cost even if it wasn't their thing. Peer pressure is very prevalent in the drug society.

For that matter, peer pressure is very prevalent in many vices. If you are at work and the company gives employees smoke breaks, many will go out and have a smoke. Some companies used to even give smoke breaks specifically every hour or so. If you didn't smoke, you didn't get the break; this would encourage one to smoke to be able to indulge in the extra break time.

I had to make a choice about this drug thing, and I did. I told my friends that how they led their lives was none of my business, but I was going a different route. This was a hard thing to do, as I didn't want to lose my friends, but my mind was made up.

I was also very much in love with Sophia and didn't need drugs to make me happy.

It was only a year or two later when my friends made similar decisions and we were one big happy family again.

As for the political question of whether or not drugs should be legalized, I am unsure what would be the best for our country. That said, I would lean toward not legalizing them. Stop the source and the use will diminish greatly.

For Nicole

I am dedicating this chapter to my daughter Nicole. She has on many occasions asked both Sophia and me how we knew we were made for each other. We have always said we didn't know. Well, Nicole, now I'm going to try and enlighten you.

For me it was love at first sight; the minute I saw Sophia, I was hooked. I was consumed with the thought of making her mine.

We had similar interests and she was easy to talk to, kept a very tidy apartment, and could cook. She seemed like a strong woman. She neither smoked nor did drugs, and she wasn't a drinker. (I guess one could say that I had double standards, as I did all three for short periods. I did ultimately quit them all, though, except for occasional drinking.)

I couldn't get enough of Sophia, and to embrace her was heaven. To this day, one of my greatest pleasures in life is to embrace her and breathe in her aroma.

She was the oldest of ten children and, like me, came from a broken family. Sophia was a great help to her mother and siblings, and provided them with financial assistance from time to time. I think her family was much more broken than mine, as I feel my family gave me more love and support than hers did. Both of our fathers were pitiful, but even so, my father pretty much just stayed out of our lives once he left and didn't cause me any additional anguish. I can't say that about Sophia's dad.

Sophia had a sugar daddy or two; they were kind of like father figures, in my thinking. They would take her out to dinner and such. I remember our first date; she liked a restaurant called The

Hacienda. We still go to that restaurant from time to time. I was so excited, but still struggling a bit with money issues. I arrived at her apartment and spotted a flowering bush by the parking lot. I picked a bouquet and as I was running up the stairs to her door, I noticed an older man parked out front.

Months later I found out the man had been Sam, her main sugar daddy. Sophia shared with me that Sam had told her he was parked out front that day and had watched this young stud pick flowers off the bush, then run up the stairs to her apartment.

Sam and I became friends later, and when Nicole was born, we called him Uncle Sam. He was a nice man and Nicole really liked him. He would call every so often and occasionally we would go out to dinner with him.

One week, when Nicole was around six, Sam did not call on his usual night. Sophia called him to see if he was okay but got no answer. We drove over to his home and found him lying on his bed with the phone next to him. He had died, but he did have a peaceful look on his face. Sam was a good, kind man.

After dating for a few months, Sophia and I decided to live together. Sophia had the nicer apartment, so I moved in with her. Those were the days! We were deeply in love and enjoyed every moment together.

Ours was a ground floor apartment, and it actually had a very nice patio with a bit of a backyard. I planted a garden and it flourished like no other garden I've ever planted. Sophia was impressed and life was good.

Sophia always thought going to church was important, and that was when I started attending the Catholic church. It was also when I found out that Catholics recite the Lord's Prayer differently than the Protestants do.

A New Beginning

Mom and Murill had bought some rental property and thought it would be a good idea if Sophia and I did the same. We thought it over and started looking at properties.

We found a large home near Forest Park, just inside the St. Louis city limits, that had been a doctor's home and office at the turn of the century. It had been built around 1901, was all brick, and had been converted to a six-unit rental property.

Sophia and I purchased it and moved into the ground floor unit. It was a neat old house with a sprawling staircase leading up to the upper units. It also had a few pocket doors that would open by sliding them into the wall. I love pocket doors—they are out of the way and kind of neat in their design.

Sophia and I made a lot of improvements to that home; many a night and weekend was spent scraping wallpaper, patching, and painting. We eventually converted the house into five units, as two of the six original units were very small.

Aunt Edith and Uncle Wilbur came to visit once while we lived there. We let them sleep in our bedroom, and Sophia cooked homemade lasagna for them. I think Aunt Edith in particular really enjoyed the stay.

✳ ✳ ✳

"Beer, I'm going to marry Sophia. Will you be my best man?"

Naturally, Beer accepted. Sophia's sister Kitty was the maid of honor.

We were to be married at St. Anthony's Church, which was near our home. The priest needed to know why he should marry this good Catholic girl to a Presbyterian, and wanted me to provide letters from friends as to my worthiness. I did.

He then insisted we go to marriage classes. After attending just one class, we realized that it just wasn't for us. The others in the class were in their early twenties; we were not only in our mid thirties, but we had also already been living together for four years. We never went back.

The priest's final request was that Sophia and I stop living together until we were actually married. I politely told the priest it was unlikely that we would do that, but that if he would marry us I would promise to raise any children in the Catholic faith. I told him further that if he would not marry us, then any children would be raised as Presbyterians; and I handed him a $100 check for his favorite charity. He married us!

The wedding did not go off without a few problems. Sophia had rented a Lincoln Town Car for Beer to take us from home to the church, from the church to the wedding dinner, and then back home in. The night before the wedding, there was a huge hailstorm, and our Town Car ended up full of dents—but it was the only one available, so we used it anyway.

Sophia had invited her brothers to the wedding, but told them they'd have to dress nicely. They didn't think it was worth the price of a new shirt, so they did not attend.

Sophia walked herself down the aisle and I remember looking toward the back of the church as she started her processional. Man, was she beautiful! I started crying and damn near cried through the whole ceremony. Naturally I had no hankie!

About the time Sophia got to the altar, in came her mom and two sisters—right in the middle of the ceremony! One sister

had a black eye and her other sister, Mary—who was a bit…
different—had dirty, greasy hands (she was a mechanic). To look
at her you would have thought she was a guy, but at least she did
have on a nice men's suit and a little fedora.

After they settled in, the ceremony progressed and I kissed
my bride.

We had the reception dinner at a very nice restaurant not far
from the church. The room we had reserved was large and had
a partition separating our group from the rest of the restaurant.
Mary came up to the bridal table a bit drunk. She told me I had
better take care of her sister. I assured her that I would.

She then walked over to the partition, grabbed the handles,
and slid both sides open. I guess she didn't know the rest of the
restaurant was on the other side. All of the patrons turned to see
what the commotion was and Mary said, "What's you all lookin'
at?"

It was hilarious—at least to me, as I knew Mary very well. One
of my buddies walked up to me and said, "Monk, would you like
me to take him outside?"

"Doug that ain't no 'he', that's Sophia's sister!"

About this time good ole Mom stepped up and grabbed Mary's
hand and asked Mary to sit with her. She did, and all was well.

We headed back to our house to take a few more pictures and
wind down with a few family members and friends. Upon arriving
home, we found a car parked in our driveway. The St. Louis
Blues' hockey arena was not far from our home, and people who
were going to the arena would sometime park on our street and
partially block our driveway. But this time the car was actually
in our driveway!

I was furious, but discovered the keys were in the ignition. I
started it up, drove it a block away to a red light, and just left it
right in the middle of the intersection.

I remember we had put Billy Idol's "White Wedding" on the stereo and were carrying on when Kitty heard the doorbell. It was a cousin of mine (one I rarely ever saw), and evidently it had been his car in our driveway. He hadn't known I was getting married and I hadn't know it was his car. We walked to the intersection where I had left it, and I'll be darned, his car was still sitting there blocking traffic.

It was an eventful wedding day, and at the very end, after saying goodbye to the last guest, I managed to close the screen door in Sophia's face. It did not hurt her badly, but it did make a bruise. She forgave me but has not forgotten... .

✳ ✳ ✳

We had some dandy tenants in the four or five years we lived at that house.

One was a young man from the country who came to the city to be a roofer. He was a mess and not well educated—nearly illiterate, in fact. He didn't know how to write, but he would get a money order every month and have us write our names on it so we could cash it.

When he moved out, an elderly lady moved in, and every week she would claim that she could smell the animals from the zoo about two miles away in Forest Park. We never smelled them ourselves (and Sophia has an excellent sense of smell!), so I just told her time and again that her lease was just month-to-month and she was free to move out whenever she wanted. She finally did, after about six months.

All in all, three of the tenants were already there when we purchased the property and were still there when we sold the property. I only had to ask one tenant to leave in all the time we owned it.

We also bought a duplex across the street and became quite the rental property owners. Both properties made us a nice profit in both rent and selling price when we later decided to sell them.

I almost made the mistake of renting to Frank, an ironworker that I had met on a bridge job. He was quite the drinker, had gone through a couple of divorces, and was unreliable in many ways. Still, we hit it off.

We stopped at a bar once on the way home from work and got plastered. There was a barmaid that Frank was intent on hooking up with. She wore a halter top, and Frank would always ask her for an unpopular brand of booze that they kept on the top shelf. She would climb up on a stool to reach it, which meant her knockers—which Frank said were the most beautiful he had ever seen—were in full view.

I remember that when walking out of the bar that night I somehow got both of my feet entangled in a wire hanger (there was a dry cleaner right next to the bar). I fell but managed to keep my bottle of beer upright in my hand. We laughed and laughed—I mean, how could anyone get both feet stuck inside a wire hanger?

Luckily, Frank later told me that he really liked me and that his moving into our rental unit would probably not be good for my marriage. I agreed.

❈ ❈ ❈

City life was not really our bag, so we decided to sell both properties and buy a nice home in a more suburban setting.

The rents we'd been receiving, plus the profits from the sales, afforded us a down payment on a very nice home. It had a spacious lot of just over half an acre, as did the rest of the homes around it. It also had 200 acres of common grounds dispersed throughout the village and a five-acre lake.

After we'd been living there for a few months, Sophia told me that on occasion she would dream that we lost the house and had to move; she would then wake up. But we still live there, and it is a wonderful home.

* * *

In retrospect, the many ups and downs, rights and wrongs, good fortune, and luck I'd had up to that point were a molding of my final casting. Like clay moldings, things can change, and different parts can be cast aside or re-evaluated in life and how one lives it.

Things I would eventually cast aside were smoking, drugs, excessive alcohol use, reckless driving, a careless lifestyle, and my motorcycle.

I thoroughly enjoyed every minute on every motorcycle I ever owned, but the time to put that activity aside was drawing near. Times were changing, traffic was worsening, the thrill the bike offered lessened, and a nice vehicle with some comfort seemed to be the best way to travel. Also, getting a ticket was less likely when driving a car than when on a motorcycle. Occasionally I think it'd be nice to have a bike again, but for just a short road trip.

Beer and Wiz bought Harleys when they were in their 50s, and they've tried for years to talk me into buying one to take on a cross-country ride. I have told them I will take my low-rider, Hemi-engine Magnum wagon and follow them. We could take turns driving the car and could even pull an empty trailer in case of a breakdown. We will see if that ever happens... .

The rare smoking and casual drugs were easy to give up. I never was that big on cigarettes and only smoked lightly for a couple of years. The pot wasn't hard to drop either. The day after my child was born, I simply threw out my stash of weed—half a bag—while driving down the highway (ironically, almost the exact same part of the highway where I'd seen the highway patrolman as I was driving sitting on top of my car and steering with my feet). I just threw it out and never looked back.

I still on occasion have a heavy foot while driving, but I try hard to be safe and look out for the other guy. I never want to hurt anyone with my driving.

As for the wild lifestyle, well, I still like to get on the edge a bit now and then. I also still like a good stiff drink (whiskey), but only on rare occasions nowadays.

The Move

With the rental properties sold, it was time to move into our new home. This house was a bit more than we'd figured we could afford, but with the profits from the rental properties, we ended up with enough for a nice down payment and an affordable monthly note.

Beer, Wiz, and Frankie were my movers. I had rented a beat-up U-Haul truck and we figured it would take three trips to get everything moved—one trip just for toilet paper and paper towels.

"Monk, what in the hell are you doing with all the sundries and paper products? Are you expecting the world to come to an end?"

"Yeah, Frank, I know there is a bunch of that stuff." My Sophia always made sure we never ran out of anything—and watch out if there was an item on sale!

We got the first load ready and headed off to prestigious West St. Louis County. Wiz was in the truck with me, and as we turned onto my new street, we passed a fairly big home, white brick with two white lion statues on either side of the main driveway, which circled through the front yard and exited on the opposite side of the property.

Wiz looked at me and I looked at him, and it dawned on us: we had been there before. Probably some ten years prior, we had been out in that area, having a few drinks and possibly a joint. Afterward, we'd gone to a deli to get something to eat. There had been a display case of bagels.

I had really never had a bagel before and eyed the display, as we'd had the munchies and been a little goofy from the pot and booze. There'd been all kinds of bagels—cheese, onion, blueberry, plain, and one that I'd scratched my head over. It had said "GAPLIC BAGELS". I'd asked what the hell a "gaplic bagel" was.

Wiz and the counter girl had come over to see what I was talking about; it had turned out the little leg of the R had broken off as they'd been, in fact, *garlic* bagels. Well, we'd laughed and laughed; I'm not sure if the counter girl had gotten our humor, but we'd left with some bagels.

Anyway, we'd gotten lost and taken a turn onto the street I was now to live on. Then, just as now, the white house had been there. It had been nighttime and there'd been floodlights on the front of the house and on those two lions at the circular drive. We'd observed that the owner must have been rich.

So here we were again, and I was moving in right down the street. At the same time Wiz and I looked at each other and said, "Gaplic bagel!" and started laughing.

I pulled up in front of our new home in this beat-up U-Haul with a Scanoe tied to the top of it. Some of the neighbors were out and about, and I could just imagine what they were saying. We figured it was something like, "Honey, look what's moving in next door!"

We started unpacking and carrying things in. We were working our butts off when my new neighbor, Harriet, came over to introduce herself. She was a nice lady and we hit it off and talked for a bit.

As my buddies were straining with some huge piece of furniture, Harriet said, "Where did you hire these great movers to move you in?"

It seemed my new neighbors weren't accustomed to doing manual labor!

Frankie overheard her and said, "We aren't getting paid, and Monk is also one of the movers; Monk, get your ass over here and help us."

Harriet was astonished, but she became a great neighbor.

A couple of days later, we got a phone call. I don't know how they got our number, but some neighbors two doors down called to ask us over for dinner and drinks. I politely told them, "Thank you, but we are right in the middle of painting and taking down some wallpaper."

"You mean you are doing it yourself?"

"Yes we are, and again thank you for the offer."

We were probably one of the youngest couples in the neighborhood and definitely one of the least wealthy. But all of our new neighbors were very nice and they learned to accept us, even with my redneck ways.

* * *

The house was structurally sound but very dated, and it needed a lot of work; the previous owners had really let it go during a long divorce process. If you were to see the "before" and "after" photos of the inside of the house, you would not think it to be the same place.

One of the first things I did was install a skylight in the family room, as the room was on the north side of the house and had dark paneling; it needed to be brightened up a bit. We'd taken the paneling down and drywalled, but the room still needed more light, as Sophia had many house plants.

I had installed a few skylights on commercial buildings, so I assumed I could handle this project. We ordered a huge skylight and I went to work figuring out how I would install it. I went up to the attic to see in which direction the roof rafters ran. However, I did not inspect the entire attic, which would prove to be almost disastrous.

I laid out lines on the ceiling to cut out the ceiling drywall. I thought I would install the skylight longways down the roof, which would create a long skylight along one side of the family room. I got my power saw out and started cutting. Not six inches into the cut, I hit a ceiling rafter. I didn't understand how that was possible, since I had seen in the attic that they ran in the opposite direction.

I went back up in the attic, and damn—they ran in the same direction as the fall of the roof in every room *except* the family room, where they ran in the opposite direction. I should have checked more thoroughly.

So I figured I would go ahead and cut out the ceiling drywall and set my saw so it would cut shallowly enough to go through the drywall without hitting the wood rafters. I probably should have used a different type of saw—or at least one with a vacuum bag—as when I had finished the cut and looked around, all I saw everywhere was fine white dust. The whole room was covered but I managed to get it all cleaned up before Sophia got home (I had purposely begun this project when she was not home, since I'd known it would create a mess!).

I overcame the rafter problem by cutting out four feet of two of the rafters and then boxing their ends in. I also attached four uprights to the four corners of the roof joists to stabilize the opening, which became very useful for hanging the drywall from the ceiling opening to the bottom of the skylight on the roof.

I was so proud!

But there was a catch-22 to having achieved this success. There was a pretty substantial main electrical wire running the length of the attic and, wouldn't you know, it ran right through the middle of the long side of the opening. There was no extra play in the entire length of the attic; the wire would have to be cut and added to.

I was sure I did not want to take on such extensive electrical work myself.

There were a couple of new homes being built not far down the street and I went straight over there. I found an electrician and told (not asked) him that he would perform the needed fix to my home. He looked at me like I was crazy but said he would do it. Three hours later I was out a hundred dollars but ready for the next step.

Now, I knew this next step would require immense precision and accuracy. I plumbed up from the four corners of the ceiling opening and made a mark on the underside of the roof. I then drilled a hole through the roof at each mark, so there were four small holes in my roof. I had made the hole in the ceiling the exact size the directions for the skylight installation had called for, and made damn sure the holes at the four corners were straight and precise.

Everything should have been a go; so I snapped a line between each hole to create a perfect rectangle the size of the skylight, which I would cut out of the roof.

Had I taken Geometry in school, I would have probably known something in my calculations was amiss. Lucky for me, I did know that one should always measure twice before making an important cut. I was just about to put the saw to the roof when this instinct kicked in: I'd better measure again.

I forget exactly how much too big the opening would have been had I made that cut right then, but it would have been a major screw-up.

My roof has a three-inch drop for every foot of roof, so the rain can run down. My skylight was four feet in length, so I guess I was probably a foot off in my measurement. My solution was to shorten the length of each side cut by one-half of the difference. It was a redneck calculation; my math schooling had ended at fractions and decimals. But fortunately, in the end, my redneck calculations prevailed.

I probably would have been very good at geometry and school in general had the system not failed me. I am slightly near-sighted, so I'd always had a hard time seeing the blackboard. I would ask every teacher in every class if I could sit near the front. Well, each and every teacher had told me we had to sit alphabetically, no exceptions! That had usually put me at the middle of each class, closer to the rear than the front. I'd figured if that was the way they were going to treat my situation, the hell with them. So I had done what I wanted in school—which was not too much!

Anyway, the last step was to place the skylight on the curb I had installed around the opening after making the cut to open the roof. I couldn't get the skylight up the ladder by myself, though.

There were storm clouds forming and the wind was picking up, with lightning in the distance. I had to get that damn skylight up there and snapped into place.

By this time, Sophia had come home, and even though she was seven months pregnant I had to enlist her help.

"Sophia, I need you to help me with this."

"Okay, Monk, what should I do?"

"You just go up the ladder, get in a safe position, and grab the end as I slide the skylight up the rungs of the ladder."

We got it on the roof and snapped it in place—just in time. *Boom!* Lightning flashed and the rain started coming down. We laughed and ran into the house, sat on the couch, and watched the storm through our brand new skylight. It has been almost 30 years since I put that skylight in, and it has never leaked one drop.

❋ ❋ ❋

"Monk, we need to fix up the yard. It's clearly been neglected for years. I want you to cut that tree down, as it is too close to the house. Then we need to put some plantings in and mulch the whole lot." Sophia really had a vision for our new yard.

I had a pickup truck and there was a nursery not far away. I bought a truckload of mulch and was just finishing putting it around when a brand new Mercedes convertible pulled up.

"Hey, you've done a nice job on this yard. Where did you get the mulch?" the driver asked.

"I bought it at a nursery not far from here."

"My name is Jack," he said, "and I would like you to get some for my home."

I thought this was a strange request, and then it dawned on me. My pickup truck, my redneck appearance, the fact that not too many of my new neighbors were into manual labor... yeah, I got it. He thought I was a hired hand.

"I'll tell you what, Jack. If you pull in the driveway I'll get your address and deliver you some mulch."

"Oh, I probably shouldn't come up the driveway. I don't know the person who owns this house."

"Jack, this is my house! Go ahead and pull in."

I got mulch for Jack and his wife, Bubbles, after which Jack had me lay it down and told me I would be his new lawn boy. Jack and Bubbles were very nice people, and I ended up taking care of their lot for four or five years.

That experience gave me an idea.

"Sophia, I'm going to get some fliers printed up to deliver around the neighborhood to see if there are any more Jacks around," I announced.

When I got home after distributing about 30 or 40 fliers, I'd already had two phone calls. Supplemental income—just what the doctor had ordered. I ended up being offered so many jobs that I had to turn some down. After all, too much work and no play is not a good lifestyle. But the added income was very nice, now that we had no rental property.

Above the Rest at the Gateway to the West

After Callaway, I did a three-year apprenticeship with Local 396 in St. Louis. This was a requirement to officially become a journeyman ironworker.

Well, in reality, it took a few more years and much more experience to become an actual journeyman; but you would technically became one after completing the apprenticeship.

Ironworkers are a proud bunch with a lot of testosterone running through their veins. It is a man's job; it's very exciting, a bit dangerous at times, and—if you're able to stay working through the slow construction times—a pretty well-paying job.

I said it's a man's job, but this was about the time that a few women joined the ranks of construction workers. There had always been strong women to take on such jobs when needed, as in the two World Wars, but now some were seeking these jobs as a career. There were only a few women when I first started out, as it was backbreaking work, but they were for the most part hard workers.

❊ ❊ ❊

Now, ironworkers have some traits that are kind of funny to the average Joe. For instance, we like our hard hats to be just so—we like to wear them "backerds"—and we also like our little stickers that display our opinions. We basically just like to have our own identities and personalities.

Of course, the idea of "personality" was taboo in the thinking of most of the office and management personnel.

"Hey, Monk, there is a safety meeting this morning."

Naturally, safety was something we all wanted, and it became a big thing later in my career as an ironworker. But for the upper echelons, it became a way to try to take away our personality and keep us under their thumbs.

The wearing of the hard hats backerds was the first of many little battles with the office and management group. They thought the only reason we wore them that way was to buck authority. Damn, authority was a concept we hadn't even considered—who cared about authority? We just wanted to do our jobs without any bull.

There were two main reasons for wearing our hard hats backwards. Number one was that they looked a lot cooler that way; yes, having that little brim on the front looked kind of geeky, and geeky and ironworking did not go together.

Reason number two was practical: if the task at hand required a little welding, that little brim on the front of the hats prevented the welding hood from being lowered. On all large jobs, we were required to wear hard hats, even while welding.

So now we had a legitimate reason for wearing them backwards, as the headband on the inside couldn't be worn comfortably if we had to keep switching our hats around when welding was required. The same scenario applied when we needed to wear a face shield for protection while performing certain tasks.

"Men, this is Herman Doolittle. He will be conducting the safety meeting today."

"Hi, guys. I will be addressing an issue that is a sore subject with the ironworkers: I'll give you some hands-on examples of why you should be wearing your hard hats with the little bills to the front."

There were moans and groans from the crowd.

185

Herman continued. "I was on a job the other day and had to walk under some scaffolding men were working on. As I passed under, a small, hot piece of metal someone had dropped hit my hard hat right on that little brim. Thank God I'd had it on forward, as it could have hit my face. This is why I am going to suggest that wearing your hard hat with the brim to the front be the standard procedure."

What a cheesy, lame way to try and take away some of our personality! I raised my hand and said, "Mr. Donothing, I mean Doolittle, could I please say something?"

"Yes, go ahead."

"Herman, you probably didn't know it, but I too was on that very job you mentioned. And I too walked under that very scaffolding, and a hot piece of metal dropped on my hard hat also. The thing that is important to know is that, being an ironworker, I was a few steps ahead of where most people would have been, and that little piece of hot iron hit the little brim on the back of my hat. Can you imagine my pain had it gone down my back? Therefore, your thinking is flawed unless you are slow to foot. Ironworkers are not slow to foot, and I think I've had enough of your weak attempt to keep us under your thumb. I'm going to go to work and make the company some profits. See ya, wouldn't want to be ya!"

I heard a round of applause as I stormed out. I was not worried about getting in trouble for my little speech, as I was a damn good ironworker. I liked to tell anyone I worked for or anyone I was trying to get to hire me that I was one of the best at the Gateway to the West.

※ ※ ※

This ties in with those stickers I was talking about. Ironworkers like their stickers, and we had many different ones.

One said "Proud to be Union", which was pretty self-explanatory.

Another one said "Git it Up". When moving or setting iron with a rig, if the rig's operator needed to lift the load, we had a hand signal for getting up on the load. Sometimes we would have a handheld radio for talking to the operator and instead of a hand signal we would say "Git it up!" or "Gittin' up".

Still another sticker said "Can't Beat it", with our Local #396 printed below. One of the many tools ironworkers use almost every day is a four- or six-pound beater. It's basically a short-handled sledgehammer. I can tell you that I beat on many a piece of iron in my days as an ironworker!

Some of these stickers were from the international union; some came from guys that were running for an officer's job in our local union. They would come up with a little saying and have it printed on stickers to hand out to the members as they went through the line to vote.

The graduating apprentice classes would also at times make up stickers. Our class decided to have a contest to see who could come up with the best new sticker.

Now, apprentice class was much like high school: there were the "in men", who had connections, and then everybody else. Needless to say, I was in the "everybody else" crowd.

I designed a sticker that said "Above the Rest at the Gateway to the West", with the St. Louis Arch on it. Between the legs of the Arch, it said "Ironworkers Local 396". On the two upper corners there were American flags that looked like they were blowing in the wind. (Almost every sticker had either a flag or a flag motif of some type on it.)

Mine was by far the best entry, but I was not an "in man".

"Monk, I'm sorry to tell you that even though we liked your sticker very much, we found it to be a bit busy."

Some forgettable design won, and I don't even recall ever seeing it on anyone's hard hat.

I did, a few years later, run for one of the more important union offices and had a couple thousand of my stickers printed up. I hadn't been a journeyman long enough to warrant such a position, but I just wanted to see how the union was run. I think I only received 15% of the vote, but everyone wanted a few of my stickers!

The Real Deal

"A man that don't mess up sometimes must not be doing nothing," Homer Bronson said to me out of the corner of his mouth. In the other corner was a stubby cigar with a thin brown line of saliva running down to his chin.

That was one of the first bits of wisdom that came to me from the mouth of a longtime journeyman ironworker.

Homer was pretty crusty and his body was pretty much broken down after many years of ironworking. He was, however, always happy—especially when playing poker at lunchtime. Homer liked his cigars, his beer, and his ice cream.

I never worked with Homer again after that job, which was the first job I had as an apprentice. The last time I saw him he was retired, and he told me he still liked that ice cream. I heard he passed away a couple of years ago.

I remember some of the first little safety tips I learned from some of the older men I worked with on my early jobs.

"Monk, it's either chicken or feathers." That was Harley Chisholm's advice to me on the ups and downs of making a living as an ironworker.

"Monk, don't do that!" said Thaddeus as I was straining to lift the end of a beam with my shoulder. "You will hurt yourself; there are tools and machinery to lift a load like that."

Thaddeus Rodeus was one of the many Rodeus who were Ironworkers; I worked with them all at one time or another. They were all characters.

Geno was one of Thaddeus's brothers; I worked with him many times. He, just like Homer, liked his booze, but instead of ice cream he liked lemon cookies. They were kind of like Oreos except they were not round and had lemon cream filling between yellow cookie chips. Geno always had at least one jumbo pack of them in the trunk of his car.

Geno was ornery and comical. One time, we were raising large rolls of insulation for a metal building we were adding a second floor to. The ground men would put a few rolls in a huge net and the rig would raise it to the lower roof for us to take out, and then we'd send the empty net back. Well, on the last load, Geno said, "Watch this, Monk."

He took that net and threw it over the side of the building. The truck driver who had delivered the insulation was standing right below. That net went over him perfectly. He was a pretty big guy, and as we peered over the edge laughing our heads off, Geno said, "We better hide."

I guess the driver didn't know Geno had thrown the net off with the intention of "catching" him. By the time the guy composed himself and looked, up we had skedaddled to the other side of the building.

※ ※ ※

There were a few mean men in the trade, too. One was a guy named Gene Helfield.

Gene and I were both older than most apprentices. Gene could get real mean, was not afraid to take on almost anyone, and usually kicked ass. I did not know Gene very well and was never on a job with him till my third year of apprenticeship.

One day on that job, some guys and I were installing rebar on the foundation part of a two-phase high-rise. The elite structural men were putting up the steel next to our part of the job. *Whirl,*

whirl, whirl, I heard passing my ear. Then, *bang*! An object hit our metal gang box.

We all looked up and saw an ironworker duck down behind the side of a beam he was sitting on. That fucker had thrown a bolt at us!

Well, I did not know who it was at the time, but I later found out it had been Gene. He liked to scare the guys on the ground every now and then.

"I'm going to go up there and kick that fucker's ass," I said as I headed up the many stringers of half-finished stairs. I was pissed; that bolt had just missed my ear, and if it had hit me in the head it would surely have knocked me out—or worse.

It was eight flights of stairs, and then another two floors of just iron. Gene and another ironworker were bolting up the iron on those two floors.

I yelled up at them that whoever had thrown that bolt was a fuckin' asshole. I got no response.

I shouted, "Whoever threw that bolt was a fuckin' punk!" Again, no response.

"Whoever threw that bolt can suck my dick!" Still no response.

"Whoever threw that bolt, your mother sucks donkey dick while taking it in the ass!"

Up popped Gene, who had been hiding behind that beam. "Monk, you better shut your mouth right now or I'm going to come down and kick your ass."

"Come on down, it's a good day to die!"

Gene got up, went across the iron to the nearest column, and slid down.

Now, my adrenaline was pumping about 100 miles per hour, but I did take a moment to assess the situation. I had just run up eight floors of unfinished iron, I had my fuckin' rubber mud boots on over my regular boots, I was out of breath, and I had just stirred up a hornets' nest. I knew I was about to meet my maker. Time to take control!

There was a thump as Gene slid down the column and hit the deck. I spotted a five-ton shackle laying on the deck. A five-ton shackle is about the size of a small horseshoe but much fatter, with a round pin running through where the open end of a horseshoe would be. These shackles are used for rigging and are quite common on job sites.

I picked it up as Gene turned to face me and began marching right toward me. He grabbed me with both of his monstrous hands, picked me up off the ground, brought me to his face, and while slobbering, with every vein from his neck up bulging and throbbing, screamed at me that he was going to kill me.

Just as I was starting to bring that shackle to the temple of Gene's ugly head, an angel appeared—literally. It was Angel Cordell, the ironworker boss on this project. I felt a hand grab mine and heard a heavenly voice say, "Gene, put him down and get back to work!"

Angel was a well-respected boss, and he made it real clear that if we didn't back down we would both be out of a job.

Gene walked away and said something that pissed me off.

"Fuck you, you big lummox. You're lucky I didn't kill you," I said.

"You little punk, I'm going to kick your ass."

Angel walked between us and promised us again that we would lose our jobs if we didn't stop it right then.

After that job, I ran into Gene from time to time, and he was always gracious about deciding not to kill me. He would just give me a mean grin and go about his business. Gene ended up in jail, and I'm not positive but I think he died in a jail fight.

* * *

On this same job I met an ironworker I came to love and respect, though it didn't start out that way.

As an apprentice, you were not allowed to misrepresent yourself as a journeyman (journeymen made more money). Well, this job was was with an out-of-town company, so they had no way of knowing whether I was an apprentice—which I was—or a journeyman.

Dodie Wynch, the same boss I'd had on my previous job, handed me my first check.

"Dodie, they paid me a journeyman's wages!"

"Yeah, don't worry about it. I told them you were a journeyman. Just take the money; you're worth it."

Well, Oscar Bixton, a younger, black ironworker, overheard the conversation and it rubbed him raw. It probably looked like a racial thing—I was getting full pay while he and two other black apprentices, "Give me Five" Joe and Gene "the King", were not.

Joe and Gene were both much older, but had become ironworkers through the minority program the ironworkers had implemented. All four of us were in the same gang, and Joe and Gene really liked me, as I did them. They told Oscar to forget about it, that I had done nothing wrong, and to just be thankful he had a job.

Oscar didn't listen, and told the pay guy in the office that I wasn't a journeyman.

Looking back, I fully understand Oscar's frustration. Not only was it true that I was an apprentice receiving journeyman's pay, but Oscar had come from a very rough and deprived part of town; he hadn't even had running water or an indoor toilet till he was 18. All the while his little part of St. Louis was crammed between two interstate highways but only blocks away from a very affluent part of town.

But at the time, I didn't know about Oscar's background, and I was pissed—I figured I was going to get in big trouble. It was break time, so I headed for the trailer. I was the only one in there when Oscar walked in. Oscar was smaller and eight years younger than me, but he had been a state champion in wrestling.

As he was about to sit down, I kicked the bench he was planning on sitting down on. We grabbed each other and out the trailer door we went, stumbling down the wooden stairs. We faced off: he knew I was older and bigger, I knew about his wrestling proficiency, and we both just wanted to keep our jobs. We parted company and the next day I decided to take a different job. I did not see Oscar for some time after that.

A few years later, Unk was injured in an auto accident. It was the norm for a collection to be taken or a raffle to be held for injured union members. I was at the Union Hall selling raffle tickets for Unk when Oscar came over.

"Hi, Monk. Sorry to hear about your uncle." He handed me $40. Most times if you got $10 per person you were doing good.

I gave Oscar 40 raffle tickets, and all wounds were healed. Later in our careers we worked on many jobs together and became good friends.

❋ ❋ ❋

Dino the Bandito was another character. He kind of resembled a handsome troll with his huge shoulders, stockiness, and cumbersome movements; but he had a twinkle in his eye and a special little chuckle when amused.

"Hey, Dino, how did you get your nickname?" I asked him one day.

"Monk, that is a very funny story. I came home one day after looking for a job. I had been out of work for months, as work was real slow at the time. My kids were hungry and my wife opened the fridge to show me it was empty except for a frozen pack of chicken wings.

"I hopped in my truck and drove to a convenience store in the next county. As I walked in, I analyzed the surroundings, and then went into the bathroom. I can still see myself looking in the mirror and pulling a ski mask over my head. I reached inside my jacket and pulled out my pistol from my hidden shoulder holster. I looked in the mirror again and said, 'It's a go!'

"Out the door I went, pistol raised, ready to get my family some money. But as I came around a display case I spotted a highway patrolman standing at the counter with his back to me. The cashier also had his back to me.

"I did a quick about-face, ran back into the bathroom, tore off the ski mask, and holstered my pistol. I looked in the mirror again; sweat was pouring down my face. I just started laughing and thanking God that that highway patrolman had been there!

"So, Monk, I gave myself that nickname. And a week later, I was hired on a job that lasted many months."

✳ ✳ ✳

Dr. Jekyll/Mr. Hyde advised me, "Monk, when you're on the iron, don't look up at the moving clouds overhead or the moving water below, or you'll get disoriented and lose your balance. Just watch where your feet are stepping or concentrate on the point you are standing or working on."

Dr. Jekyll/Mr. Hyde, as I liked to refer to him, was probably one of the all-around best ironworkers I ever worked with. He could make the prettiest welds I've ever seen. He was extremely agile on the iron and was also a very good connector.

Connectors (there are usually two connectors working together) are the guys that put the pieces of iron together as the building is being erected. One connector signals the crane operator while the other, perched on some iron that's shaky at best, guides the new piece in place. He then inserts a connecting bolt or two into

195

the connection, which holds the piece in place till the bolt-up guys come to finish the connection and tighten everything up. Two good connectors can keep the ground guys (hook-up crew) running their butts off to keep the flow of new iron streaming into the air as the building rises to new heights.

Mr. Hyde and I were the same age and worked on many jobs together over the years, but we did not always get along. But he was a veteran and had fought for our county, so I always kept that in mind and looked up to him even when we were feuding. I could tell that the war had hurt his psyche, and I watched him go through various phases in life; but regardless of whether he was in the Dr. Jekyll or Mr. Hyde mode, he was always one of the best at the Gateway to the West—a true journeyman.

One of my first and also one of my last jobs as an ironworker involved working with Mr. Hyde.

On an early job in my career I remember he was landing some decking onto a floor that had just been connected and bolted up. I was a few bays over but I watched as a load of decking came at him and he had nowhere to go!

(We were in the heart of downtown St. Louis and things were tight. The operator of the rig couldn't see the men below or where the decking was being landed, so the workers used handheld radios to communicate with the operator.)

I don't know if there was a communications breakdown or if the signal man did not see Mr. Hyde, but that decking was headed right at him. It knocked him off the iron and he fell two floors down. Luckily he landed feet first in an area that had not been welded down and in which there was no steel. This enabled the decking to give and bend a bit, thus lessening the impact. Still, Mr. Hyde was off work for a few weeks. He came back still limping a bit, but he fully recovered.

On several jobs we came close to blows, but we never actually fought. One year, Mr. Hyde and I attended the ironworkers' annual fishing tournament. He was in Dr. Jekyll mode that day. We were sitting on the dock discussing a poker game we had participated in a few weeks earlier. I had beaten him with a very good hand. He hadn't had enough money to call me, so I'd let him call me with the understanding that he would pay up the next day if he lost. He'd lost.

The next day he'd brought $30 worth of pennies to pay his debt and thrown them down in front of me.

"There's your fucking $30!" he'd said.

"Fuck you," I had replied. I'd taken those pennies and thrown them as far as I could.

So we were sitting on the dock when Mr. Hyde threw a hundred dollar bill on my lap and said, "Monk, I'm buying, you're flying." (When work was good, money was no object; and during those days there was lots of overtime work available.)

I took the money and headed out to the corner liquor store at the end of the dock. I gathered up $105 worth of beer and paid for it. I think I had about five cases of canned beer on each shoulder as I walked down the dock back toward Mr. Hyde and the rest of the guys.

When I got back, I dropped the cases in front of him and said, "Here's your fuckin' beer, and you owe me $5." He took it well; we all had a good laugh and a lot of beer.

Mr. Hyde was one of the best at the Gateway to the West!

* * *

There were so many nicknames among the ironworkers.

There was Big Arms, a former bouncer with some pretty nasty facial scars.

Bucket Head was, to my knowledge, the only Jewish guy in our local union. I worked with him on many jobs over the years. He had a big head, both literally and figuratively.

There was Nick the Prick; I never called him that, as we were friends, but he was usually the boss so naturally there were those who did not like him.

There were two brothers I didn't care for whom I nicknamed the brothers Grimm. They were always whining and spending more effort not working than they would have if they would have just done their jobs.

There were a dozen Reds, Whiteys, and Leftys. One Red was the ironworker superintendent of a huge St. Louis company. He was "the man" in town. I worked for this company and him for many years. Later, I always told him that he had made me a rich man—and he had!

Red's son, who was a very good ironworker in his own right, got the nickname of Pinky. Why? Because he just wasn't quite Red yet!

He hated that name, but what could he do?

Then there was the Duke, who was a perfect specimen of a man; in fact, when I first met him, he told me he was a man's man. He was from Mississippi, where his family members were sharecroppers, but to me he sounded like he was from the Caribbean—maybe Jamaica.

You didn't want to mess with the Duke, as one prejudiced, inbred bully of an ironworker had found out when he'd made a racial statement at a union meeting one night. The Duke was waiting for him after the meeting and put his sorry ass on the ground with one punch after telling him he shouldn't have said that.

And there was Rhinestone, a hard-drinking, heavy-smoking ironworker. He would always take a drag on his cigarette, knock off the ash, and then say, "That's the ticket."

One time, while working on a tower, Rhinestone was hit with a large electrical shock which the doctors said killed him. The thing is, he also fell about 50 feet, and when he hit the ground he was alive. The doctors said the impact probably got his heart beating again. Either way, he was a lucky man to survive that incident!

* * *

Pancho was around 60 when I started working for him. I don't know why they called him Pancho, as he wasn't Mexican, he was Filipino.

Pancho was a highly-regarded ironworker. He could walk the iron as well as or better than any ironworker I ever worked around. We were setting bar joists, which are like smaller versions of trusses used in making high-rise floors and warehouse roofs. These were very long bar joists that were sitting, shakily, on about eight inches of bearing on each end.

Pancho was a little ticked that we were reluctant to go out on the joists before they were welded down, but he understood that we were pretty green. Since he was rather boisterous and fun-loving, he decided to give us a little show. Off he went across a joist. That damn iron was shaking and wiggling and he looked like a drunk stumbling down the street. "Look, men," he said (he always called us "men"). "There ain't nothing to it!"

Pancho had a couple of sons and I worked with them both, especially Bernie. We called him Baby Panch. He didn't mind the nickname, as he loved his dad.

* * *

There was only one Big Bopper. He was a mountain of a man with a deep, rich, theatrical voice and was very entertaining. He also thought he was a ladies' man. He would use some cheap hair dye to keep his hair jet black, and if he got to sweating there would be black streams running down his face.

Pancho, Big Bopper, and I were on a high-rise job in downtown St. Louis. Next to us there was a glass building so close that we could see the office girls working inside. The girls would put up signs in the windows saying "Hi" or stuff like that.

One day, Big Bopper and Pancho decided to have a little fun. Bopper found a three-foot section of pink air line that was at least twice as big around as a garden hose. Bopper, who was wearing overall bibs as it was a little chilly out, took that section of pink air line, put it in his bibs, and stuck one end of it out the back of his bibs between his shoulder blades.

Big Bopper and little Pancho started off across the iron to a point right across from an office with about 20 girls. Pancho was almost glued to Bopper's back and had a large glass of water. The Bopper kind of looked around "innocently" and groped around the fly of his bibs for a bit, then pulled out that pink hose like he was taking a leak. Pancho, who was hidden from the office girls, was pouring the glass of water into the hose coming out of the back of Bopper's bibs.

The rest of us were back on the deck trying to hold back our laughter. Immediately, the girls start putting signs in the windows: "I love you", "Call me", "I'm free for lunch", and more.

We had such fun. It was hard work, but we always made sure fun was a part of it.

✳ ✳ ✳

An ironworker, unlike some other tradesmen, could either solicit his own jobs or go down to the hall, where companies would sometimes put in an order for a good man or men to take on a job. From time to time, I caught some pretty neat jobs working out of the hall.

I got to the hall very early one day.

"Hey, Monk, I've got just the job for you," said Lonnie. Lonnie was one of our business agents; he would dole out the jobs that were called in.

"How's that, Lonnie?" I asked. Usually whoever had been out of work the longest got the first crack at a job. But I was the only one in the hall and the company was in need of a man pronto.

"Monk, this is a tower job. Have you ever been on a tower job?"

"No, I haven't. What's it all about?"

"Southern Tower and Erection out of Suffolk, Virginia, is putting up a communications tower that will be almost twice as tall as the St. Louis Gateway Arch."

"Damn, that must be over 1000 feet!"

"That's right, Monk. Do you want it?

"Yeah, I'll take the job. It sounds interesting."

I met the crew of men from Virginia and Harold, the boss, gave me the lowdown on how we would go about putting the tower up.

"Monk, first we will assemble the tower on the ground in 50-foot sections, and then we will paint each section alternating red and white."

"Sounds like a plan!" But I was most excited to see how we would erect it.

"That's at least a month away, Monk. It will take some time to receive, assemble, and paint the tower."

Well, a month later we had the sections assembled. "You told me we would paint this puppy dog," I said.

"That's right. The paint will arrive the day after tomorrow. You'll have the day off tomorrow with a full day's pay."

"No kidding!" I said.

It turned out that Harold wanted me to take his number one hand, Kenny, fishing in one of the Ozark streams the next day.

Well, I had never gotten paid for fishing before, but it sounded good to me.

Kenny and I slayed the smallmouth bass the next day. It was one of the best fishing trips I had ever gone on, and I was paid a full day's wages for it!

The next day I showed up for work in the rattiest clothes I owned, as Harold had advised me to do.

"How are we going to paint this thing?—Or maybe the better question is, why is the painters' union letting ironworkers paint a 1000-foot tower?"

"Monk, it's all part of our project package. The painter's hall is aware of our plan."

"Okay, so, what now?"

"Over there are some terry cloth mittens that are long enough to go up to your elbow, and 40 five-gallon buckets of white and red paint. We will put on the mittens, dunk our hands in the bucket, and slather it on the sections."

The next week and a half was great fun! It was kind of like the food fight in the movie "Animal House", but we did get it all painted.

The next day there was heavy rain, so we couldn't start erecting the tower. We were standing on top of a steep ridge overlooking the area where we park our vehicles. I had just bought a new four-wheel-drive pickup truck, and boy, was it pretty.

"Monk, I doubt that pretty little truck could even make it up to where we are standing, and I know you won't get it all muddy to find out. Tell me, do you own the truck or does the truck own you?" Harold said.

"I tell you what, Harold, that 'pretty little truck' will make it up this ridge with no problem, and I damn sure own it—it doesn't own me! I'll need five bucks from each of you if I make it up this hill, as my pretty little truck will need a trip to the car wash when I get done. If I don't make it up the hill I will give you each five bucks."

The group agreed so I went down, got in my truck, and didn't even bother turning around to build up speed. I just engaged the four-wheel-drive, shifted into reverse, and backwards up the hill I went. I cleared the top of the hill—in reverse—and hit the ground, slammed on the brakes, changed gears, and started after the guys. Mud was flying off the tires; the guys were running in all directions but I sprayed mud on each and every one of them.

I hopped out of my 'pretty little truck' and said, "I guess I own the truck," and reminded them they all owed me five bucks. Yes, we always had fun on our jobs.

❊ ❊ ❊

I called Red and nabbed a job building the new football stadium in downtown St. Louis with a major contractor. This contractor had many other jobs in progress at the time and the first week or so I just filled in on the welding gang; we didn't seem to have a foreman over us.

On a job this size, safety was always a big deal, but at times it was impossible to comply with the rules. One of the requirements was to be tied off anytime we were within six feet of a fall zone. Now, we were not big on tying off, especially if it seemed stupid. I mean, we were used to being in the air, on shaky iron, and in dangerous positions.

There was an apprentice carpenter I was working with, as the job we were doing required a composite crew of carpenters and ironworkers. Buck was his name and he was a strong young man.

"Buck, Red wants us to hook on to this ten-ton piece of precast and move it out to the next section of deck. It's in the way where it is now sitting. Richie the operator is in the rig and he will move it for us," I said.

We put the rigging on the precast and I got on the radio to tell Richie to get up on the load a bit to tighten the rigging up.

"Richie, you need to boom up on the rig before you lift it."

"Can't do that, Monk, as I am boomed up all the way right now."

"Okay, how about backing up a bit? You're over-boomed, and the load will swing away when you get up on it if you don't."

"Can't do that either, Monk; I'm boxed in with some other equipment right behind me."

I looked over a couple of bays and saw Red and the head safety man eyeing us. They didn't have radios so they didn't know what was going on. I had known Red long enough to sense that he was wondering what the heck the holdup was.

Buck and I were standing on opposite concrete piers, with concrete stringers spanning the opening between the piers which the precast was sitting on. The precast had a step out, which would allow me to raise it one foot to see how much it would swing out before it came to rest on the next precast step out one foot down.

"Richie, I want you to get up on the load real easy so I can tell how much we are over-boomed."

"Okay, Monk."

Up it came, and when the step out was cleared, sure enough the whole slab took off and came to rest at the lower step out. It caused the pier and concreted stringer to jolt a bit, but I figured we could raise it without the whole slab of precast taking off wildly if we did it slowly. I figured even if it swung out more than I anticipated, it would also lower a bit, which would drag on the concrete stringer and slow the swing down so we would be able to control it.

I look over and saw Red and Bill, the safety guy, scratching their heads trying to figure out what the problem was.

Now, there was a safety cable strung out the length of the concrete stringers and about a foot off of them. Buck and I had to only reach out a bit to hook off our safety lanyards to that cable.

"Buck, I am going to get up on the load now, and when I do this whole slab is going to swing out."

"No, it won't."

"I'm telling you, it's going to swing out; steer clear and we won't get hurt."

Just as Richie was getting up on the load, I saw my lanyard hooked to that damn safety line. I yelled, "Buck, unhook your lanyard! I'm unhooking mine."

But Buck didn't get his unhooked. Out swung the precast. It hit the safety line but was also scraping along the pier. I looked over at Buck and saw him holding on with a death grip to some rebar sticking out of the pier he was standing on. He was still hooked to the safety cable and his lanyard was stretched to the limit; his safety harness was pulling away at the back and cutting into his front side.

I jumped up on the slab, raced across, and unhooked his lanyard. Just then, the precast took off another few feet, taking the safety cable with it, and then settled down just like I had figured it would; it was now gently swaying back and forth.

Richie was screaming over the radio, "What's going on?!"

"Richie, all is good. Get up on the load and boom it down to the next bay." I looked at Buck and said, "I told you it was going to swing out!"

Buck was still a little on the white side, but grinned and said, "So you did." I glanced over at Red and Bill; they just tipped their hats and walked away.

The next day the carpenter foreman on the job walked up to me, handed me some keys and a radio, and said, "You are the ironworker foreman."

I asked, "Who says?"

"Red says."

* * *

Our company was a huge company that did many large projects all over the country. In fact, in taking on this football stadium job, they may have overextended themselves. The work wasn't getting done quickly enough to meet the completion date.

So Big John was hired to pick things up. He was six foot eight inches tall and 380 pounds of pure ego.

Now, Big John had built a couple of huge stadiums, and he knew how to get the ball rolling. He just put everyone on massive overtime hours, started future phases of the job before the first phases were complete, had cement trucks lined up for blocks and blocks, and in general had everyone tripping over each other in a mad frenzy. It got pretty crazy.

There was always graffiti on the wall of the Johnny on the Spot. Once Big John came, it was mostly about him. One particular work of art portrayed rigs swinging in all directions, cement trucks dumping loads, and guys with wheelbarrows running all around, while laborers were busy dealing with concrete pours that had been mispoured in all the confusion. The caption read, "Thanks for all the extra money, Big John. I bought my wife a new stove, my kids new bikes, and myself a new boat; I just wish I had a day off to use it!"

As the stadium job grew, I—now the foreman for the ironworkers—started getting more men. It became necessary for me to make a few of the men crew foremen. I had never been on a job of this size and had never made anyone a foreman before.

"Danny, I want you to run the imbed crew, and I'm going to get you foreman's pay."

"That's fine, Monk, but then you should be getting general foreman's pay."

I agreed with him and called the office to make Danny a foreman and to raise my pay to the general foreman rate.

"Hi, this is Shirley in payroll."

"Shirley, this is Monk at the stadium job. I want you to start giving Danny foreman's pay, and I am making myself general foreman."

"And on whose authority should I make this change?"

"On my authority, Shirley."

"How long is this to be in effect?"

"Until I call you or until someone above me tells you differently."

"Okay, Monk, it will all take effect this payroll cycle."

The next day I was at the south end of the stadium and happened to catch sight of Red. He was on the north end and headed my way. A football stadium is pretty big, so I was able to keep a good distance between us without making it look like I was trying to avoid him. But he finally cornered me and asked, "How are things going, Monk?"

"Oh, pretty good, Red, but this job is starting to get really big. Oh, by the way, I made myself the general foreman."

"Yeah, I heard something to that effect." That was all he said.

So I was officially the ironworker general foreman and rather new to being so in charge, much less running a project of that size. I had been having trouble getting the necessary temporary electric power and procuring some equipment I needed to keep up with the new demands. My company contacts didn't know me, and my needs were basically ignored while foremen on the other large projects got their orders because they were company men with the ties and contacts I lacked.

I had approached Mario, who had been the job superintendent prior to Big John, with my needs and he had just kind of shrugged me off. I'd gotten a little huffy with him and he'd gotten in my face in front of my men to let me know he was an important man with the company.

But with Big John in charge, things were different.

"Monk, why in the hell aren't your men welding on the field level connections? If you can't handle the job I will find someone that can."

"Tell you what, Big John," I said. "You go ahead and do what you think is best. But unless the new guy can squat down and shit you out about 5000 feet of welding lead and a few new banks of electrical power, well, he probably won't do much better than me in the keeping up department."

Big John was a lunkhead, but he was reasonable. "What do you mean?"

"John, I have been trying to get those things for the last three weeks, and so far I don't have the pull to get what we need for my men and me to keep up."

"We'll see about that!" John said. And damn, the next morning I got to work and there were a dozen electricians frantically hooking up some new electric banks.

Big John called me up to the office. "Monk, there is a load of brand spanking new welding lead due to hit the job site any minute. It should be enough to reach around this stadium four times. Do you need anything else?"

"That will do for now," I said. "I will keep you posted on any future needs."

"Well, Monk, if you need anything else, just tell Mario and he will see that you get whatever you need." I turned around to see Mario, the former head honcho, sitting in a little cramped corner of the office and looking down at his desk. Mario didn't stay around much longer; I'm sure the company took care of him and sent him somewhere else where he could bask in his power.

Not too many of the company men liked Big John, but I must say he sure got that job buzzing, and he and I got along quite well.

I did manage to tick him off big time on one occasion, though, and the whole job site was privy to the showdown.

Like I said before, Red was the main man in St. Louis, and he was also the head ironworker for the company I was working for. Red kept me employed through some lean times, and I owed him my allegiance for that in addition to the fact that he was a fellow ironworker. Big John was just a hired gun from out of town; he could get a big project in line, but Red had the experience and full knowledge of all aspects of ironworking that Big John didn't.

On large projects, all foremen and office personnel carried two-way radios for communication. Those radios could get a worker in trouble at times if he wasn't diplomatic in what he said. Occasionally the radios would get accidentally turned on, and that always resulted in comedy or tragedy, depending on the radioer's rank in the food chain.

The other large projects in town were winding down, and it was time for Red to assume his rightful position and for Big John to move on. But Big John had that ego thing and I got caught in the middle.

"Monk, this is Red," I heard over the radio. "I need you to turn the rig over to me for a while."

I saw Red and his crew of men at the top of the stadium and waved at him. I had been setting precast risers, per Big John's request, to get them off the ground so more could be delivered.

"Okay, Red, the rig is yours," I replied.

"Monk, this is Big John," blared the radio. "What are you doing giving the rig up?"

I looked a couple of bays to the right and saw Big John standing on top of some risers with his hands on his waist, his body language the epitome of superiority.

"You just keep setting those risers," Big John ordered.

"Monk, this is Red. I am taking the rig," Red repeated.

What was I supposed to do? I figured I could play that game too. I picked up my radio and broadcast over the air—for all to hear—"Who is number one on this job? Because I damn sure know it isn't me."

There was a slight moment of silence and then Red came over the air. "Monk, I am number one."

"That is what I thought, Red. The rig is yours."

A couple of hours later I ran into Big John.

"Monk, you're lucky I wasn't anywhere near you when the number one thing came up. I would have strangled your ass!" he said.

"I'm glad I wasn't near you too," I said, "but it did clear up an issue for me. Sorry, but I gotta go do some work." Big John was a good guy, but Red was number one!

✳ ✳ ✳

Over the years, engineers and safety men were always my biggest headaches. I would generally try to get along with the engineers, and many of them were nice guys, but they always wanted to know why things were not going as planned.

My usual response to an irritating engineer or a wise guy was, "Well, you know, just because it works on paper doesn't necessarily mean it works in the field." Then I would just walk away rather than argue, as I didn't have to answer to engineers. I was a journeyman ironworker and a member of Local 396.

Ironworkers only took orders from another tradesman (usually just another ironworker).

Some engineers were a little jealous when they found out how big our paychecks were. With all the overtime, it was not unusual for an ironworker's check to dwarf an engineer's. They just couldn't grasp the union wage idea or the concept of working conditions as laid out in our contract. They figured they had a degree and we were just workers. Well, we had a degree, too, with our three-year apprenticeships!

Vladimir was a new engineer for our company. He was from Russia, had a neat accent, and didn't know "union" was a word in the English language.

Red called me one night to inform me that Vlad was going to be the head engineer for our job. He asked that I work with him and teach him the ropes, including the concept of the union.

I grew to really like Vlad, but we butted heads often.

The first day Vlad hit the job was a Saturday morning (overtime).

"Monk, we are to get twelve truckloads of precast today."

"Yes, Vlad, I am aware of that, and my crew is here and waiting for the trucks to arrive."

"Vat vill they do till the trucks get here?"

"Well, I brought them in to unload the trucks, and we must be ready the moment they show up. Therefore we will be in the change shed waiting for their arrival."

"Monk, the trucks vill be late! Don't the men mind waiting till they arrive?"

"No, Vlad, they will not mind. They are on the clock."

"Vat! You mean they are getting paid to sit?"

"Yes, they are."

"Is there not something they can do?"

"Vlad, all the work is up there on the structure; the trucks will be down here on the ground. The minute they show up we have to jump into action so the city streets will not be clogged up. The truck drivers will also expect to be unloaded immediately so they can be on their way. If I send the men up to work it will take at least an hour to get the equipment out and figure out what to do, and about that time the trucks will probably show up. My crew is scheduled to unload trucks; that is what we are geared up to do and that is what we will do."

"But aren't your men getting paid overtime?"

"Yes. It is Saturday, an overtime day."

"Vell, do they work harder on overtime?"

"No, Vlad, they do not work any harder."

Clearly it was taking Vlad some time to get used to this.

"Monk, I just got a call that the trucks are here."

"Yes, Vlad, I just received the same call; and as you can see, my men are anxiously awaiting their entry into the stadium."

We got a couple of trucks unloaded and then it was time to take a break. (Most jobs had a morning break and a noon lunch.)

"Monk, why are the men sitting down?" Vlad asked.

"They are taking their morning break; give them ten minutes to grab a donut and a cup of coffee and they will be back on the job."

"Do they get paid for this break?"

"Yes."

We got all the trucks unloaded. Vlad was impressed with our ability to unload so quickly and have all the precast landed and secured in an orderly fashion.

"Monk, I like your men. They are very good workers."

"Yes, Vlad, they are indeed!"

Monday came, and it was time to start setting the precast. Now, I usually had the prints indicating where each piece was to go. The prints had come in with the trucks, and Vlad had gathered them all up. He thought he was going to run the show. I figured I would let him decide which pieces to set first, as I wanted to see how much he knew.

"Vlad, we have a problem up here. It seems the wrong piece was sent up, and now we will have to take it out."

"Monk, that is unacceptable. Why did you set it in the wrong place?"

"Well, Vlad, there is an old Russian saying that goes, 'A picture is worth a thousand words.' I need those damn drawings! Tell you what. I'll send a man down for the drawings, and you probably need to go sit at your desk in the office while we do the work."

Vlad was trying to accept our union ways, but he was curious as to why I made a fair amount more than the other ironworkers.

"I'm the general foreman, Vlad. That means I'm responsible for what does or does not get done, for what is done right or wrong. I must keep the men working and happy and have their respect. That is why I get the big money."

"Monk, would you mind if I observed you for a day to understand?"

I agreed, and the next day Vlad came over my radio, "Come in, Monk."

"This is Monk."

"This is Vlad. What are you doing?"

"We are setting a stair tower for access to the top deck so my men can weld up there."

"Oh, okay."

Soon I heard Vlad again over the radio. "Come in, Monk."

"This is Monk."

"This is Vlad. What are you doing now?"

"I'm helping the men string out cable to the welding banks."

"Oh, okay, Monk."

A little later, Vlad popped back on the radio. "Come in, Monk."

"This is Monk. Is that you, Vlad?"

"Yes, what are you doing now?"

"I am walking to my shed to get some drawings for a little project we are going to do later today."

"Okay."

I was starting to get a little peeved, as this was all going over the air for everyone to hear. It was time to play my own game.

"Come in, Vlad," I said.

"This is Vlad."

"This is Monk. I'm running up the stair tower to check on my men."

"Okay."

A few minutes later, I radioed Vlad again.

"This is Monk. I'm with the safety gang and we are putting up some new safety cable."

It was now time for me to visit the Johnny on the Spot and get rid of some coffee. The Johnnies were all made of green plastic.

"Come in, Vlad."

"Yes, this is Vlad."

"Yeah, Vlad, this is Monk. I'm in the little green house and I'm shaking it, boss."

There was radio silence for a bit and then Vlad came back.

"Monk, I don't think you have to call me anymore, as I can see that you are a busy man."

I really grew to like Vlad, and I think he came to approve of the union way.

* * *

Bill, the safety man, was another headache. I never really took a liking to him, and the other men on the job didn't appreciate him much either. He had the authority to give a worker a couple days off without pay if he caught him breaking a safety rule.

The guys gave Bill, who was a bit rotund, the nickname of Pork Chop.

When it was really hot and humid, our safety glasses would steam up and make it hard to see. But Pork Chop was adamant that we always have our safety glasses on.

Occasionally men working at the very top of the stadium with not a chance of something falling on their heads would take their hard hats off. Hard hats are necessary, but they can be uncomfortable and cumbersome at times. Pork Chop would peer out his office window with binoculars to try and catch someone with his hard hat or safety glasses off.

What really ticked me off was Pork Chop's insistence that we throw away any electric cord or welding lead with the slightest abrasion. I understood the issue with electric cords; whenever one got too beat up to be fixed with electrical tape, we would throw it away on our own anyway. But Pork Chop was unrelenting; the slightest nick and he would unplug it, even if it was being used at that moment, and throw it away.

Welding lead is very expensive, and commonly has many abrasions. It's almost impossible for it not to get beat up and it usually doesn't take very long. It really isn't dangerous, as it will only make a spark if a bare spot comes in contact with metal; it happens all the time.

Pork Chop, however, had no problem throwing away $1000 worth of welding lead because of just one small nick. We went round and round: he would throw it away and I would go retrieve it later.

He was also relentless in catching workers not tying off when needed. I had no problem with this, although the rules for tying off were way too stringent. Pork Chop actually caught me out on the iron not tied off once. I didn't even have a safety harness on. I had just walked out on a large beam to unhook the rubber hose to the cutting torch for two of my men working on the floor above. It was wedged in a joint, and rather than their having to come down to free it up, I had yelled up that I would get it.

I turned around and there was Pork Chop.

"Monk, you are off the job without pay for two days."

I thanked him, as I hadn't had a day off in over a month. He caught a little heat for giving me that time off, but I was one happy camper those two days.

I was standing with Red a few weeks later when up walked Pork Chop.

"Red, your men have got to stop calling me Pork Chop. They even call me Pork Chop over the radio. It's disrespectful."

I almost fell off the building laughing my ass off and Red said he would take care of it.

Red got on the radio for the whole job site to hear and broadcast, "This is Red; I want everyone to stop calling Pork Chop—I mean Bill—Pork Chop."

That was the only time I ever heard Red be so humorous. I will never forget Pork Chop and the look on his face when Red said that. People did stop calling him Pork Chop—over the radio, at least… .

Unions

Most people either think highly of unions or hate them. There are many reasons for both views.

Me, I just know that I was proud to be a journeyman ironworker for Local 396 in St. Louis. Not having had much of an education, I was thankful for the excellent training and pretty damn good salary that I as a union man could earn.

Are unions all good? No way. Do unions always do what is best for the company? No way. Do unions sometimes guard and protect unworthy employees? Damn right!

But even given all that, for the most part, unions are necessary and good for the country. In the late 1800s and early 1900s, working conditions for the average worker were abysmal. Wages were usually pitiful, safety was unheard of, and an average workweek was 50 to 60 hours. Unions led to the improvement of these conditions.

Unions also usually have good health benefit programs that pay doctors and hospitals their high rates, which in turn helps to offset the costs incurred by people who receive medical care and never pay (for whatever reason).

I remember when our union first got an eye care benefit, and let me tell you, it was one hell of a benefit. There was a large eye care company in town that had started off with just one location. It just so happened that the doctor starting up this practice was so anti-union that he was erecting his building non union, which in St. Louis in the late 1970s was not the norm.

I was an apprentice and was sent out to the site to picket. The doctor, seeing me on the sidewalk, came out, cursed at me, called the police, and wanted me arrested. Naturally, the police informed him I was perfectly within my rights to be there.

About two years later, I decided I needed to get some glasses, as my eyesight was just bad enough that I thought they would be helpful. Many of my fellow union members told me about this great eye care company that had four offices scattered around town.

I got the address of the one near me on Clarkson Road, and I'll be damned if it wasn't the same one I had walked picket on. It seemed the good doctor's practice had blossomed and he had opened three more offices. I'll be damned again; that same good doctor was who I would be seeing that day.

After the exam, I picked out one of the most expensive frames and chose all the upscale lens options. The doctor told me that not many eye plans offered what my plan did. I asked him if he had a large clientele of union patients. He said he did, and noted that their insurance always came through, with little hassle for his office workers. I asked if my insurance was better than what he provided his office girls, and he admitted that it was.

"Doc, you probably don't remember me," I finally said.

"What do you mean?"

"I am the young man you called the cops on who was walking picket on your new building two years ago. I'm so glad to hear that union members have made you and your practice so successful. I won't hold the incident against you."

This doctor now has about 20 offices in and around St. Louis.

※ ※ ※

Now, my best buddy is not a real champion of unions either. He was always fearful that they would try to make his shop union. I can't say I blame him, as a small business owner would be in a tough position to fight a union.

"Monk, my employees always turn down the chance to join a union, as I already pay them at or higher than union scale."

Yep, another reason unions are good—they bring up the non-union pay scale, if for no other reason than that non-union employers fear becoming unionized. Wages equal taxes paid to our government; taxes provide money for running the country. Prosperity encourages prosperity, and prosperity equates to a higher standard of living.

The opposite is true of a dog-eat-dog mentality of getting everything as cheaply as possible. Capitalism is designed to be most efficient if everyone is both working and a consumer. That is the only thing wrong with capitalism—it is go, go, go; don't let up!

Finally, be they good or bad, unions have been a major part of our country. "… in order to form a more perfect *union* . . . " (hm, that phrase rings a bell!), *United* States, *Union* Army, and so forth… .

✳ ✳ ✳

I have been accused of being non union on a couple of occasions. Once was when I made a resolution at a union meeting to do away with our annuities.

Our officers had spent many years trying to get an annuity to supplement our pension plan when retirement came. The first few years, our annuity usually gave a decent return on investment.

Then came a couple of years when we lost money. Most investment advisors were making money for their clients; I had a little personal portfolio that I administered myself that was making money. And yet our annuity advisors were getting a nice payday for themselves while losing our money.

The day of the vote on my resolution came, and the pressure for me to back off came pretty strongly from a couple of our officers. The meeting came to order and the ringers chosen to speak against my resolution came to the mic and attacked viciously.

When it was my turn to speak, I said, "Fellow members, I am not against having an annuity. What I am against is having some 'fat cats' smoking cigars and lounging on the beach, while collecting payment for ill-advised investments with our annuity."

I had a speech all made up. It was a fictitious little fable and it went something like this:

"Boys, my pappy used to go to Africa to collect animals for zoos throughout the United States. Pappy took me with him once on a trip to collect monkeys.

"'Dad, how are we going to catch those monkeys?' I asked.

"'Monk, we will find out where the monkeys sleep and where they gather in the morning to forage for food. We will then throw grains of rice on the jungle floor for the monkeys to eat; they like rice. We'll do that for a few days, and then we'll hollow out a bunch of coconuts, leaving a hole just big enough for the monkeys' hands. We will stake the coconuts to the ground and allow the monkeys to shake the rice out of the coconuts for a few days. The next step will be to walk out into the clearing as they are gathering the rice, and we will grab them.'

"'But Dad, won't they just run away?'

"'No, Monk, they will try but they will not. You see, the monkeys will not leave until they grab a handful of that rice. The holes we cut out are just big enough to for them to get their hands in, but when they make a fist to grab the rice, it will be too big to pass back through the hole. Nevertheless, they will want that rice and won't let go.'"

I then turned to the men in the meeting and said, "Boys, it is time to let go." There was silence.

A vote was then called for, and though my resolution ultimately failed, many members came up to me after the meeting and thanked me. And a few months later, another resolution was submitted that would have allowed members to choose to self-direct their investments or have the union's advisors continue directing their investments.

Looking back, though, I don't know if my actions and the resulting options were for the best. Few laymen really know how to successfully invest money.

Once we got the option of directing our own investments, there were about fifteen funds we could get in and out of just by calling the fund office and re-allocating our portfolios.

There was this one high yield/high risk fund that many men invested in; in fact, there were three or four funds that were very high yield but risky.

Now, I pretty much tailored my annuity cautiously. I diversified, but put nothing in the high risk funds.

The first few months, guys were going crazy watching their high risk funds multiply by large percentages. The change shed was like a gambling casino with all the talk of funds and stocks and profits. Nick, a guy I nicknamed "Mustard Face" who was an "in man" in the union, would get out the newspaper, look up his fund, and then gloat about how much money he was making.

Everyone knew that I had chosen a more cautious investment plan, and Mustard Face would go down the columns to my chosen funds and yell out, "Wow! Your funds have increased a half of a percent this month. Let's look at mine now. Monk, look, mine have increased 8% this month and 17% the last three months." He would lay it on each and every day.

What wasn't so funny was that this was mid-1999, just prior to the first major market correction of my investing life. By mid-2000, many guys invested in those high risk funds lost 50%—some even lost 80%—of their entire annuities. These losses were pretty substantial, as at that time we were probably contributing $3 per hour of our pay into the annuities. We had been contributing for years, and with all the overtime we'd had in the last years of the '90s, many men had accumulated $100,000 or more in their annuities.

I felt kind of bad, knowing that it had probably been my resolution that had prompted the union to allow the members to self-direct their annuities. Mustard Face was one of the many who lost much of what they had contributed over the years.

✳ ✳ ✳

This experience got me to thinking that the self-direct plan for Social Security that President George W. Bush was pushing would probably have ended up just as tragically. The average Joe doesn't know squat about investing. The banks and a certain political party would have loved to push that through. You can bet the house that the big money guys would have made a killing on average citizens directing their Social Security accounts! Thank God that hasn't happened yet.

I have a friend, Mark, who lives up in the Northeast, and one time when I visited him he took me crabbing. You basically take some simple traps and a bucket out to the ocean tidal pools, and trap and then collect the crabs.

"Mark, how are we going to keep these crabs in the bucket?"

"Don't worry, we won't lose any, as crabs are a lot like people."

"How's that?"

"Well, you see, if one of the crabs starts to climb up the side of the bucket, there is always another crab that will reach up and pull him down."

Yep, he was right; just like crabs, there are always people just like that. If the average guy tries to get ahead, the money guys will always be scheming on how to take his hard-earned cash.

The politicians owned by these money guys will also do what they can to screw the little guy.

The crabs, at least, don't realize that they are pulling down their fellow crabs in trying to climb to the top themselves!

Danger

Ironworking can be a pretty dangerous job, and I've seen and been a part of many unfortunate instances. Safety was a subject of constant disagreement; either the company was pushing it down our throats, or the men were trying to get the company to spend dollars so the job would be safer for them. It was an ongoing battle.

The job that sticks out the most for me was a bridge we were building across the Missouri River with a contractor called American Bridge.

This was my first experience with building a bridge. The first day for me was just after the winter ice was beginning to break up. The job had been shut down for a month or so, as it had been a very cold winter and the ice in the river had delayed the arrival of some of the steel members that had been shipped by barge.

"Men, some of you are new to this job, and some of you are returning from the shutdown. All of you need to be at a safety meeting after lunch today so I can discuss what I expect."

Chisholm or Boss is all I ever called that guy, and I always assumed Chisholm was his last name. He didn't talk too much, but we could pretty much tell what he wanted from his body language.

Boss had never worked for any company except American Bridge, and building bridges was all he wanted to do. Rumor had it that as a young man, Chisholm had once fallen off the upriver side of a work barge, been sucked under by the current, and miraculously come up gasping for air on the downriver side. Over the course of his life, he had probably been involved with every element of building a bridge, and for the last 20 years he'd been the boss man.

* * *

Barges are a key component of building bridges. There is the ringer barge, which is a flat barge secured to the riverbed with large steel spuds at each corner. The spuds are secured to the sides of the barge with large hollow tubes; the spuds slide through them and sink into the mud and gunk at the bottom of the river. This keeps the barge in place so the current doesn't move it. The ringer barge needs to be stable, as the main rig for setting the steel members sits on it.

There are other barges involved—the open-top barges full of steel to be erected, and another flat barge for storing bolts and equipment. On this particular job, this barge also had a large metal storage container we used for a change shed and break room.

* * *

The Duke was my partner on this job. I had never met him before, and he introduced himself as Lonny Owens (like Jesse Owens) and told me he was a man's man. Indeed, The Duke was a chiseled specimen of a man.

"Say, young man, look at this." The Duke was holding a piece of iron shaped like a big banana cut in half longways but only an inch thick at most.

"What are you going to do with that, Duke?"

"It will make a good plow shear for my folks back home in Alabama."

I, having been on the farm in Georgia and seen many old plow shears, replied, "Yes, Duke, I must agree, that could be used for a plow shear."

The Duke looked at me with a big smile, his dark skin glistening, the veins in those powerful arms pulsing, and said, "I will take it home to my parents' farm." It did not take much to put a smile on the Duke's face.

I had heard of him from other ironworkers' tales, but now I was working with him myself and I thoroughly enjoyed our time together.

* * *

Our foreman, Jon Nosey, decided we would go to the far bank to work on the approach at the other end of the bridge. The only way to get over there was to get in the skip box and have the rig swing us over and land us on top of the structure.

A skip box is an 8-foot by 8-foot steel box-like piece of equipment, used to move things from one point to another. It has four cables—one on each corner—that are all attached to an iron ring. The rig has what is called a headache ball (a large round metal ball with a connection on the bottom for a heavy duty hook and safety clasp). The headache ball probably weighs around 200 pounds, and it basically keeps the cable of the rig tight so the cable doesn't tangle in the drum of the rig when lowering or raising a load.

We put the ring to the skip box on the hook under the headache ball, hopped in the skip box, and off we went. There were five of us in the box as we were lifted up, up, and away. The ringer rig could reach from one side of the river to the other, and we were probably 80 feet up, swinging to the approach iron on the far side of the river.

We were required to be tied off while in the skip box—although in a few short years, riding in a skip box would no longer be allowed at all. Heck, we used to stand on the headache ball while grasping the load cable and have the rig swing us to wherever we wanted to go. Sometimes two or three of us would be crowded on the top of the headache ball with just enough room for each of us to have only one foot on top of the ball. The rig would swing us to a point on the iron and off one of us would scamper; then it would swing to the next point and someone else would disembark. We were sometimes referred to as "cowboys in the sky".

Anyway, the tie-off practice at this time was just a 5/8-inch rope lanyard woven around our work belts with a metal hook to attach to a cable or, in this case, one of the cables attached to the skip box.

Now, there was much barge traffic while we were constructing the bridge, and when a tow came by it would usually cause a large swell that would rock the ringer barge. A tow consisted of up to eight or ten barges lashed together and pushed by a towboat. We were always supposed to be notified when a tow was passing.

Jon instructed the operator to let one man out of the skip box and then swing the rest of us a bit farther out. As the skip box settled on the iron, I unhooked myself and stepped out. Just then, the skip box started hopping up and down. Two more guys jumped out as the skip box tipped on the edge of the iron. The Duke was the only one left in the box.

The operator, seeing the skip box about to slide off the iron, got up on the load. The Duke was flung out of the box. It seemed like slow motion; I watched as the Duke fell over the side of the box, the rig got up on the box, and then the Duke got snapped back up because he was still tied off to the cable on the skip box.

Our work belts, at that time, had a "quick-release" buckle. They too were outlawed a few years later, though I always kept mine. The quick-release feature had a double catch. When the Duke got snapped up, only the first catch opened, and he was hanging bent in half like an upside-down V. If the second catch opened—and it could have at any moment—he would fall 80 feet to the cold river.

Duke slowly raised his hand to his waist, where the safety clasp was still holding, and threaded the little stiff leather tab back through the guide and closed the quick-release mechanism. The skip box was still swaying violently as the Duke then slowly pulled himself up the safety lanyard and got back in the box.

The operator, seeing all was well, raised the skip box, waited for the water to calm, and then lowered the Duke to the iron. Duke had a big smile on his face and suggested we take a break and clean out our undies.

For some reason, the operator hadn't been notified that the tow was coming. He normally would have seen it coming, but since we were working on the other side, his back had been to the main channel. By the time he'd seen it, it had been too late. But all was well, so no harm done.

✳ ✳ ✳

The Duke and I were landing steel on the riverbank with another rig when out of the corner of my eye I noticed a commotion on the ringer barge.

"Duke! Look over there!" I shouted.

The whole mast of the ringer rig was coming apart, and parts of the boom were raining down on the barge. Men were running in all directions.

This all lasted maybe 45 seconds and then all was calm. It was amazing that no one was hurt, as the pieces of the boom would surely have struck killing blows had they hit anyone. I had never witnessed anything like that incident and still haven't to this day.

It seems the operator had done what is called a low-ball swing while turning the rig from the bridge back to the barge. The top of the spuds that anchored the ringer barge had a metal hoop for attaching the rig when raising or lowering them. The hoop was probably a 12-inch opening, and the hook on the headache ball probably took up 8 inches of that opening. The chance of threading that hoop with the hook was probably a million to one; I doubt the operator could have done it in a thousand tries.

And that is what had happened. When the hook had caught the hoop with the rig still swinging, the only possible result was catastrophe. Down the boom had come, like a splintering Tinkertoy. The operator was fired on the spot.

* * *

I learned and experienced a lot while working with the Duke. I really liked him, but he had some demons which in the long run got the best of him. It was sad to see Duke's downhill spiral.

He bounced back once or twice, but I think in the end the demons won. I really don't know for sure, as we were from such different environments and had different lifestyles.

* * *

Another time, a guy named Happy and I were reaming out some connection holes on some iron to be set.

Connection plates would be incorporated into these holes, and they had to be lined up so the connectors could easily insert the bolts. Many times we had to drive some iron pins into the holes to help with getting everything to line up. These pins were used over and over, and the ends would get knarled at times.

Happy was furiously swinging his beater and pounding those pins. I just happened to be looking in his direction and suddenly it looked like his arm was getting riddled with bullets. Blood started spewing out from his wrist up to his elbow. We were astonished!

Evidently the impact of Happy's blows had caused a piece of the knarled end of the pin to break loose. It acted like shrapnel, skipping up his arm and tearing skin along the way.

It was not a serious injury, but it was very enlightening. We both agreed later that the damn safety glasses we were required to wear were probably a good idea… .

❋ ❋ ❋

Cocky, the steward on this job, was concerned with the river rising due to the melting snow up north. He told Chisholm we needed a larger safety boat. (All bridge jobs required a safety boat to be just downstream from the bridge, in case someone was to fall. Nets were sometimes used at that time and are almost always required now.)

"Cocky, the river will go down in two weeks, and with the time it will take to get a larger safety boat, it would not be worth the cost," Chisholm replied.

Cocky was adamant. "Chisholm, look at all the flotsam coming down stream. If one of those large trunks of driftwood hits that small jon boat, it could be disastrous."

"It ain't gonna happen."

The safety boat was manned by two men, an operator and a laborer. The operator was responsible for running the boat, and the laborer's job was to get the man out of the water, should someone fall in.

Usually at lunchtime the operator would take the laborer to the shore to pick up some food for guys that hadn't brought lunch that day. The safety boat would always came to the upriver side of the storage barge to let the laborer off (since we would sit in the break shed on that barge).

We were sitting at the break table when someone yelled, "Man overboard!"

Out we went to the deck top of the barge. A huge tree trunk had hit the safety boat and tipped it over.

We saw the operator in a safety vest floating along the side of the barge, pointing at the laborer and yelling, "Get him! I'm okay!"

The laborer was a 20-year-old kid whose wife was expecting their first child in the very near future. He was not wearing a life vest and was fully clothed in some winter overalls.

The boat was nowhere to be seen, but the portable gas tank for the motor was floating just ten feet behind the young man.

"Turn around and get hold of that tank!" we shouted.

Our job site also had a towboat for moving our work barges, and it was manned by two very experienced riverboat men. They had already jumped into action and were headed our way. We ran down the side of the barge, shouting for the young laborer to grab that gas tank. He finally saw it and started swimming in its direction.

He looked like an Olympic swimmer as he struggled to get to the tank. I still cannot believe it to this day, but as good a swimmer as he looked to be, he did not move one inch closer to the floating tank. That is how powerful the current was. I had never really realized the power of moving water, much less the power of the Missouri River at near-flood stage.

One of the men on the barge grabbed a life ring and tossed it to the young man. It landed just behind him. He turned to swim to it with the same results.

Between his heavy work clothes and the cold water, the laborer was running out of energy and went under. A friend of his ripped off his coats and boots and dove off the barge to try to rescue him. The thought of jumping in after him had never occurred to me, but even if it had, I don't know if I would have had the courage to do it.

The towboat was nearing the poor laborer. The deckhand on the towboat had a very long pole with a hook on it, much like a shepherd's staff in a Bible story. The captain was very adept at maneuvering the towboat, and we were very hopeful that all would end well.

Up the laborer popped from the water.

"He's over there!" we screamed, pointing.

The deckhand ran to the other side of the tow while the captain brought the bow around. Out went the pole as the deckhand yelled, "Grab it!"

The young man just missed grabbing it and went under again. The captain put the tow in reverse and kept backing up with the hope that the next time the laborer came up they would be in position to rescue him.

I looked toward the end of our barge and saw one of the ironworkers kneeling at the edge saying a prayer. We all kind of joined in and the young man popped up again. But he was only up for a few seconds before he went back under and we never saw him again.

The tow did rescue the friend who had jumped in, and then headed off to find the operator, who had floated a mile or so downstream.

The young man's body was found two weeks later, and shortly after that his wife had their baby.

We all went home early that day, and the next morning we had a safety meeting. Miraculously, a new and much larger safety boat was sitting on the side of the bank. Cocky just shook his head and walked away.

✳ ✳ ✳

Operators are an integral part of ironworking, as much of the work requires the moving of heavy objects. I always figured the operator is the king of the rig and has the last say.

While working on the stadium job, it was determined that one of our rigs was due to get new brakes for the load line. These brakes would slow or stop the descent of the load.

Now, I knew that when new brakes were installed, they needed to be burned in. This meant a load (usually a concrete weight) would be put on the headache ball and raised and lowered a number of times until the operator deemed the brakes properly burned in. Sometime the maintenance crew would perform this procedure instead of the operator.

Lowell, a very respected and experienced operator, was the operator of this rig. I needed to move a large picking beam to the deck I was working on. There was a crew of rodbusters working on the deck where I would be landing the picking beam. My cousin Billy was on the crew, and I informed his gang what was going to happen.

"Billy, Lowell is going to swing our picking beam over here, so let your men know to keep and eye out, as it will be overhead."

"Okay, Cuz."

It occurred to me to remind Lowell of the new brakes on his rig, but I was sure that Lowell did not need me to tell him how to perform his job.

My men on the stadium floor hooked up the picking beam; Lowell got up on the load and swung it to the deck where we were standing. As it traveled above Billy's crew, a whirring noise came from the rig. I saw the beam lowering at a pretty fast speed.

"Billy, watch out! I think the rig has lost its brakes!"

It all happened so fast, but Lowell was able to swing the beam between my men and Billy's crew before it crashed to the deck.

"What the hell happened, Monk?" Billy asked.

"Cuz, I guess the new brakes were not burned in. Is everyone okay?"

Everyone was. We thanked our lucky stars and I radioed Lowell that he might need to burn in those new brakes.

* * *

Rigs and rigging are definitely safety concerns. Sometimes, though, the danger can be quite hilarious. While adding some new bays to the Chrysler assembly plant, one of the funniest things I ever witnessed happened.

I was working on the iron probably a couple hundred feet away from a ground crew sending iron to the connectors. Now, when iron is sent up, it has to have what is called a tag line attached to at least one end of the iron. The tag line enables the ground crew to get the piece pointed in the right direction to make setting the piece easy for the connectors. Sometimes the connectors have to grab the line to make the final correction, but it is imperative to stay clear of the tag line when getting up on the load.

The hook-on man signaled for the rig to get up on the load. He was letting the tag line run through his open hand when the tail end of the line wrapped around his leg. The operator watching the load rise did not notice what was going on with the end of the line. It must have wrapped six or seven times around the guy's leg, and up he went with the load.

I was looking on and wondering what was going on. The iron was about 60 feet in the air, with the hook-on man dangling upside down 20 feet below the iron and a good 40 feet off the ground. The only thing keeping him from falling to the ground was the tag line wrapped tightly around his leg.

Finally the operator saw him and stopped raising the load. But the sudden stop set off a reaction to the tag line, which started to ever so slowly unwind from the man's leg. The operator started lowering the load, the hook-on man waving his arms and screaming to get back down. I was in awe as I watched the line unwrapping.

Luckily, the line had wrapped several times around his leg, and by the time the line fully unwound, the guy was only five feet off the ground. He immediately got up and moved away from the line.

You had to be there to appreciate it, but it was priceless.

No one got hurt, which is amazing, as tag lines usually do not have weight on them and are generally not tied to the iron very securely. And many times the tag line is old and weathered, since it's just used for directing the swing of the load.

I have often thought that God is looking over the ironworkers.

* * *

Doug was a friend that I worked with early in my career. Like many ironworkers, he had a nickname.

"Hey, Lulu, it's pretty damn cold down here under the deck. Let's get these bolts sorted and get back up top, where the sun is shining," I said.

"Yeah, I'm ready to get the heck out of this freezer too."

About this time we heard a scream and saw a body falling through an opening in the deck two floors above. Watching a man fall and bounce off the iron on the way down is not a nice sight. It's crazy the way accidents happen.

The man that had fallen was called Scout, as he had been in the Army and had been a forward observer in Vietnam. It seemed a stack of decking had been landed on a floor opening, effectively hiding the opening. Scout and another man had been unstacking the sheets and spreading them out in the open bays. When they'd walked forward holding the last sheet, Scout—not being able to see the opening—had stepped right into it.

Just that quick; he was there and then he was gone.

Scout did survive the fall, but he never worked the iron again. Years later I saw him and he was using a cane to help him walk.

* * *

Dave was an exceptionally good hand and had been a Navy Seal. He was also very comical. Some of his humor was a bit sophomoric, but his delivery overcame any other shortcomings.

We were refitting the lower railroad level of the Eads Bridge, which was the first cantilever structural steel bridge to span the

Mississippi River. This required busting out old rivets from the 1870s and replacing the old deck beams.

"Hey, Dave, how are we going to get these rivets out?" I asked.

"We will have to use a tool called a helldog."

"Why do they call it that?"

"You'll see."

A helldog is a 40-pound tube-shaped air tool with a drive pin activated by air pressure. When you pull the trigger, all hell breaks loose. You grip it with all your might as the pin pushes the rivet out of the hole it was put into 120 years earlier. The helldog rattles your bones, the sound is deafening, and the air line powering it is spewing a greasy, watery mist from the fitting right behind the trigger you are pulling. I still have a small contusion on my chin from one of those rivets breaking apart and bouncing off my chest.

"Monk, the best way to handle that tool is to attach a rope sling to it and let it hang on your shoulders while it is banging out those rivets. I'm going to the next bay to work with John and Bitter Man." (I forget his real name, but everyone called him Bitter Man as he'd supposedly had a bitter divorce and had an equally bitter personality.)

"Okay, Dave, I've got this helldog all figured out. I will persevere."

It had been decided that safety nets were better than having two men in a safety boat in case of a fall, and this job was one of the first I was on that was completely netted. The whole underneath of the bridge had safety nets. They were sometimes 20 to 30 feet below the iron we were working on, but they would keep a man from hitting the river. I remember thinking they were kind of stupid, as you would be lucky not to break your neck if you fell that far.

Someone yelled, "Dave's in the hole!" ("In the hole" was a term used when someone fell.) I looked up from the iron I was working on to see men running to where Dave had fallen.

Dave had somehow slipped while moving a pick board. He'd hit a few iron members on the way down, which had knocked him out. I looked down to see him sprawled face down in the safety net. I could see the raging river flowing underneath the netting, and at that moment I realized that without those nets Dave would have been gone. No unconscious man could survive a plunge into the raging Mississippi.

The fire department's rescue team had been called, and the three paramedics that showed up were hesitant to go down to get Dave. One was a female and she said if two of us went with her she would go down to tend to Dave. We agreed, and down we went so she could check his vitals.

The only way back up was to strap Dave to a gurney board. We hoisted him up and started carrying him down the bridge. I wasn't sure how bad Dave's injury was, but his body was just jiggling around on that gurney as we trotted to the end of the bridge. I didn't have a good feeling as I looked down at his face.

Someone said we should get Dave's car keys and have one of the guys drive his car home. At that moment I saw one eyelid crack open. At the same time, Dave cracked a sly little grin and said, "Don't let Tommy drive my car." Tommy had just had a minor accident. We all burst out laughing.

Dave fully recovered, but it took a couple of years in a brace. Those Navy Seals are tough!

Cally

His name was Cal, but we all called him Cally. Cally and I worked on a few jobs together and he was a prince. He would do anything for anyone and he loved being an ironworker. He came from a long line of ironworkers. He was as at home on the iron as a squirrel in a tree.

Cally was highly respected. At the same time, though, he was just a kid in a man's body.

We were in downtown St. Louis working on the Southwestern Bell Building, and I headed up to a sixth-floor work platform on the outside of the building. I took the elevator up and climbed out a window onto the platform.

"Hey, Monk, I heard you were on this job." It was Cally.

"Did you come all the way from the ground up that iron?" I asked.

"Yeah."

Cally had just climbed up six stories of temporary iron that the work platform sat on. He'd come up the column and over the safety rail, and jumped down onto the platform. He was smiling and happy to be alive; this was going to be a good and long job.

* * *

We had a lot of fun on that job. Cally loved the sports page and read it at break time every day. The St. Louis Cardinals were always a hot topic, and the subject of Red Schoendienst's salary came up. I told Cally that I was sure Red made $500,000 a year. This was probably the mid 1980s, and $500,000 would have been a lot of money for an assistant manager.

"No way, Monk!"

"I'll bet you five bucks he does."

We climbed in a window and found a working telephone in an office. I called KMOX and asked for the sports desk.

"We have been having a discussion about Red Schoendienst's salary, and I say it's $500,000. My buddy says there is no way an assistant manager gets that kind of money," I said.

"Well, your buddy would be right about any other assistant manager, but Red has been a player, manager, and now assistant for the Cardinals, and Augie Busch is a generous owner. Tell your buddy you are right."

Cally took me out to lunch that day.

I'm not sure of the exact figures, as it was a long time ago, but the gist of the story is correct.

* * *

"Hey, Monk, the oiler on our rig wants one of us to climb to the top of the boom and grease the head roller."

"Why does he want us to do his job for him?"

"He's kind of old, and since we're in the city, they don't have room to lay the boom down. He can't climb up there; he would never make it."

"Fine, but why don't we just have the operator swing over to our work platform? We can take it up to about the 20th floor and I will climb out on the boom and grease it."

I hopped onto the boom and headed to the top. The operator raised the boom to get away from the building as I was climbing up. It's funny, but while climbing up the boom with my eyes on my goal, there was no problem. I reached the roller, greased it, attached the grease gun back to my work belt, and headed back down.

But as I descended, I looked to the ground as the operator lowered the boom and swung it to our work platform. I froze. Looking down at the ground a couple hundred feet below while swinging on a boom was something I had never done before, and I was scared.

I told myself to get a grip and get over it. Fortunately, I managed to do that. I hopped off the boom on to our platform.

"Wow, that looked neat, Monk! Were you scared?" Cally asked.

"Oh, maybe a little," I replied. I never told him I had frozen for a short time.

* * *

When that job ended, Cally and I moved on to different jobs. Cally went to a large job putting on a new addition.

There were no cell phones then, but somehow the news that Cally had gone in the hole spread like wildfire. Evidently he had lost his footing while working on the iron. He'd only fallen maybe 40 feet, but he had hit the concrete slab the iron was being set on.

The tragic part was that the safety nets waiting to be hung were lying on the very slab that Cally had fallen onto.

It hit everyone hard. I was definitely upset but did not know Cally's family all that well. I wrote a sympathy note, put it in an envelope, and delivered it to his home. I don't know who answered the door, but I handed him the note and said I was so sorry.

I've never seen such a turnout at a funeral. I got there at four in the afternoon and there was a line coming out of the church and going down the sidewalk for two blocks. I was told it had been like that all day. There was still a line when I left two hours later.

Cally's family greeted each and every person that day. I held back my tears as I greeted his brothers. It was hard for me to speak to his children, and I lost it after giving his wife a respectful hug. He was such a good person.

Sometimes You Get the Bear; Sometimes the Bear Gets You

Close calls are part of being an ironworker; they are exciting and really get your heart pumping at times. They are probably good for your health, and definitely keep you alert and on your toes.

While working on the Butterfly House in Chesterfield, Missouri, I managed to pucker my butt while setting some iron.

"Monk, those are some really nice new work gloves you've got there. Where did you get them?"

"Jim, I was working at UE (an electric utility company) and they gave these gloves to all their employees. I figured I was a temporary employee, plus my electric bill helped to pay for them, so I acquired two pairs for myself."

Jim was our operator on this particular job, and a very good operator at that. I worked with him many times. But no matter how good he or I or anyone was, there was always that little error that can be perilous.

We were setting iron at a pretty good pace, and I cut loose of the rig from the piece we had just set. It had been a pretty small piece, so the headache ball was right next to me. I raised my hand to signal for Jim to get up on it and get another piece as we were smokin' the job. Everything was fitting and we were slamming the iron in place.

Jim got up on the ball and I'll be damned, the hook caught the cuff on my new leather glove and up, up, and away I went! In a flash I was probably ten feet off the iron and fifty feet in the air. Before I could say a word, Jim set me back down on the iron like a feather.

At the end of the day, Jim said, "Those surely are some very nice gloves." We couldn't believe they'd held me up like that without even one stitch breaking!

❉ ❉ ❉

On another job downtown, I worked with Oscar. Occasionally we would call him "Oscar Mayer" or just sing "Oh, I wish I were an Oscar Mayer wiener". He liked that, as the man had one hell of a wiener! He used to always tell everyone that he only had three inches. He would pause for a moment and then say, "But I measure mine from the ground up!" We would all laugh and Oscar would just smile.

I loved Oscar. He was a pleasure to work with, was not afraid of working hard, and always wanted to do a good job. He was not real educated, but he was very smart and a quick thinker.

One time, we were going to hoist a work platform from the second floor up to the roof. To get to the second floor we were using a long extension ladder. We went up the ladder and hopped over the safety rail onto the floor of the work platform.

"Hey, Oscar, how do you think we should hook up the rigging?"

"Why don't we just sling the chokers around the electric motors on each end?"

"Yeah, that sounds good. Let's get up on the rig a bit to make sure the weight of the motors will not make the platform tip."

We made the check and Oscar said, "Looks good to me, Monk. Let's go back down the ladder and get out of the way."

We jumped over the handrail and shuffled down the side of the platform to where the ladder was resting. That was all it took; with us on top of the rail and the heavy electric motors also near the top of the platform, the weight caused the whole platform to roll like a log. Before we knew it, we were both kind of running on the sides of the platform and anywhere else we could get footing. I felt like I was in a cartoon.

The ladder went back and was falling toward the sidewalk. Pedestrians and the operator were screaming. All I could think about was that damn ladder; it was extremely long and rather expensive. I was responsible for it, as I had borrowed it from another trade on the job. I yelled down to one of the guys to grab the fucking ladder.

The platform leveled out and stopped rolling. Oscar and I were hyped. I yelled down to the operator, "Are you okay?"

"Am *I* okay? Hell yes! The question is, are *you two* okay?"

Oscar and I turned to each other and laughed. "Monk, I didn't know your old white ass could move that quick," Oscar observed.

✳ ✳ ✳

Washington University in St. Louis always has some new building going up, and I had a job there. I was working for a company I did not really like, but work was slow, so I figured I would just bite my tongue and make some money.

We were going to erect a tower crane, which is a rig that sits atop a square steel tower and can turn 360 degrees. They are sometimes called whirlybirds, as they can keep turning in the same direction round and round.

The boom section is much longer than the counterweight section and there is a cab at the top of the tower just in front of the counterweight section. The boom must be long enough to reach the outside walls of the building, so the larger the footprint of the building, the longer the boom section has to be. The tower section is always taller than the building that you are erecting so it can clear the highest part of the building. Sometimes the tower starts out short and is raised higher as the building gains height.

We were getting ready to add a section to the boom.

"Hey, Monk, the guy who usually connects the boom sections is off sick today. Do you think you can fill in for him?" asked Jerry, the steward.

"Well, Jerry, I've never done that but I'm pretty sure I can."

"Okay, then you head up the tower and the electrician foreman and I will do the rigging."

"Why would we have an electrician helping with the rigging?"

"He is the job superintendent as well as the head electrician, and he says he is running the show."

This is exactly why I do not like working for this company, I thought to myself. But I figured if it was okay with our steward then it was okay with me.

There was only one way to get to the top: a series of iron ladders welded to the inside of the tower sections. About every 40 feet there was a little platform where you could catch your breath before continuing on to the next platform. I figured I had plenty of time to get up there, as it would take them a while to rig up the boom section.

The operator's name was Sonny.

"Hi, Sonny, I'm Monk. How are we going to go about doing this?"

"It's easy; they will hook on the boom section, I will raise it in place, you will make the top pin connections, and I will ease off on the rig to let the bottom pin connections line up. You pin the bottom and then I will let up to loosen the rigging."

"Sounds like a plan," I said. "But what's the holdup down there on the ground?"

I radioed Jerry to see what the problem was.

"Monk, it's going to be a while, as the rigging the electrician ordered is too short. We are going to have to shackle another pair of chokers to the rigging to make it long enough."

"Great… are you sure he knows what he's doing?"

"Yeah, this should make them long enough."

A few minutes later, Jerry came back on the radio.

"Okay, Sonny, this is Jerry. We are ready and you can get up on the load."

Sonny did so.

"Damn! Sonny, get back down. The chokers are sliding along the boom. Monk, we are going to drive a pin in front of the chokers so they can't slide."

After a few more minutes, Jerry said, "This should work. Get up on it, Sonny."

Finally the boom section arrived and I drove in the top two pins. I signaled Sonny to lower the boom slowly to line up the lower pins.

"It's not coming down, Sonny; I want you to lower it."

"Monk, I am, but the rigging is hung up on those pins they drove in to keep the rigging from sliding."

Damn, we couldn't come down and I had already put the top pins in. I radioed down that I would have to drive those keeper pins out and I didn't have the slightest idea where they might end up—just somewhere 100 feet down on the ground.

"Jerry, heads up down there," I warned. I hit the pin with all my might and out it flew; the boom section quivered a bit and I grabbed a crossmember. The pin actually ended up on the street in front of the project.

"Okay, Jerry, I'm going to drive out the other pin."

Bam!

Nothing.

Bam!

It moved an inch.

I gave it my all; it flew out and at the same time the boom shook like an earthquake. One of the pennant lines dropped about three feet. My shoulder was two feet below and took the full brunt of the impact with the two-inch steel cable.

My radio was blaring. "Are you okay up there?… Come in, Monk!"

"I'm okay, but I think I have injured my shoulder," I said before inserting the two bottom pins and heading down.

Jerry and the electrician foreman met me at the foot of the tower. "Say, man, I'm sorry about that rigging," said the electrician foreman.

"Forget about it," I said. "I need to see a doctor, though. I think my shoulder is hurt."

"Why don't you just go home with pay and see how it feels tomorrow?"

"Tell you what, buddy. I do plan on getting paid the rest of the day, and if your company has a doctor they would prefer me to see, I suggest you find out who he is right now!"

I was lucky. They sent me to a doctor who had just started a partnership with a bunch of specialists. He was a great doctor, but he was getting paid by the company, not me. I guess he figured I was just trying to get out of work and earn a little compensation. He X-rayed my shoulder and gave me some pills. I wasn't too impressed with his work, as I was sure I was hurt, but I told him, "You are the doctor, so we will do it your way for now."

At my next appointment, I told him that he was the doctor but we were going to do it my way. I demanded an MRI. The results showed a torn AC.

From then on, he was a great doctor.

"Monk, I'm going to schedule you at St. Mary's Hospital for an operation to repair your AC. I will see you there next Thursday."

✳ ✳ ✳

When I checked in at the hospital for the surgery, some nurse who looked like Rosie O'Donnell came in to shave me.

"Why are you going to shave me? The doctor said the incision will be on the top of my shoulder."

"Yes, that's right, but I must shave around the area."

"Okay…. Why are you lathering my chest and armpit?"

"Look, I'm just doing what I'm supposed to, so be nice. When I get done with you, you will know what it's like to be a woman."

A couple of days later I got the picture. There's nothing worse than stubble under your arm. To this day I think Rosie just enjoyed being a masochist.

"Hi, Doc!" I said when I was wheeled in for the operation. "You remember which shoulder you're going to cut, don't you?"

"Yes, Monk. The one that looks like a newborn baby's butt. I see you have been to Rosie's part of the world."

The best part of getting operated on was the drugs they put in my veins. Man, it was like "Strawberry Fields Forever"! I surely can see how someone could become an addict.

It was dream time and the doctor did his thing. I remember nothing except a foggy memory of being rolled down the hallway to my room after the procedure.

I was peacefully resting in la-la land when someone—I guess a nurse—walked into the room. I had just begun regaining my senses and just barely had my eyes open enough to make her out. She was maybe 30, with sandy-colored hair in tight waves and cut on the shorter side.

She walked to my bedside, and I closed my eyes, thinking she was just going to look over my chart. I figured I was still feeling no pain and couldn't care less what she was doing.

Or so I thought. I felt her pull the sheet up at the side of the bed, and before I knew it, she was fondling my privates. I remember thinking it was a pretty good dream. I cracked my eyes open to see what the heck was going on. The woman looked down at me and, startled, squealed and ran out the door.

I hope she got her rocks off, cause I didn't. I probably should have reported her, but I never told anyone till many years later. She was probably one of those angels of death roaming the hospitals, putting people in misery to death. Who knows? I just know you never know what happens when you are put under. You are at the mercy of the hospital staff.

I was put under one other time, and the "Strawberry Fields Forever" feeling was the same. I remember telling the anesthesiologist a joke and about halfway through it I was out. I was getting a procedure to my throat and I had a dream (probably wasn't a dream) that two guys were holding me down and I was struggling. When I woke up there were two pretty stout young black men smiling and looking down at me. I asked them if they'd had to hold me down for the procedure. They said they most surely had, and that I had been quite a handful. We all had a good laugh.

Anyway, the shoulder operation had gone well and I was ready to go home. I had parked my car out in the garage even though they had told me I wouldn't be able to drive till the day after the surgery.

"Now, you know you need someone to pick you up, sir, don't you?" asked the nurse.

"Oh, yeah, I was told that. I will call my wife and she will come and get me."

"You need to call her now so we know someone will pick you up."

"She will not be home for another hour, so I will call her then."

The nurse left and I called one of my buddies and told him I would be calling him back in an hour and to just ignore whatever I said.

An hour later, I told the nurse I would call my wife.

"Yes, babe, I will meet you on the north entrance and you will be here in about a half an hour. Got it. Bye, babe." Of course, I was making it all up.

"We will have Kathy the candy striper walk down with you and wait at the exit till your wife gets here," the nurse said.

Damn, how was I going to get out of this?

Kathy and I were down there for about 20 minutes when I walked out the door and gave a wave at a passing car.

"That was my wife," I said to Kathy. "I told her I would meet her at the west parking lot. Thanks for keeping me company, but I can make it from here." Kathy let me go. Whew!

I headed to my car, jumped in, and took off. I hadn't gone three blocks before the urge to throw up overcame me. I pulled over and let it go right in the middle of traffic. I then realized why they hadn't wanted me to drive. Once I was finished, though, that was it; I felt great the rest of the day.

❊ ❊ ❊

At my next appointment, I told the doctor my shoulder felt pretty good but I had lost a lot of muscle. He put me on the phone with Elizabeth, a nurse for the insurance company.

"Hello, Elizabeth," I said.

"Oh, you can just call me Beth," she said. "I will be overseeing your rehab. You should be back to work in a week or two."

"Really? The doctor told me it would take eight to ten weeks to fully recover enough to go back to ironworking."

I was getting the feeling that Nurse Beth was really just a paper nurse, with her only function being to get me off the books.

"Beth, the doctor said that after the operation I should get therapy. I would like to go to St. Luke's Sports Therapy program. It's a little over a mile from my house, and I went there once before and got good results."

"I actually have you signed up for a work hardening program in St. Charles," Beth replied.

"St. Charles? Man, that is a 20-mile trip one way. I can walk to St. Luke's. I also think a work hardening program is what you do after therapy."

"Yes, but I think you are in good enough shape to forgo the therapy."

Now, I had heard about these work hardening programs. They were basically for guys who were faking an injury and—in cases where the worker really was hurt—a way for the insurance company to save some money. But I wasn't faking and I damn sure wasn't going to suffer because of their little game.

I could see where this was going, so I figured I could play along and teach them a little about how to play to win.

"Okay, Beth. What days will I go to this program?"

"I have you signed up for Mondays, Wednesdays, and Fridays."

"Fine. When will you pick me up? And should I call you when I'm finished each day or will you just stick around?"

"Oh, no. You can just drive yourself."

"Beth, I can't do that. My arm is in a sling."

"Oh, you should be able to drive if you are careful."

I lied and I told her I had a stick shift and it would not be safe. I said I had asked the doctor if I could drive and he had said I'd better not.

"I'll tell you what, why don't you just have your wife drive you?" Beth suggested.

Now, Sophia probably could have driven me, but I was playing the game. "Damn, she works on those days. I guess you can just send a cab to my house."

"We can't do that," Beth said.

"Then I guess you are going to have to think of some other way for me to get to St. Charles. There is always the option of St. Luke's; I can walk there from my house and the exercise will do me some good."

Beth hesitated. "I will have to call the office and get back to you."

The next day Beth called. "St. Luke's it is," she said. "I have you set up for four weeks of therapy and we will see how things are after that."

St. Luke's was great. My therapist was Joan, the same girl who had worked with me before. She was good and had a schedule for working the stiffness out of my shoulder, after which we would work on strengthening my upper body to get me back in fighting form. Joan said it would probably take eight weeks and that after the first four she would talk to Beth to get the other four weeks.

Three weeks later, I got a call from Beth telling me I had an appointment with the doctor so he could release me.

"What are you talking about?" I asked. "It has only been three weeks."

"Yes, but I am required to schedule you an appointment."

"Fine, when should I go?"

"I have you scheduled for tomorrow at 10:00."

I got to the doctor's office the next day and was sitting in the waiting room. I noticed a woman in a business suit carrying a briefcase. I had never seen Beth, but I knew that had to be her. She ignored me and I played like I didn't notice her. She didn't realize I was about to put the hammer down on her little game.

The receptionist called me in, and I saw Beth getting out of her chair as I passed through the door. I was escorted to an examining room, and again I saw Beth; she was heading down the hall toward me.

The nurse sat me on the examining bed and started taking my vitals, and in walked Beth. She introduced herself to the nurse and turned to look at me.

"Hi. I guess you are Beth," I said.

"Actually, only my friends call me Beth. My name is Elizabeth."

"Oh, excuse me, Elizabeth, but you are the one that said I should call you Beth. Don't you remember that? Well, it doesn't really matter. What I need to know now is what are you doing in my examining room?"

"I have the right to know your progress."

About this time the doctor entered the room.

"I'll tell you what, *Beth*, you may have the right to know my progress, but I have the right to not have you in my presence. You should probably leave right now!" I demanded.

Beth looked at the nurse, who confirmed what I had said. Beth turned and looked at the doctor; he gave a nod of approval, and Beth stormed out of the room.

I was sitting on the examining bed biting my tongue to keep from laughing and the nurse was doing the same thing. The good doctor said, "Monk, it seems like you are feeling your oats."

"Yeah, Doc, I am much better. My therapist said she will call you to get those other four weeks of therapy, and then back to work I will go."

That is just how it went down. Beth was pissed and I was happy. Paper nurses!

"What a waste of money," is what came out of my mouth as I passed Beth in the waiting room on my way out. "I think I will call your company and tell them they could save a ton of money if they got rid of you!"

I would never do that, but it sure got her pissed.

That's how you play the game!

※ ※ ※

I hated doing rebar, but there wasn't a lot of work and I needed to do something.

A lot of rebar jobs require working around carpenters. In my experience, ironworkers and carpenters together usually resulted in a few disputes. As men, we generally liked and respected each other; but conflicts on jurisdiction were common. Rebar also often required working in the mud and dirt.

I just did not like working with rods or carpenters all that much.

We were installing some ground rebar beams and were knee-deep in mud. Trigger, a clown with a big mouth, was constantly spewing out some garbage that got on everyone's nerves. He was incredibly annoying, and I just happened to be working in the same ditch as him.

He kept yelling out, "Trigger man! 'Bang! Bang!'" He was black and I tried to ignore him, but if he said it once he said it a hundred times, and I couldn't take it anymore. He was on one side of the ditch, I was on the other, and the rebar beam was between us. I leaned over the beam and put my forehead to his, looked in his eyes, and started screaming those same words.

That was all it took. He jumped over the beam and took a swing at me with his claw hammer; he missed and it flew out of his hand. He was quick and got another swing in, just grazing the side of my face. My hard hat and safety glasses flew off as I grabbed him by the neck. We were rolling in the dirt and neither of us could land a good punch.

Next thing I knew, someone had me by the waist and another guy had a handful of my hair, and they were pulling me off Trigger. I could see they were both carpenters and I figured I was in trouble.

I thought, *I'm going to hurt this guy before I get my ass kicked.* So as they pulled me away, I stuck two of my fingers in Trigger's nose while grabbing his upper lip with my other two fingers. I can still see his grimace as I dug my hand into his flesh while I was being dragged away from him.

I jumped up as my hand left Trigger's face, and the two carpenters that had pulled me off stepped back and showed no aggression. I guess they'd just figured they should break us up. Trigger was pissed, but he didn't push it. The fracas was over as quickly as it had started.

A few minutes later my boss came by, gave a little chuckle, and said, "Can't you ever stay out of trouble?"

I just grinned, but Trigger shut his mouth for the rest of the job. Everyone was happy about that.

Cancer

"Hey, babe, have you noticed that spot on your leg is changing color?"

"Yes, Monk, I should have it looked at. I will make an appointment for next week."

After the appointment, Sophia informed me that it was cancerous in nature, but could be easily removed with only a small scar which would go away in time. I was very relieved.

But a few months later, after we discovered Sophia was pregnant with what would be our second child, she came home from the doctor with unsettling news.

"Monk, the doctor has found something he doesn't like, and the pregnancy is in jeopardy. I will be going in for tests to figure out what is wrong."

Cervical cancer was the diagnosis, and I was devastated. I couldn't even imagine how Sophia felt.

We went to a specialist to find out about how to deal with it.

"Sophia, you have a few options," the specialist said. "You can have chemo and/or radiation. But you are young, and sometimes these options create problems down the road. The other option is for me to operate and remove part of your reproductive system. The test indicates that the cancer has not spread to your lymph nodes, and this is good. However, you would no longer be able to conceive after the operation." The doctor then proceeded to hold up a model of a female's reproductive system and show what he would be removing.

Sophia and I were just listening and not saying much until Sophia asked, "Doctor, will we be able to have sex after the operation?" That thought had never entered my mind, but bless her for thinking of us post-operation. The doctor assured us all would be as it was, except for the ability to have another child.

I called my mom and sister in California to tell them the news and I lost it. I started crying like a baby but composed myself enough to get the bad news out.

"Monk, you will need someone to watch Nicole while Sophia is in the hospital and recuperating, as you will have to work. I am willing to come help," my mom offered.

"Mom, that might not be a bad idea," I said. Sophia wasn't too thrilled about it, but it worked out pretty well, and Mom only had to spend a week with us.

The night before the big day, Sophia had to endure many pre-operation rituals to cleanse and empty everything in the digestive tract—what fun for her.

The next morning I kissed Sophia goodbye as the nurses rolled her off for surgery. I sat in her room for the next three or four hours waiting for her to return.

A nun came in and offered to pray with me. I'm not too big on praying with an audience, nor have I ever had someone join me for an event like this. I'm also not Catholic. I declined her offer; I felt kind of bad and the nun probably thought I was a heathen, but that was my decision.

Finally a nurse came in to inform me that the operation was over and had been successful. They rolled Sophia back in and I rushed to the bedside.

No one had ever told me that Sophia would be pumped with fluids for the operation, and when I saw her, I burst out, "What's wrong with her?" She was all puffy and looked like someone completely different. Sophia later told me that even though she had still been kind of out of it, she remembered my saying that, and that it had hurt her feelings.

I had gone for most of the day without food, and Sophia was asleep, so I went to the cafeteria. When I returned, Sophia was awake and hungry; that's my girl! However, she still was not allowed any food, and she was a little ticked at me for eating in front of her. Damn, I couldn't win for losing... .

We went home a couple of days later, and Sophia's recovery was pretty quick. I can still see her walking around in the backyard in her nightgown with a bag of saline (or something) hooked to her, with our little Nicole following her in diapers. It was both a good sight and a little funny at the same time.

A month later, with Sophia always the one to worry that she would no longer be able to please me, said, "Monk, do you think we should try doing it?" That sounded good to me; and just like the doctor had said, all was as it was. Very nice.

Over twenty years later, the cancer has never come back. It would seem the doctor was a good doctor and knew his business. Thank God.

The Simple Life

Sophia is a pretty competitive person, and our daughter Nicole was about old enough for competitive sports.

"Monk, I think I will volunteer to coach the girls' basketball and softball teams, as the association is looking for a few new coaches," Sophia said.

They were looking to have double teams for Nicole's age group, as many new kids were signing up. What they did not say was that the A team did not want to take in new kids because then they would have less playing time. So Sophia would be coaching the ragtag group of new kids who appeared to not be real good at sports.

I told Sophia I would help her and her assistant, Russ, coach the girls.

Russ told Sophia, "Our team doesn't have a lot of skill, but the three girls you will pitch are pretty darn good. I've been catching for them and Sarah, Jessie, and your Nicole can fire that ball in and throw strikes too. Nicole has an awesome changeup."

"Yes, Russ, we probably need to really practice fielding and hitting, as those will be our weaknesses," Sophia observed.

After three weeks of intense practice, our team was looking pretty good.

It's pretty much common knowledge that children's sports teams are all about the parents—my son this, my daughter that. "Why is my son not starting?" "My daughter wants to pitch."

But there was very little squabbling within Sophia's teams, as the parents were just happy their kids had been able to get on a team in our league.

Ours was a Catholic league, and in many parts of the country, Catholic leagues were the foundation for many a kid growing up. Only six of our girls on the team were from our church; the rest were either Jewish or Protestant.

Our first game came and it was a close one.

We started out by giving up four runs in the first inning. But slowly we closed the gap, and when it was 5-6, our power hitter, Emily, came up with two girls on and two outs. Emily slammed one to right center, between the two outfielders. Both of the girls on base went home, and Emily tried for an inside-the-park home run. She was thrown out by a mile at home, but we were ahead 7 to 6.

The other team had one last chance to bat. Sophia had taken our ace pitcher out earlier in the game, so it would be up to a girl named Sarah to save the win. She walked the first two and the lead runner stole third. The next girl up hit it on the ground, right back to Sarah. Sarah grabbed the ball as Sophia yelled, "Throw it home!" Just in the nick of time she threw it to our catcher, who tagged the runner and then noticed the second runner was right behind her. We caught her in a rundown and got her out too. Sarah struck out the next batter to give us the win! The fielding practice had paid off.

We went on to have a pretty decent record and were tied for second in the league. If we could win the next two games, we would be the champs!

※ ※ ※

Our next opponent was our sister team: the A team.

The A team had some really good players, and we knew we would have a battle on our hands. The coach hadn't expected our team to be at all successful, and he was a bit apprehensive about our upcoming game. And he definitely did not want a female coach beating him! But Sophia had every intention of winning this game and the next.

On game day, we were really holding our own against the A team.

"Monk, do you see that? The girls on the other team are standing in the base path and not allowing our girls to advance freely," Sophia said.

"Yeah, I've been noticing that, but I thought it was just accidental."

"I think the coach on the other team has instructed his players to do that."

"You should alert the umpire," I advised.

"I did, but his sister is on the other team, and I don't think he wants us to win either."

"Well, in that case, we should probably tell our girls to just run over anyone blocking the base path. Emily is on base; tell her that."

Emily was our biggest and strongest player. She was very mild-mannered and not too aggressive, but she did like to win. Our girls knew the other team was not playing fair and we knew the umpire could not fault our girls for running through anyone blocking the base lines. Those are the rules; it's unfair to block the base paths.

Our next girl up hit a grounder past first base. Emily rounded second and found the shortstop standing in her way. Emily lowered her shoulder and charged forward; the shortstop retreated just as Emily made contact. No one was injured, but Emily had made a statement!

The A team coaches were angry and they asked the umpire to call Emily out. As much as he probably wanted to, he did not. The coaches were very vocal in their displeasure and I couldn't hold my tongue. I yelled back, "We have the right to a clear base path unless someone has the ball to tag us out. You should know right now that we will run over anyone blocking the path!"

I got some pretty icy glares, but we were in a church league, after all, so that was as far as the hostility went. This incident kind of put the momentum in our favor, and we went ahead by two runs. All we had to do was keep them from scoring more than one run.

Nicole was pitching, and the calls were not going her way. She walked the first two batters. The next batter was the A team's slugger; she looked about five years older than the rest of the girls and was quite the athlete. She swung viciously at the first pitch, and missed. Strike one. She made contact on the next pitch; it was a powerful shot—almost out of the park—but it went foul. Whew, strike two.

I figured Nicole was probably worried about her next pitch. She looked down at the mound, pulled her cap down, and threw the meanest changeup I've ever seen. The slugger looked like a clown trying to connect the bat and ball and damn near fell on her face. Strike three. Our team's parents were cheering and clapping.

We still only had one out, though, and with two on base, we weren't out of it yet. The next batter hits a pitiful squibbler down the third base line. But a hit is a hit, and the bases were loaded with only one out.

The A team had many good batters, and the next one up was another one of their best. Nicole burned one in right across the plate. The batter made good contact and hit a line drive right at my daughter's face. In a flash, Nicole raised her glove and caught the ball in the webbing. She took a quick look at the ball, spun around, and fired it to Emily at first base. The runner didn't make it back in time. A double play!

The whole grandstand of parents on our side got up and gave Nicole a standing ovation. We won!

✻ ✻ ✻

It was championship game day and we were hoping for the best. Our opponent was another powerhouse team and the coach was a very good one. His team was always in the hunt, and we know our chances of winning were not good.

It started out as a pitching duel. As the game progressed, each team managed to score a couple of runs. By the last inning we were trailing by one run. But as the home team, we got the last at-bat so we still had a chance to win.

Our girls struggled at the plate, but we managed to get two weak singles and ended up with two runners on with two outs. It was down to our last batter, April.

"April, we know you can hit this girl, so just go up there and make contact. If you make contact, we have a chance," Sophia encouraged.

April was a sweet girl, and at times she had power. But she was not real interested in sports, and her parents were probably the only reason she was on the team. Nevertheless, she had moments when she really shone.

The count was full and the pitcher threw an outside screamer. April leaned out and made contact. It was a slow liner right over the first baseman's head. Our runners were on the move; we just needed one to get home to at least tie the game. They were rounding second and third, and things looked good.

"April, run, run, run!"

April was very pleased with herself for having made contact, and as she skipped down the first base line it looked like she would beat the throw. But at the last moment she stopped skipping, came to a halt, and made a bunny jump on to first base. The ball got there just as she was starting that cute little hop onto first, and she was out.

It had been a good game, and we'd had the champs sweating till the end. What a season. Sophia was beaming, even after defeat. The parents were all happy and life was good.

※ ※ ※

Basketball was the same scenario as softball: we had the ragtag team. Neither Sophia nor I knew anything about basketball, and we had a learning season our first year and only won a few games. But by the end of the year, we were improving.

When the second season came around, our girls were at least in shape and knew how to handle the ball. Sophia had a few plays and had decided to go with a zone defense.

Our first game was very close, and one of the girls on the other team actually made a shot into our basket near the end of the game. We ended up winning by two points, the errant basket by the other team being the deciding factor. There was some complaining from the other team, but what could we do about it? We'd won.

We improved throughout the season and actually became the team to beat. Sophia's strong competitive nature rubbed off on her girls. Sarah was our star, Emily commanded the boards, and Nicole was very adept at getting turnovers and a few fouls along the way. We went on to take the West County Championship that year.

※ ※ ※

Volleyball was a new interest (and would eventually take the place of softball, as they were both played during the same season once junior high started). Sophia decided to coach the volleyball team too.

As with basketball, she knew nothing about the sport, and these new parents were a bit apprehensive about Sophia's ability to coach the team. She didn't know any of the terminology or even how to properly substitute players.

"Monk, I'm not sure how this will go," Sophia confessed to me.

"Oh, don't worry. You will figure it out."

I strung a line up in our back yard, hung a net, and painted some boundary lines. The girls would come over and even though the net was a little higher on one end (as the yard was not level), the practice helped and they became a pretty solid team.

❋ ❋ ❋

It was time for Nicole to go to junior high school. She wanted to go to Visitation, a private all-girls' school. It was—and still is—a pretty expensive school, but she was our only child, so we bit the bullet.

I remember the convocation night when all the new parents met each other. I was looking around and thinking that as far as finances were concerned, I was definitely the lowest man on the totem pole in that group. But we were holding our own, socially speaking; I managed to hide my true redneck nature and, as I have been told, I clean up nicely.

A Dr. and Mrs. DuBonet introduced themselves and asked, "And you are Dr. who?"

Yeah, right. My cover was blown.

"It's a pleasure to meet you, but I am unfortunately not a doctor; I'm the magnificent manipulator of molten metal."

I caught Dr. DuBonet off guard with the magnificent manipulator stuff. He probably figured I was a lawyer for some steel conglomerate, so I fit in again, just in time for crumpets and tea.

I must say, the upper-class parents were—for the most part—always easy to get along with, as long as you did not beat them in a sport.

✳ ✳ ✳

It was a yearly tradition for the the Junior Varsity girls' volleyball team to play the Varsity team in a pre-season 2-out-of-3 exhibition match.

Now, the Varsity coach had no idea that Sophia was actually planning on winning this game. And there were a few hoity-toity Varsity parents who thought that their girls were the cat's meow.

Our girls jumped out to a fast start and won the first game. The Varsity girls were not too worried, as they really hadn't tried that hard. They may have even planned on losing the first game. However, they were not going to let us win another game. It was hard-fought but they took the second game.

One game to go, and our girls had been showing some real spunk. But there were over 100 years of pride in the team's way, as the Junior Varsity team had never beaten the Varsity team in this exhibition game for as long as the school had been around. Nonetheless, she had faith. "Girls, we can do this!"

They jumped out to a big lead and never looked back. The Varsity girls broke down; they could see impending defeat and just completely fell apart. I was sitting in the stands next to the hoity-toities and they were hot. How could this woman who knew next to nothing about volleyball trounce their daughters?

Alas, all good things come to an end. When Nicole made the Varsity team, that was the end of Sophia's coaching days. Nicole was pretty good at volleyball, and her senior year, her team went to the state championship tournament. They came in third, but that banner hanging in Visitation's gymnasium is possibly the school's only state banner in volleyball to date, and it has Nicole's teammates' names as well as hers on it. It will hang there for another 100 years.

* * *

Beer and Frankie called and said, "Let's all go to Hidden Valley tonight."

"Tonight? Are you nuts? That's a ski resort," I replied.

"Yeah, Monk you are right, but they are going to have a Midnight Madness Run tonight. It should be crazy; we should go."

"Okay, we'll go," I said, "but Sophia has never skied before."

"They have a beginners' tow rope and a bunny run; she'll be okay," Beer and Frankie assured me.

I helped Sophia get her skis on and took her to the tow rope. She didn't do too badly, but the other bozos that would fall in front of her would cause her to wipe out. She made a couple of runs down the bunny hill and then retreated to the loft for hot chocolate.

Frank and I headed for the lift.

"Monk, I'm glad you guys came. This is going to be awesome!" Frank said.

The runs were a little icy but I hadn't skied for over a year and I thought this would be great. Frank's wife was already at the top of the lift and we saw her coming down the hill.

"Frankie, look, did you see that?" I asked. Frank's wife Pat had taken a bad spill right below us.

Pat yelled up, "Frank, I think I broke my arm."

"Damn, I can't believe it; I haven't made one run and now I will have to take her to the hospital!" Frank groaned. Frank and Pat left and it turns out that she had indeed broken her arm.

Other than Pat falling and getting hurt, it was a good night.

Critters

We have only had one dog, and it was one an old boyfriend had given Sophia a few years before I'd met her. It was a small Poodle named September. She was a good dog but died while Nicole was still very young.

Sophia loved that dog, but September grew old and was losing her sight.

"Monk, wake up!" Sophia said one morning.

"What's wrong?"

"I let September out and I think she strayed and can't find her way back. We have to go look for her."

Out the door we went and we started combing our neighbors' backyards.

"She can't have gone very far. Don't worry, we will find her," I assured Sophia.

About this time I heard a tires squealing, as if a driver had slammed on the brakes. I also heard a high-pitched yelp.

"Sophia, you look back over there. I am going to check out the front yards."

I walked down the street a bit and saw something in the road. It was September, and she had clearly been run over. It was a pretty bad scene; her whole body was flattened. Her head was intact but her jaw was broken and her face looked pretty gruesome.

I walked back to the garage and got a black plastic trash bag and a snow shovel.

"Monk, what are you doing?" asked Sophia.

"You keep looking. I'll be right back."

I scooped up September and put her body in the bag. Then I headed to the back of our lot and started digging a grave for September.

"What are you doing, Monk?" Sophia asked again.

"Babe, September was run over and I am going to bury her."

"Where is she?"

"She is in the bag, and you do not want to see her. We will bury her and say a prayer for her."

Sophia was crying and really wanted to see September one more time, but I convinced her to just bury her.

✳ ✳ ✳

Sophia liked all animals, so one day I brought her a baby crow. I had been working on the Eads Bridge and found a crows' nest in one of the cross members. There had been three babies and I think two of the babies had kicked their sibling out. It was an ugly little thing with its fluffy baby feathers.

"What is that?" Sophia asked.

"It's a baby crow that was kicked out of its nest."

"I'm not going to take care of that thing."

"That's okay, babe. I will take care of it."

"What are you going to feed it?"

"I don't know, maybe some milk and rice or earthworms."

"Crows don't eat rice, they need meat!" Sophia said.

"Well then I will feed it worms."

The worms did not work out too well but it really didn't matter, as Sophia took over the duties of raising our crow. Chicken liver and cut-up hot dogs is what she fed her. (I say "her" because Nicole named the crow Sally.)

I hung a swinging perch from a tree limb, and that is where Sally would spend the day. It was funny, as almost every time something went in Sally, something would come out the other end. It must have been some pretty good poo, as a patch of luscious green grass flourished right below that perch.

Sally was such a good crow. She would follow Sophia around the yard as she tended to her flowers. I would put her on the glider on Nicole's swing set and they would both swing. Sally was also very vocal and would talk to us while swinging or following us around.

I made a tall cage on the porch for Sally to stay in at night so she would be safe. Whenever we would say, "Sally, it's time to go night-night," she would walk over to her cage and hop in for the night.

Sally finally got all of her feathers and was now looking like a full-fledged crow. Eventually she became very adept at flying. She would fly up on the roof and Sophia would call for her—"Sally, Sally." Down Sally would come and land on our outstretched arms.

Sally no longer wanted to stay in her cage at night and would fly to the back of our lot to spend the night in the trees. It would be her Waterloo. She would walk down through the yard instead of flying down to get breakfast, and one morning, I heard a bunch of crows squawking and carrying on. I went out to investigate and found Sally dying on the ground by our wood wagon. A damn cat ran off as I approached. Apparently the wild crows had heard Sally's cries and come to her rescue, but it was too late. Sally was gone.

I saw that cat a week later and ran in to get my bow. I let an arrow fly and just missed killing that damn cat. It was a smart cat, as I never saw it again.

＊＊＊

Wild critters were always nearby. A fox started coming around and Sophia would put some scraps out for him. It got to where we would be sitting at the dinner table looking out to the patio and there the fox would be. He just lay there calmly waiting for some scraps. Eventually he would allow Nicole to come out and throw him some food, though we never allowed her to get too close, as he was a wild critter.

I was sitting at the table one morning and our fox was resting under a large pin oak by the patio. All of a sudden his ears stood up and he looked to the back of our lot. There was another fox, and this was our fox's territory!

He got up and headed toward the intruder.

I have never seen anything like two foxes fighting. I could hear this clapping like castanets and couldn't figure out what it was. It turned out to be their teeth as they snapped them together for intimidation. What really surprised me was that they stood on their back legs and pawed at each other with their front legs. They fought for a good ten minutes, their teeth clicking, and 90% of the time they were standing upright on their back legs. Finally our fox chased the intruder away.

Seeing them standing on their back legs reminded me of the drawings I had seen from ancient Egypt. Everyone has probably seen these drawing depicting jackals standing on their back legs and pawing with their front legs. I always thought it strange that they were drawn that way. I now realize it was a natural depiction and was probably Egyptian art glorifying war.

＊＊＊

We had an abundance of squirrels too. They could get quite troublesome and cause damage to the house and wood deck. I did not really want to kill them, though, so I bought a Havahart trap. I would catch them and take them for a ride to a nearby wooded park, where I'd let them go. I can't tell you how many I have trapped over the years, but it is definitely in the hundreds.

My most memorable squirrel experience was really strange. I took a squirrel I had caught to the park and stopped under a large tree near an open field. I opened the cage and shooed the squirrel out of the cage. Off he went through the field. Out of the corner of my eye I caught a shadow above; it was a hawk that I guess had been in the tree I'd parked under.

Down he glided toward the squirrel that was heading to the woods at the end of the field. *Bam*; the hawk struck the squirrel and they both rolled through the grass, fur and feathers flying. The hawk had missed with his talons; the squirrel got back on its feet and was off to the races again. The hawk composed itself and took flight, again headed for the squirrel.

About this time I noticed a group of wild turkeys walking the edge of the wood line. They had some young ones with them, and I can only assume they thought the hawk was after their babies. The adult turkeys made straight for the hawk, who saw them just as he was about to go for the squirrel again. At the last moment he broke off his attack and veered away.

The turkeys settled back down, and it sure looked to me like that squirrel wiped his brow, said "Whew!", and headed to the woods. I was thinking that the pot I'd smoked years earlier must still have been affecting my mind; I couldn't believe what I'd just seen!

We love our critters—fox, raccoons, opossums, deer, and birdies.

Almost Paradise

Fishing has always been a big part of my life. Like the old saying goes, if you give a man a fish, he will eat that day. If you teach a man to fish, he will always be able to eat and feed his family. But my friends and I rarely eat the fish we catch. We just enjoy catching them and releasing them immediately so they can live to fight another day.

When we'd bought our home, one of the selling points for me had been the large community lake surrounded by woods on two sides and open common ground on the other two sides. I'd figured it would be a nearby escape from the everyday work routine.

It turned out our lake was indeed full of fish, and with no homes directly around it, it felt almost like being in the country. There were deer, turkeys, raccoons, water birds, and turtles.

I had a small boat I would launch which enabled me to fish off an island in the middle of the lake. I have fished many bodies of water in my life, but the largest bass I ever caught was just a few feet off that island.

* * *

During a very cold spell one year, the lake froze over.

"Nicole, how would you like to go down to the lake and walk out to the island?"

"That would be great, Dad!"

"Now, you must always be very careful on ice, as if it is not thick enough, you could fall through and very possibly drown."

"Why is that?"

"Well, if you fall through, there is nothing to grab on to to pull yourself out except more ice. With wet hands, it would be too slippery to get a hold. The water would also be very cold and it would not take very long for hypothermia to take over. Your body would slow down and the cold would impede your ability to move."

"Okay, Dad, I won't ever get on ice without you," Nicole promised. We walked out to the island and took some pictures.

❋ ❋ ❋

I learned a little about turtles at that lake too.

One day I was in my boat and heard this hissing noise and saw some splashing. I paddled over to see what was happening. There were two large snapping turtles, and I can only guess that they were mating, as they totally ignored my presence. (Usually a turtle will leave or go underwater when you approach.)

These two were making a ruckus and rolling around in the water. It went on for a good ten or fifteen minutes, this rolling around and hissing. I didn't know which one was the male and which was the female, but when they finished their lovemaking, one of them just looked exhausted and stayed floating in the water while the other one slowly swam off. They both looked happy and satisfied.

❋ ❋ ❋

There was also a clear stream called Wild Horse Creek not far from our home. When we first moved in, it was fairly pristine, with few homes near it. I would usually walk it in waders, but occasionally I would take my kayak.

One day while wading, I got out of the water to just sit on a log. I was sitting on that log enjoying the peace and quiet of the forest when I heard *creeek, creeek, crack.* I looked around to see what that noise was.

Creeek, crack, swish, boom, bang!

A huge tree that had probably died some years earlier decided it was time to fall. I watched it come down just in front of where I was sitting, taking branches from living trees as it came crashing through the canopy.

In all my years in the woods, that was the only time I ever witnessed such a sight. With so many trees in so many forests, this must happen fairly often; but no one has ever told me of seeing such a sight, so I figure I am just a lucky soul to have seen nature doing its thing in this way.

Of course, I am also lucky that the tree was out in front of me instead of next to me. Life is strange and full of mystery.

✳ ✳ ✳

"Hey, Frankie, you should wade Wild Horse Creek with me sometime."

"Monk, I've seen that creek, and I can't believe there's anything in there worth fishing for."

"I'm telling you, it's full of fish, and it is a very clean creek. It flows for about fifteen or twenty miles and empties into the Missouri River. The closer you get to the Missouri River, the bigger the fish get. The upper part has some nice smallmouth bass and the lower sections have some nice largemouth. In between you will catch both."

"Okay, I'll go," Frank agreed.

To get to the water, we had to descend a steep bank. Frank decided to go to the bathroom before coming down, and I started fishing. Almost immediately I caught a nice smallie. With my next cast I got another smallie!

"Frankie, you better get down here before I catch them all," I announced.

By the time Frankie got down the bank, I had caught five nice bass.

"We better wade on down a ways, as I have probably caught every fish in this area," I said.

The next deep hole we came to looked real fishy. I had good luck but Frank, not so much.

"Monk, I don't get it. Why are you catching everything and I'm getting nothing?"

We fished for a couple of hours and then Frankie yelled out, "Man, did you see that?"

"What's that?"

"Monk, I just saw a monster bass take off from the shore and he is headed your way."

I'll be damned; a couple of casts later I hooked a big 'un! It was probably at least six pounds.

"Monk, I'm sick of seeing you catch everything. Let's head back," said Frankie.

"Okay. Yeah, we've had a good day."

At least, I had!

❈ ❈ ❈

Another day, another river.

Missouri has many Ozark streams, and I sometimes go fishing by myself. One of my favorite streams is the Bourbeuse River. It is very pristine in some stretches, and many times I will go the whole day without seeing anyone else.

My Sophia doesn't really like to fish, and she isn't too big on insects and bugs either. But one day, she said, "Monk, I might like to go fishing with you."

"Fine with me. We can go this weekend."

"Is it okay if we take September?" (This was before she had been hit by the car.)

"If you want to."

We got to the river and it was a fabulous morning. Sophia and September were in the front of the canoe, and Sophia had brought a magazine to read.

"Won't you want to look at all the wildlife instead of reading?" I asked.

"I guess so. I just brought it in case I get bored."

"I don't think you will get bored," I assured her.

There was a high bank with a gradual slope not too far from the put in, and on this day there were probably 30 hogs lounging on that bank. I had never seen them there before, and it got me to thinking about my days in Georgia.

"Sophia, you know, I used to be a pretty good hog caller when I lived on the farm. Let's see what those hogs will do if I give my best call."

I started calling—"Sue piggy, sue piggy, woo piggy, woo piggy"—and I'll be damned, immediately 60 ears stood straight up! It was funnier than all get out. Those hogs started up the bank frantically in search of food. They were slipping and sliding; some actually fell into the river, squealing and splashing. I guess my hog call worked just as well in Missouri as in Georgia.

We laughed and laughed and I kept up my calling as they headed up over the bank—I guess they were going to wherever they got fed?

That excitement was over and I started to fish. The Bourbeuse is a slow, clear, beautiful little river, and as we passed some logs in the water I caught a few. I've always loved throwing topwater lures as the fish will come up, blast out of the water, and inhale your lure.

"Monk, that was a big one. Maybe I should try," said Sophia.

"Do you know how to cast?"

"Well, no… ."

About that time it started clouding over and a few minutes later it began raining. Sophia and September, luckily, were under an umbrella, but they were still getting wet. I was still fishing and the rain seemed to have gotten the fish to really start biting. I probably caught a dozen fish before it stopped raining.

"Monk, do you think I should try to catch one now?"

I was thinking, *She has never cast a fishing rod in her life, and this is not going to be pretty.*

"No, babe. They have stopped biting. We should probably head back to the car and go home."

That was the first and last time Sophia ever went fishing with me. We did go on a canoe trip once, but no camping. Sophia needs at least a cabin with running water. Actually, the Ritz is more her style.

❊ ❊ ❊

Who would have ever thought that computers and the Internet would lead me to my favorite fishing hole? With the many search engines and the ability to actually pan over and view virtually any area in the country, it was now possible to seek out new waters.

I began my search just focusing on waters I already fished, and explored them through the Internet as if I were in a hot air balloon.

I then started trying to find waters that I had fished when I was young. I found an old quarry just off the Missouri River that I'd used to go to when I was in my twenties. Back then there had been a railroad track running between the river and a high bluff that ran for miles. The quarry had been hewn out of that bluff, probably at the turn of the twentieth century. The railroad track has since been taken up, and the right of way was sold to the state of Missouri to form a hiking and bike path from Kansas City all the way to St. Louis. It is called the Katy Trail and is a very nice pathway.

I figured I would start my Internet viewing at my old quarry and pan the Katy Trail to see if there were any other bodies of water along the way. I did not have to look too long, as only a few miles upstream there was another quarry. This one was much larger but farther off the trail and surrounded by woods. I decided to check it out in person.

Vehicles are prohibited on the Katy Trail, so I threw my off-road bicycle in the back of my vehicle and headed out to the parking lot a few miles from the new quarry. I figured the new water was two or three miles from the parking lot. Up and down the trail I went, looking for any sign of this new body of water.

I actually passed it a couple of times before, through the trees, I spotted what looked like a rock cliff. I went through the woods and up a small rise. When I got to the top of it—wow! What a sight!

It was beautiful. The water was very deep and clear but aqua in color, and 90% of the whole body of water was surrounded by 50- to 100-foot sheer rock walls. The top of the rock wall was ringed with large oak trees, as that was where the forest ended.

I took a few pictures with my phone and named it "Almost Paradise".

Fishing this newfound Mecca required a boat. Fortunately I had a kayak and a canoe. But how would I get my kayak from the parking lot to Almost Paradise?

I went home and purchased two replacement wheels for a push lawn mower and made a small axle with a V in the middle; it looked good. Next I set my kayak on the axle, with the bottom keel of the kayak sitting in that V, and strapped it down. I could then pull the kayak by the handle on the front of the kayak, and the wheels allowed me to walk along at a nice pace.

I loaded my kayak and contraption onto my vehicle and headed back to the parking lot. Then it's down the Katy Trail I went, pulling my kayak. It was a 28-minute march to get to the water, but as I soon found out, it was well worth the effort.

On my third cast I caught not one but two bass. They both hit my lure at the same time and I hooked them both.

I could tell it was going to be a good day. I was right. Within three hours I caught around fifty bass.

❊ ❊ ❊

I was thinking I needed to get my buddy Larry to come to Almost Paradise with me the next time, as he wouldn't believe how good it was.

Larry agreed to come, and we used my contraption to carry my canoe. Larry observed that the trek from the parking lot was hard work, but I assured him it would be worth it and that he was going to be amazed at the beauty of it all. So off the path and over the rise we went, pulling the canoe through the trees to the only part of the lake where launching was possible.

"Monk, I'll have to admit that this is truly a beautiful hidden secret. Now let's see if we can catch some fish," Larry said.

It took about ten minutes to get the first bite. Larry was steadily catching bass cast after cast. He turned around to me in the back of the canoe and said, "I can't believe it, I've made ten casts and caught ten bass. This is truly an amazing place."

We went on to catch thirty or forty bass apiece.

On another trip with Frankie, the results were the same. He observed, "Monk, I'm not looking forward to that walk back, but this is indeed the best fishing hole you've ever tricked me into going to with you."

* * *

The best part of Almost Paradise is that for the four or five years I've been going there, I have never encountered another human being once I've exited the Katy Trail and gone through the woods. I have seen signs of human presence—a beer can or two, and one year I found two foam noodles floating on the water. I guess there are a few youngsters that may swim there on occasion! But I have never seen anyone on or near the water.

Almost Paradise does have a couple of undesirable aspects. The most obvious is the 28-minute walk to get there. The other biggie is those sheer rock walls. From time to time a rock or two will dislodge and come falling down. It's kind of like the trees falling in the forest; it happens frequently, but you rarely experience it in person. Still, even a small rock falling 50 or more feet and hitting you on the head could be serious trouble.

One day while in my kayak by myself, I noticed a rock hit the water not far from me. Funny thing, but the rock did not sink. It struck me as odd, but I figured it was a round piece of wood instead of a rock. A few minutes later I noticed the rock was moving. I decided to check it out.

As I got closer, I saw a small head sticking out of the water. It turned out the rock was actually a turtle—and he wasn't a water turtle. Poor little guy must have walked off the cliff and fell all the way to the water. I guess that is why he had just floated for a bit; hitting the water had probably knocked him out.

"Come to Daddy," I said, and I leaned over and plucked him from the water and put him in the back of the kayak. We fished for another hour or two and he did not catch a thing. We left and I placed him on the side of the Katy Trail and headed off for my 28-minute trek back to the car.

Teen Years

Our Nicole was such a pleasant child—until the teenage years came around.

I don't know what it is about those years, but I now know how my mother must have felt. She always told me, "Just wait till you have your own children. I hope they give you the same grief you are giving me." Well, she got her wish. Nicole was still a joy to have, just a bit trying at times.

"Defiant" was probably the best way to describe Nicole's new tendencies. I hadn't been defiant with my Mom; I'd just done what I thought was fun. Nicole also had the fun period, but it came after the defiant phase.

"Mom, Dad, no one goes to bed by ten on a school night…. Mom, Dad, everyone sleeps till eleven on the weekends…. I hate math; it's stupid." These were the initial disagreements.

What had happened to the little girl who was happy with horseback rides and playing "The Redhead"? (That was a game we'd made up; I was a monster Nicole called the Redhead. We would play out in the yard for hours. There was no rhyme or reason to the game, but she loved playing it.) Now the fun and games had turned into a battle of wills.

Some of Nicole's new friends were a bit questionable in Sophia's and my view, but then they too were teenagers. It probably is best not to tell your children who they should choose for friends, but there were times when we were not sure this was the correct path. And once a car entered the picture things really got complicated!

* * *

His name was Andrew, but I always referred to him as Slasher.

It seemed Slasher would on occasion slit his wrist (but just barely). All of Nicole's close friends felt sorry for him and would come to his aid. Now, he probably did have a few mental issues, but I always figured the cutting was his way to get attention, as they were really just small scratches. Slasher had a nice home and two parents but I didn't know much more about him.

He would call at all hours of the night and keep Nicole on the phone till the wee hours of the morning.

"Nicole, we understand your concern for Slasher, but the late night calls have to stop."

"Dad, he needs to talk."

"Fine, he can talk up to 10:30 at night. After that he needs to talk to his parents."

Sophia and I had a phone next to our bed, but we kept the ringer off, as the other phones in the house were loud enough to hear when a call came. Still, in the bedroom, it could be hard to hear the phone.

One night, I was asleep and dreaming, but I kept thinking that Nicole was calling us and leaving a message on the answering machine in the front room. I woke up just as Sophia was getting up.

"Monk, do you hear that? It sounds like Nicole is on the answering machine."

"Babe, it's three in the morning. But I thought I heard the same thing."

About this time we heard the phone ring and before we could answer, the answering machine picked it up.

"Mom, Dad, answer the phone," the voice said. "The cops have me and want to talk to you."

I grabbed the phone. "Nicole, is that you?"

"Yes, Dad, and you need to come get me."

"Nicole, where are you and what are you doing out at this time of night?"

"Here, talk to the officer and he will explain." Nicole handed the phone to someone else.

"Hello, is this Nicole's dad?" a new voice said.

"Yes, what is going on?"

"Well, I observed your daughter driving through the neighborhood with just her parking lights on, so I pulled her over. She is only sixteen and past her curfew. I need you to come and get her, as I can't let her drive."

"I'll be there in ten minutes," I said.

When I got to the police station, I asked Nicole why she had been driving with her lights off.

"Well, Dad, when I left our home I thought you might see the lights if I turned them on. After that I just forgot they were off," she explained.

"But what are you doing out and why would you leave the house without telling us?" I asked.

"Andrew needed me to come to his house to talk."

I sighed and asked the officer if it would be okay if Nicole followed me home. He said that would be fine. When we got home, Sophia and I told Nicole to never do that again, and we all went to bed.

✳ ✳ ✳

"Monk, where are you going?" Sophia asked.

"I'll be right back," I said.

I got in Nicole's car and drove it a few blocks to a church parking lot not far from home and then walked back.

I told Nicole that I had sold her car to a guy I worked with. She actually took it pretty well.

I left that car parked at the church for a week, and then invited Nicole to take a walk with me.

We walked to the church and headed to the back parking lot.

"Dad, look, there is my car!" Nicole said.

"Yes, that's your car. And if you ever do anything like that again, I will sell it."

Nicole ended up telling me that she had taken the car out in the middle of the night one other time. I asked her where she had gone.

"Well, I always wondered about that speedometer. It says 120 miles per hour on it, and I wanted to see if it would go that fast."

"What?" I said.

"Yes, I took it out on Highway 40, but I could only get it to do 110."

"You're kidding, right?"

"Nope, I really did do that."

"You are damn lucky a policeman didn't catch you! That would have been one expensive ticket."

Nicole did go on to get a few speeding tickets over the next few years, but of course, given my own history with speeding tickets, who was I to talk?

College Life as a Parent

Nicole is a pretty smart cookie, but is rather lazy when it comes to studying. She also has a very good memory; she can read something once and pretty much remember it all. She could even hear an easy piece of music on the piano once and then play it two weeks later. I don't think her memory is really photographic, but it is indeed good.

Her memory is what got her through high school. Visitation Academy is a prestigious and private all-girls college preparatory high school. There were some pretty bright girls enrolled there, and at least half of the students were studious and really strived to succeed. Nicole and I had different views of success, which was a foreign word for her.

Nicole did manage to graduate in the top 30% of her class and earned a nice scholarship to a state college.

Sophia and I tried to get Nicole to attend a college that was fairly close to home, but she was determined to get as far away from us as possible while still staying in Missouri.

Her first year was a breeze, and I spent barely a fourth of what her high school tuition had been. In that first year she made some new friends. Some were good, and others were good but lazy. Nicole always seemed to gravitate to the lazy, carefree crowd. They were almost always nice kids, and usually very courteous, but the zest for success was not present. That word "successful" still has a totally different meaning for Nicole than it does for Sophia and me.

The second year was not good. Nicole gave up her scholarship to transfer to the University of Missouri. She still received a Bright Flight scholarship for the remaining three years of college, but the scholarship she had given away had been substantially greater. What the hell; she was our only child so we spoiled her and let her walk away.

Nicole did graduate with a good grade point average, and she had a happy three years at Mizzou.

* * *

Boys will be boys, and girls will be girls. Nicole and her friends were at the age of girls in heat and boys on the prowl. It was not so different from when I'd been young, but every new generation has its own thing.

Sophia and I have some friends that occasionally travel out of the country, and they like for us to live in their home while they are gone so we can care for their dogs. The home is very nice and has acreage, a nice pool, and a hot tub. I call it "the five-million-dollar house"; we also sometimes call it "the big house".

These friends always tell us to just act like it's our home while they are gone, and we've had a couple of parties and gatherings there over the years, as it is the perfect home for entertaining.

One summer while our friends were gone and Nicole was home from college, she asked, "Hey, Dad, do you think Mom would let me have a party at the big house?"

"She'll probably be okay with that as long as you tell your friends that this is not our home so they will have to be very respectful and well-behaved. How many of your friends will be coming over?" I asked.

"Oh, probably no more than eight, maybe only six."

"That sounds good. I'm sure Mom will be fine with that number."

Sophia gave her blessing with the stipulations that the party end by two in the morning and that they clean up any mess they make. Nicole agreed.

"Nicole, do you want me to take the cover off the hot tub for your party?" I offered.

"Dad, a hot tub is for old people. We will be fine with just the pool. But could you turn the heater on the pool up a little, in case it gets cool at night?"

"Okay. But are you sure your friends won't want to use the hot tub?" I asked.

"I'm sure, Dad."

The kids showed up, and after a little talk with Sophia and me, they headed down to the party room and pool. Sophia and I reminded Nicole that things had to end at two, no later.

A bit later Sophia and I went to bed, after reminding Nicole and her friends to keep it quiet and not disturb the neighbors.

Around 2:30, Sophia woke me up.

"Monk, it is 2:30 and I can hear the party is still going on."

"I'll take care of it. You go back to sleep."

I figured I would flick the pool lights on and off a few times so Nicole would know to shut things down. I then headed down to the party room on my way out to the pool. The lights were off in the party room, but I knew my way around. Out of the corner of my eye I saw a shadow move across the room. I figured someone must have been using the bathroom. I saw another shadow; it looked like someone had gone behind the couch.

I turned on some little accent lights that were pretty dim but gave enough light for me to see what was going on. I walked over to the couch and looked down to see a guy named Blake. He was naked as a jaybird and kind of reminded me of Chris Kattan, who used to be on "Saturday Night Live". The character he played was like a monkey and he would walk around in a squatting position eating an apple and then spitting it out. That is what Blake reminded me of, except he was naked, and Kattan always had on a gold pair of tighty-whities.

I said, "Hey, Blake, how's the party going?"

He just stayed there squatting and naked and said, "Oh, it's going pretty good."

I chuckled and walked to the back door leading to the pool. I could see four heads sticking out of the hot tub.

"Hey, Nicole, I thought you said your friends would never use a hot tub."

"Dad, what are you doing out here?!"

About this time two naked girls and two naked boys jumped up and started putting on their clothes. I just laughed and told Nicole it was past two and she needed to close the party down.

When I got back to the bedroom, Sophia asked if I had told Nicole to stop the party. I said that I had and that her friends would probably be gone in a few minutes. But I didn't tell her exactly what had gone down, as I figured if I had, she wouldn't have been able to go back to sleep. It was many years after Nicole finished college when I finally told Sophia about Blake and the hot tub. She laughed, but I don't think she would have laughed that night.

Morning arrived, and Nicole came out to the pool to pick up a few loose beer and soda cans.

"Did you have a good time last night?" I asked her.

"Yes. Dad, why didn't you let me know you were coming out to the pool?"

"Didn't you see the lights go on and off a few times? I did that so you would know I was up and that the party was over. You didn't seem to get the hint, so I came down."

"Oh. I was wondering why those lights were flickering. What did Mom say? Is she mad?"

"No, she is not mad, as I did not tell her." Nicole was grateful for that.

✻ ✻ ✻

I guess Nicole took after me in many ways, especially in the speeding ticket department. She had a lead foot, and was always in a hurry.

"Nicole, do you understand that driving is a privilege, not a right? You will get your license taken away if you get too many tickets. You can join the service like I did or you can slow down. You do not want to lose your license! But if you get a ticket, let me know, and we can maybe get a lawyer to fix it."

"What do you mean, 'fix it'?"

"Well, if you pay a little extra, a lawyer can sometimes get your ticket changed to a non-moving violation, which means there will be no points put on your license," I explained. "Just let me know if you get a ticket."

"Dad, I have two tickets right now."

"What? When did you get them, and why didn't you tell me?"

"They were both stupid tickets and I shouldn't have gotten either of them. The cops just like to give college students tickets."

We found a lawyer and got one of them fixed. That girl, though… there would be a few other lawyers needed before she finally realized that the driving privilege meant slow down, don't tailgate, be smart.

✻ ✻ ✻

Around the time of Nicole's college graduation, she gave me a phone call.

"Dad, I probably won't move back home, as I think it is time for me to go out on my own."

"That's fine! I am happy for you."

"I am also going to apply for Mizzou's School of Law. But don't worry; I will get student loans for school and to live on. You will not have to pay."

"Nicole, I would prefer you not get a student loan, and definitely do not get a loan to live on! Your mother and I will help and you can work part-time to help with your living expenses, just like you've done the last two years."

"Dad, everybody gets loans; I want to do it myself without your help."

"I'll tell you what," I said. "You get a loan for the first semester of law school, and we will pay for your portion of your rent (she was going to live with roommates). If you do well the first semester we will then talk about what to do for the rest of law school."

First semester went according to that plan. Second semester was about to start when Nicole called.

"Dad, I'm near the bottom of my class, I don't really think I want to be a lawyer, and you are probably right about the student loans. All my friends are deeply in debt, and a couple that have graduated can't find jobs."

"Nicole, if that is how you feel, then don't waste any more time and money. Come on home, look for a job, and then you can move out, as I know you don't want to live with us anymore."

But times were tough for job-seekers from 2008 through 2012, and Nicole couldn't find a good job. She did a little waitressing, tried retail, and even delivered pizzas. She kind of liked the pizza gig, as the hours were good—30 per week—and the pay was decent—$400 to $500 per week. Still, that was not enough for her to live on her own. And she wasn't happy back at home with us.

❋ ❋ ❋

"Mom, Dad, I'm moving to Amherst, Massachusetts," Nicole announced one day.

"Why there? How are you going to afford to live?"

"Well, I have some friends that I will live with, and I will get a job, as it is a college town so there should be work. I'm going, so don't try and stop me."

"Nicole, I can't stop you as you are an adult, but are you sure you want to do this?" I asked.

"Yes. I plan on leaving next week."

"Will you let me drive up with you? Amherst is over a thousand miles away."

"Dad, there won't be room for you with all my stuff."

"Well, Mom and I could load up my car too, and we could follow you up and help you move in. Better yet, I could rent a car dolly and we could tow your car with my Dodge Magnum power wagon. It's got a Hemi and it can do the job."

"I don't know, Dad. I think it would be better if I just went by myself."

"Nicole," I said, "if I tow your car you will not have to purchase gas. If Mom and I go we will buy food along the way. This will save you a lot of money, which you don't have much of to begin with. Plus, on the way back, Mom and I can stop at Niagara Falls, as we have never been there."

Nicole agreed, and I rented the car dolly and loaded up Nicole's car. The dolly was quite a large contraption with wheels that were wider than my car. The warning notice on the dolly said not to exceed 55 miles per hour.

"Monk, it will take us forever to get there doing 55!" Sophia said.

"Babe, I am sure we can do 65, and it should only take about twenty hours of driving to get there."

"The notice says 55!" Sophia objected.

"Okay. We will see how it goes, and if 55 is all we can do, then that is what we will do. I am quite sure the Hemi will not even know Nicole's car is behind us. The only thing we have to be careful of is braking. The Hemi has disc brakes all around, but they are not designed to stop two cars, so we will have to keep a safe distance from any car in front of us. If we do that, all will be fine."

We were all loaded up and off we went!

"Monk, surely you don't think you will drive the whole way. Also, you are going too fast," Sophia said.

"Babe, my car is doing just fine, and I'm only doing 60."

"It says 55."

"Yeah, and we are doing 60."

We were about halfway through Illinois, and things were running smoothly. I was actually just following some semi trucks that were doing 65, and we were keeping a good distance.

"Sophia, this is great. We will just find a truck to follow all the way to Massachusetts."

"I think you should pull over and let me drive for a while."

"Babe, we have only been driving for three hours. I am fine."

We got to Indianapolis and it was time for gas, food, and potty. At that point, Sophia insisted on driving.

"Okay, but let me get us back on the highway, as there is some construction, and I don't know if you can handle this dolly in tight turns."

"I will drive, and I can handle the turns and construction," Sophia countered.

"Okay," I agreed.

We got back on the highway and I sat back to rest a bit. I looked out the window and saw that we were passing a truck. A little further and we passed another truck. I looked over at Sophia and the speedometer.

"We are doing 69!" I said.

"Monk, I know, I know. But I just want to get around these trucks, as I don't like following them."

I sat back and kind of chuckled to myself, wanting to say, "Fifty-five!" But I was very happy to be going a bit faster, so I bit my tongue.

"Monk, your car sure has a lot of power; it doesn't feel like we are towing anything."

"Yep, just be sure to keep a safe distance and all will be fine." About that time I felt the passing gear kick in and we left another truck behind. "That's my girl, and my Hemi!" I said.

Sophia made it to Cleveland and then I took over the driving again. The next stop was Erie, Pennsylvania, and then the state of New York. I never realized how large a state New York is. We were now on a toll road, and naturally each fare was almost doubled, as we had two vehicles. Oh well.

At four o'clock in the morning we pulled into a very nice rest stop to catch a couple of hours of sleep. A quick shave and tooth brushing, and it was off to the races again.

Upstate New York presented a different kind of scenery—lots of water, lots of open country, kind of sparsely populated. I was amazed at how old everything was. I had never been to the East Coast, other than for layovers while flying, and I just couldn't believe what I was seeing.

We made it to Amherst, and although it seemed like a nice little city, it too was old. Even Nicole commented that things were a little ghetto-looking. We got to Nicole's new home, unloaded the car from the dolly, and helped Nicole move in her stuff. We met her friends, and they seemed nice, but the apartments seemed a bit run-down. I noticed that some of the residents seemed a little rough around the edges and I didn't like it. Still, this was what Nicole wanted, so what could we do?

* * *

A big hug and kiss, and Sophia and I were back on the road. We hadn't gone five miles down the road before I started crying.

"What's wrong with you, Monk?" Sophia asked.

"We just left our daughter off in the ghetto and you ask what's wrong?" I said.

"She will be fine!" Sophia said.

When the evening came around, Sophia asked whether we were going to stop at a motel for the night.

"Of course, but I want to get a little closer to Buffalo so we won't have far to drive in the morning to get to Niagara Falls," I said.

"Why do we have to get to Niagara Falls early in the morning?"

"You do realize we still have the dolly back there," I said.

"Oh, yes, how could I forget that?" Without Nicole's car loaded on it, that damn thing made such a racket. *Clankity-clank.*

"We will be lucky if we can find a place to park with the dolly on back," I said. "That is why I want to get there early."

We soon found a motel, ate, and crashed. I have never seen Sophia look so tired. We had been on the road for about 28 hours with only two hours of rest in the car.

Morning came, we had a little breakfast, and off we went.

We passed through Buffalo and crossed a bridge over some of the water destined for the falls. After crossing the bridge we saw a very small sign on the shoulder of the road that pointed the way to Niagara Falls. It seemed like a pretty small sign for such a well-known destination.

The road was also worse than you would expect, given that it led to one of the marvels of the world.

"Sophia, this can't be the way to Niagara Falls. We are in a run-down part of town; it looks like anything but the yellow brick road to Oz. I have to find someone for directions."

I spotted a woman who looked down on her luck on the sidewalk and we pulled over.

"Excuse me, could you tell us how to get to Niagara Falls?" I asked.

"If you just keep going in the direction you are headed, you will get there."

We headed back out and the road got worse. There were potholes everywhere; *clankity-clank*—the dolly was our constant companion. We were in an area that reminded me of the worst parts of East St. Louis. I simply couldn't believe this was the way to Niagara Falls.

Finally, we arrived at our destination. Niagara Falls was magical and beautiful; it was like the parting of the waters, as different as night and day. Nice buildings, flowers, restaurants, and a parking lot that had a space I could get into with the dolly that would also be easy to get out of, even if the lot filled up!

The falls were just down the sidewalk, and we crossed a couple of pedestrian bridges crossing the water that was rushing to the main event. We met a couple from Canada on the first bridge and took each other's pictures. The rushing water leading up to the falls was almost as breathtaking as the falls themselves. The noise of the water increased the closer we got, and there were a few rocky islands in the middle of the torrent with the rushing water swirling about them. As we rounded the last curve in the path, the noise of the falls plus the mist from the cascading water overwhelmed all.

There were some observation points jutting out from the rim along the side of the falls. Some truly great pictures can be taken from there; all of mine looked like a professional had shot them! If you have never seen Niagara Falls, you should go. It is not expensive but it is incredible.

Clankity-clank; we got back on the road and headed to St. Louis.

"Sophia, we should be home in about twelve hours."

"Monk, there is no way we will get home that soon."

"Babe, we only have a little over 700 miles to go." It was pedal to the metal and five miles per hour over the speed limit; we actually made it in eleven hours. Had I known we could get to Niagara Falls in eleven hours I would have not waited so long to go!

✳ ✳ ✳

Back at home, reality set in.

"I guess we will not see our daughter for a long time," Sophia said. "I hope she will at least call every week."

That was an unrealistic thought. Nicole had never been one to call very often. She'd always said, "Dad, if you don't hear from me, then that must mean all is good." I probably deserved my anguish, as I hadn't been one to call my mom too often when I was young either.

Months passed and Sophia and I were getting used to the idea that our little girl was gone. Then one day, the phone rang. The caller ID said it was Nicole!

"Hi, sweetheart, how is it going?" I asked.

"Well, Dad, not too good. I need to come home. Things here are not working out and it would probably be better if I came back. I will probably leave early next week."

"Nicole, I don't really want you driving back by yourself."

"I've driven more places than you can imagine; I will be fine."

"You're probably low on money, though, right?"

297

"Well, yeah, but I have enough to get home."

"Tell you what," I said. "Why don't you let me rent the dolly again and come get you? Mom will not be able to make the trip this time, so it will just be me. Maybe we could take the southern route home and catch a glimpse of New York City. I have never been to New York City and I would like to see it. We could spend a day there and I will foot the entire bill. You can save your money. It might take a while for you to find a job once you get back home."

"Okay, Dad, I guess if you want to it might be fun."

When Sophia heard of the plan, she said, "Monk, are you really going to rent that damn dolly and go back up there?"

"Well, I thought about flying, but there would not be enough room for both of us and all her stuff in the car. I could rent a trailer for her stuff and pull it with her car, but a one-way rental is actually more expensive than renting the dolly here and bringing it back to St. Louis. I will admit I'm not looking forward to the drive up there, but the return trip will be fun, plus I want to see New York City. You can come along if you want."

"Monk, I think not. I really don't like long car drives, especially the kind you are famous for. I can't take 24 hours on the road with a two-hour nap in the car."

"Babe, I'm semi-retired, so what else do I have to do? I can arrange my schedule and make the whole journey in three days." And so it was settled.

Only in America

This is about how it went:

I called my broker and told him to buy. Eight days later, I called and told him to sell. I took the short-term gain and used it to go retrieve Nicole and her car from Massachusetts. With the remaining profits—minus the ten percent I knew Uncle Sam would want at the end of the year—we stopped in New York City and showed the residents what true rednecks were like.

Only in America! But caution—the buy/sell scenario can go in the opposite direction just as easily as the profitable direction... .

* * *

I had decided that Nicole and I would take the southern route home, so I figured I would take the southern route on the way up too. That way I would be somewhat familiar with getting through New York City.

In Youngstown, Ohio, I really got the feel of some of the older areas of our country. It is probably a very nice city, but in Youngstown and a lot of the places I went through after that, it seemed like things were pretty old and crumbling. I guess I was in the Rust Belt?

Pennsylvania was the next leg of the trip. I had never driven through Pennsylvania; what a surprise! The western portion had these ferns growing along the highway. The whole forest floor was covered with these ferns; very interesting. I got out of the car for gas and sensed that I was at a slightly higher elevation.

Much to my surprise, I discovered that Pennsylvania is basically one long mountain with many picturesque rivers and many small nooks with little farms nestled in the valleys. It appeared that many of the farmers were Amish, as I could see their carriages sitting next to the horse stables or in front of the farmhouses. Only in America!

I was getting closer to New York City, and the traffic was picking up. I had planned the trip to hit the city in late afternoon, thinking the traffic would be coming out rather than going in.

Wrong! All was well until I hit the George Washington Bridge. I was in my Magnum wagon, towing the car dolly. Things were getting crazy and people were jockeying for the best position in which to approach the coming tollbooth. I didn't know what lane I should have been in, but I had the power to surge ahead of most any vehicle on the road. Love that Hemi!

Tolls… the East Coast is big on tolls, so if you're ever driving around there, bring money—cash—in all denominations. I had that covered, as I am big on cash.

I could see the tollbooth attendant ahead and noticed he was very animated. I gave him a ten and he yelled something at me. I told him I was from St. Louis and that the sign said $10.

"You have that trailer and another axle with another set of tires. That will cost you another $5," he explained.

"Okay. Can I ask you a question?"

Horns started honking at me. Oddly, this honking seemed to calm the attendant; it seemed to make him happy that we were holding up the traffic. We had a nice little conversation and he advised me that on my return trip with Nicole's car on the dolly, we would have to pay a $20 toll. The guy behind me was probably wishing he hadn't cut in front of the guy behind him; now he was stuck in my lane.

There is no "good traffic time" in New York City. An hour later I was finally across the bridge and in a tunnel, suffering from exhaust fumes. So far I was not too impressed with the city, though to be fair I wasn't really surprised by all the traffic either.

On to Amherst. How fortunate I was, and how smart I had been, it turned out. I casually looked across at the traffic going in the other direction (out of town) and they were at a dead stop. Ten miles down the road and I looked again, and the oncoming traffic still wasn't moving. Yep, those cars were stopped for ten straight miles.

I had been right! Coming in to the city in the afternoon had been a smart move. The traffic lessened a bit and I exited to get gas. There was a service truck for a local contractor next to me and I asked the driver how in the hell his company made any money when he must have spent all his time in traffic en route to a job site. He agreed that it was a problem.

I hit Connecticut and had to stop at a rest area. I had driven that far with no rest. I crawled in the back seat and crashed for three hours. Feeling fresh after waking up, washing my face, and brushing my teeth, I continued on the way to get my daughter.

When I arrived, we loaded her stuff into her Focus and got it onto the dolly. I met two of Nicole's friends before we left and the last thing I heard her say to them was, "I'll be back!"

❋ ❋ ❋

We headed off to New York City. Yeah, I had been up for 42 hours with only those three hours of sleep at the rest area, but I was determined to see the city. We figured that by the time we got there it would be eleven at night—perfect, no traffic.

Wrong! Once again I found the cars on the opposite side at a standstill for ten miles.

We entered the city (after paying another toll, naturally). In Manhattan we discovered that all we needed to know to get around was uptown, downtown, and the thirties, twenties, etc. There were no parking meters (that I saw).

There weren't too many parking spots either—even in these wee morning hours—especially for a Hemi with a Focus hooked to its rear. Yeah, we made Missouri drivers look real bad, as I parked in numerous spots that probably weren't parking spaces. But I figured if I got a parking ticket, who cared? The cops were real nice, as they witnessed many U-turns (*clankity-clank!*) on my part.

I even found a spot to park only a block from the Empire State Building. What a letdown, though. Here I had been expecting this pristine, beautiful piece of architecture. Nope; it's just a tall concrete building with a ten-story spiral at the top. The spiral was well-lit and kind of pretty, but without that spiral it would just be an ugly concrete building. At street level, it's just regular old storefronts.

One of them was a Rexall drugstore with a huge poster of the Statue of Liberty in the window. Across the street was a bus stop with another poster of the Statue of Liberty. I got the message—the Statue of Liberty is a sight to see. As we learned later, it's also something of an elusive stop.

Lying on some concrete steps across the street from the Empire State Building was a very well-dressed drunk passed out. He was at 31st Street and 5th Avenue (not "Street"!), a hoity-toity part of town; I guess that was why he was dressed so nicely.

We went back to Houston Street, where people were out and about. They pronounce it "House-ton", not like the city in Texas. Pronunciation issues caused us more than one U-turn!

On the whole, the residents were very nice and cordial, and just observing all the characters in the play was a real trip for me.

We decided to have some authentic New York pizza (which ended not being too different from authentic St. Louis pizza). Nicole accidentally stepped back into a table (not hard to do—everything in New York is so close together!). Three young black dudes were sitting there and wanted to know what the hell she was doing getting in their turf!

Well, I give my best Atlas pose and my Rocky Balboa lip curl. The sense of aggression diminished a bit. Whew! Nicole and I would have gone toe to toe with them if necessary (she's tough and strong), but God was with us. I should have called my broker; I was on a roll luckwise.

Cabbies and yellow cabs were everywhere! There were at least 1000 yellow cabs zigging in and out, barely avoiding accidents with each maneuver. Crazy! I'm not kidding; it was three in the morning and 1000 cabbies were going crazy. It was like being in the middle of a hornets' nest. I have to say, the fare that was printed on the side of their doors—$3 to get in and 50 cents for each quarter of a mile—seemed reasonable. One could probably travel all of Manhattan for $20 plus a tip. The cabbies were not impressed with my rig and were very aggressive.

Nicole and I were really impressed with the trash system. It seemed like there were no alleys and few dumpsters in Manhattan. At about one in the morning, businesses and apartment tenants started putting their trash out on the sidewalks. No trash cans, just white plastic trash bags. Within an hour, almost every inch of sidewalk in all of Manhattan was covered with these white trash bags. But not to worry; at 2:00 came an army of garbage trucks and crews. Wow—Manhattan after hours, what an experience!

✳ ✳ ✳

We figured it was time to head out to New Jersey, as we thought the Statue of Liberty was accessible from that side of the water (I guess the Hudson Bay?) off of Highway 95, which runs up and down the whole friggin' East Coast!

The map said there was a 495 bridge. Everyone knows that all major interstate highways (such as 95) will have an alternate route with three numbers, such as 495.

One would think that getting directions to the 495 bridge to get to the Jersey side would have been easy. But you would have thought that I had asked how to get to Timbuktu! Everyone said the same thing: if we told them the name of the bridge, they could direct us. I repeated that the map called it the 495 bridge and that it connected to Highway 95 on the Jersey side.

Confused looks galore! Even the cops were bewildered and said they were not familiar with Jersey. Damn, I thought I was asking about a street and bridge that was connected to Manhattan! Didn't these people ever leave this island?

We decided we would try the Holland Tunnel instead of the 495 bridge, as we had seen signs for it. We found it and after waiting our turn (three streets merged into one at the entrance to the tunnel), we were greeted by lights and a siren. A nice and, I must say, rather handsome representative of the NYPD stopped us to inform me that trailers were not allowed in the Holland Tunnel. He said we had to take the Lincoln Tunnel. *Clankity-clank*; another U-turn, and the Easter egg hunt continued.

We came across four Latinos. They were kind of like the groundhogs in the KIA Soul car commercials. They were a bit interesting, but they did lead us to the Lincoln Tunnel. You guessed it: the ramp from the tunnel was closed.

So we had to take the New Jersey Turnpike. More tolls; I advise you to keep those $20s handy. (You might need two $20s if you have a Ford Focus tied to your tailpipe!)

We couldn't find one sign directing us to the Statue of Liberty! Truly amazing! We gave up on finding it, but fortunately Nicole and I had taken some pictures of each other in front of the poster of the Statue of Liberty at the Rexall drugstore. It had been a large poster so the effect was good.

I would highly recommend seeing New York City. It was actually very entertaining. I was a bit disappointed by some of the sights I had heard about all my life, but the overall experience was well worth the craziness. I will go again when I have more time.

* * *

I had been awake for 47 of the previous 50 hours (I hadn't known I could still do that), so we found a motel and caught some Zs.

When we hit the road again, Nicole and I took turns tolerating each other's music. (She and I had both brought our iPods.) The cell phone was next to us, the computer was plugged into the cigarette lighter, and wires were running everywhere! Only in America!

Finally, I had my daughter trapped for 1000 miles. Retirement (technically semi-retirement, I guess) had allowed me this luxury. We discussed life and all its ups and downs, needs and perceived needs. Life was good!

* * *

You would think the story was over… nope! When we were 90 miles from home, I was explaining to Nicole how to drive and not to drive, and what to do and say if you get pulled over by the police. I looked toward the median of the highway; it was two in the morning and hard to see, but there was Smokey!

We were in a convoy of about six vehicles, including our Hemi and Focus. We were all doing 80 in a 65 zone. I said, "Oh, shit, Nicole. We are going to get a ticket!"

I had pulled over and stopped before Smokey had even gotten out of the median onto the highway. His tires were throwing rocks and grass as he frantically accelerated in an effort to issue someone a ticket. Smokey saw me pulled over and stopped the chase.

"Nicole, do you see him back there?"

"Yes, Dad."

"What is he doing?"

"I can't tell."

We waited a few minutes and I decided to get out of the car.

"Sir, what are you doing? Get back in your car," the cop said.

"Officer, I was just wondering what you were doing and if you were okay."

I told him I was guilty and gave him my license. I explained that we were coming back from Amherst, Massachusetts, and that I had been discussing life with my daughter while not paying much attention to my speed.

He said, "Well, I had no idea which one of your group I was going to pull over, but when I saw you stopped, you made my decision for me." He then said he was not going to give me a ticket and to be careful. I practically kissed his feet, wished him well, and was upset that my broker was not at the office. I was definitely on a roll!

I got back in the car and said to Nicole, "I can't believe it; he didn't give me a ticket!"

"Dad," she said, "if that would have been me, I would have gotten two."

I replied, "Well, I don't have a nose ring... ."

Only in America!

Same O' Same O'

Nicole found a job within a few days of getting back home and started to save the money she made, as Sophia and I had told her she could live with us for free. We knew she wanted to be on her own so that seemed like the best way to prepare her financially for it.

It hadn't been two months when Nicole informed us she was headed back to Massachusetts.

"Mom, Dad, I will make it this time. I will live with my friend Heidi and we will get our own place. I know I can get a job and I will be fine. Heidi is going to fly down here and visit for a couple of days and then we will drive my car back. It will be a month before we move into our new place, so I will live with friends again for that month."

We kissed her goodbye and off she went again. True to her word, she found a job and moved into her new place. At that point, she asked if I could bring the rest of her stuff out.

"Nicole, how about those two stuffed chairs in the basement, do you want those too?"

"They won't fit in your car."

"Yeah, but I've got my little utility trailer. They will fit on that, and I won't have to rent anything. I will also take a different route through Pennsylvania so I won't have to go through New York City and will skip all of the toll roads."

"Dad, you should take the Scranton exit off Interstate 80. That's the way Heidi and I came back," Nicole advised.

A week later, I had my little trailer loaded and wrapped up tight to keep the weather out and was ready to hit the road again.

"Monk, do you want me to pack you some food? I can cut up some apples, pack some cereal, and put a little milk in a cooler for you," Sophia offered.

"Babe, all I need is a couple of those biscuits left over from yesterday and some bottled water. I will get coffee and pull over if I get tired. I love you and will see you in three days."

The first couple of hundred miles through Illinois and Indiana were always the worst, as there was not much scenery. So I left at nine in the evening. I like driving at night, as there is less traffic and less road work. The only thing I do not like about driving at night is the deer. Those damn things are constantly being hit; I always see many lying dead on the side of the highway. I always wonder how the drivers who hit them come out of the collision. I hope I never find out!

❊ ❊ ❊

Cell phones are truly amazing. It was eleven at night when I was somewhere in Illinois and only 9:00 in California, where Mom lived. I usually call her up whenever I'm on the road, and this time was no exception.

"Hi, Momma, I'm on the way to Massachusetts again and thought I would call you."

We marveled at the fact that I could be driving through the cornfields of Illinois and talking to her in California. I mean, almost the second a word came out of my mouth, it went into her ear. Who would have thought this possible fifteen years ago?

"Now, Monk, you be careful. I don't want anything to happen to you."

"I'll be fine, Mom." We were beginning to sound just like Nicole and me when she was on the road. Yes, what goes around also comes around.

Mom was getting up in years; she was 86, I think. There were a lot of sayings she shared with me while us kids were growing up. Ones like, "You catch more flies with honey than with vinegar"; or, "The wheel that squeaks the most will get the oil." Her favorite song was "Que Será, Será"; whatever will be, will be.

I really enjoy these talks with Mom while traveling the country, as I occasionally find out things I never knew about her. She grew up in a small town in southern Georgia, and her father owned the town's only bank. It was one of the few small banks that had not gone under during the Great Depression.

"Monk, my daddy was smart. He always said to never buy anything you couldn't afford," my mom shared. "He wasn't too big on credit or the creation of Social Security, either. He always said a man should provide for his own retirement, and should not rely on the government. Daddy always took me to the bank with him and taught me how to count money, balance the books, and treat customers. When the run on the banks occurred, he greeted the people of the town and assured them that all of the bank's loans were solid.

"'Trust me, do not take your money out. This bank will survive,' he told them. It did, and the townspeople admired him.

"Monk, you remind me of my daddy."

Mom's father had died of tuberculosis when she was only eleven, and her mother had died two years later.

A real eye-opener for me was a story she told me about the town sheriff. Now, I never heard my mother speak one word about guns or weapons in my whole life. But then she told me, "Monk, one day the sheriff pulled up in front of our home looking for Daddy. He wasn't home, and we got to talking about his revolver. The sheriff told me that being a girl meant that I probably could not shoot and hit anything.

"There were about six streetlights in town and one of them was across the street from our home. I told him I bet I could shoot out the streetlight. He handed me his weapon, and I took aim and blasted that streetlight. He was amazed, and then we realized what we had done! We never told anyone how that light had gotten broken… ."

Mom was never too athletic, and she has sensitive skin, so she has always been careful about getting out in the sun. She told me that her 70th high school reunion was coming up and that all of her close friends had passed away. Only the athletic ones and some of the jocks were still alive. (I guess all that exercise had been good for them.)

Then Mom told me that she had been a cheerleader! "We did not have regular cheerleader attire, so we would wear a black top with a white turtleneck underneath it. If it was hot, I would not wear the turtleneck." Yup, I always found out new things when talking with Mom!

"Monk, you know God only takes the good ones. I will probably live for quite a few more years, as I will need a lot more time to get good," Mom said.

We had been on the phone for a while and I figured I should get back to focusing on driving. I told Mom I loved her and we hung up.

❊ ❊ ❊

By morning I was in Pennsylvania. I stopped for gas and looked at my now-familiar map that shows all the different routes I've taken from St. Louis to Massachusetts. I decided not to get off at the Scranton exit Nicole had suggested, but to go a little farther on

Interstate 80 to the town of Stroudsburg. It looked like a shorter route that would connect me right to Interstate 84.

Trust me, do not ever take this "shortcut"! I have never, ever been on a narrower, curvier, or more twisty road in my life! I eventually come out on 84, the highway that cutting through Scranton would have taken me to.

Nicole was living in Easthampton, and once again I was struck by how almost everything on the East Coast seems old. Easthampton is not too big on signing its streets, either; but I managed to find Nicole's and Heidi's home.

It was a pretty run-down three-story apartment. Nicole and Heidi had the whole second floor, and the inside was actually very nice. They even had an extra bedroom with a nice new carpet. I slept like a rock in there.

In the morning, we had breakfast and then spent the day together. Another kiss goodbye and I was off and running, the pedal to the metal. This time I cut through Scranton like my daughter had told me to!

All Things Come to an End

Sophia and I were getting a little older, and we decided it would be best to enjoy our lives while trying not to worry about our daughter. This gave us time to enjoy our own wants and desires.

I reconnected with some of my father's family and attended my cousin JuJu Babe (that was her nick name)'s daughter's wedding. Cousin Billy's mom—Aunt Mary Jane—and her two other children, Debbie and Fred, also attended. We shared a table and had a really good time.

Each table had these little place settings with girlie things and there were a few silver teardrops scattered about. They were a bit sticky on the back, and Fred placed a couple cascading down my cheek to make it look like I was crying, as I'd told him how I had cried at my wedding. They stayed on the whole night, and by the end of the night half of the guests were sporting teardrops. Much wine was consumed after a very nice meal.

Sophia also reconnected with some of her family, just in time to sing a couple of songs for her niece's wedding. My Sophia can bring a tear to your eyes with her singing. She was in the balcony and I was sitting up there with her, but off to the side. As her voice cascaded down to the wedding ceremony guests, all heads turned to see where the wonderful sound was coming from.

Family is important, and I was happy to see Sophia reconnect with hers.

❊ ❊ ❊

We've always enjoyed having a roaring fire in our fireplace during the cold spells in good old St. Louie. Our fireplace is a huge one, with tight-fitting glass doors and a blower that could pretty much heat our home.

"Babe, we should purchase a wood-burning stove insert for our fireplace. It would use one-third the amount of wood and do a much more efficient job of heating," I suggested.

After much discussion, I talked Sophia into purchasing a Buck Stove insert. She was not too happy with the new rustic look, as her style is more contemporary, but by the second night of heating with it she was in love. We love a good fire, and the stove has a nice glass door, so we are still able to see the fire raging. It is also a breeze to clean out compared to the fireplace.

※ ※ ※

We recently made a trip to Florida, and naturally, we stopped in Georgia. Lynn is now a state Senator, and he and Nan have many grandchildren, with another one on the way.

Now, all politicians should be like Lynn. He just enjoys serving his constituents and doing what is right. He takes no pay for his service to the state of Georgia. What a guy, what a politician!

I am one lucky guy, as all of my friends and family are good people.

We also visited with my brother Cheeks and his wife on this trip. Cheeks's two daughters are now grown, and at that time, one was about to be married.

We went out to dinner at a Cajun restaurant with Cheeks and his wife, Carole. I saw a beer named Purple Haze on a fluorescent sign that kind of took me back to my younger days. I asked the waitress to bring me a bottle of that Purple Haze. Jimmy Hendrix would have been proud of me. Surprisingly enough, it was pretty good beer, and I later found out a few places in St Louis also sell it.

❋ ❋ ❋

Sophia and I are planning a three-week trip to Italy, kind of like the honeymoon we never took. We are planning on starting in Venice, then renting a car to travel much of the country, zigzagging across and down most of Italy. We will visit the northern lake country, the Italian Riviera, Tuscany, Pisa, Rome, Sorrento, and whatever else time will permit.

Life is good!